Also by Kristina Douglas

Raziel

Demon

Warrior

KRISTINA DOUGLAS

THE FALLEN:
REBEL

WITHDRAWN

Pocket Books

New York   London   Toronto   Sydney   New Delhi

Pocket Books
A Division of Simon & Schuster, Inc.
1230 Avenue of the Americas
New York, NY 10020

This book is a work of fiction. Names, characters, places, and incidents either are products of the author's imagination or are used fictitiously. Any resemblance to actual events or locales or persons, living or dead, is entirely coincidental.

First Pocket Books paperback edition April 2013

POCKET and colophon are registered trademarks of Simon & Schuster, Inc.

For information about special discounts for bulk purchases, please contact Simon & Schuster Special Sales at 1-866-506-1949 or business@simonandschuster.com.

The Simon & Schuster Speakers Bureau can bring authors to your live event. For more information or to book an event, contact the Simon & Schuster Speakers Bureau at 1-866-248-3049 or visit our website at www.simonspeakers.com.

Manufactured in the United States of America

10 9 8 7 6 5 4 3 2 1

ISBN 978-1-4516-5592-6
ISBN 978-1-4516-5595-7 (ebook)

For my mother

CHAPTER
ONE

I COULD FEEL IT WASHING OVER ME, and I lay motionless, frozen with dread. Not now. Not again. I began to fight it, struggling, the entangling sheets trapping my body, and I ended up on the hard stone floor as pale mist filled the small confines, my heart clenching in dread. Could it be Thomas? Dear Thomas, dead for seven long years, now come back to give me another unwanted warning? He'd always watched me a little too closely—was he still doing so?

I could hear soft whimpering, and knew it came from me. No, it wasn't my dead husband. This was nothing more than the mist that always shrouded Sheol, keeping it safe from the ordinary world. Like Thomas, there was no malice in it, but it brought the visions that plagued me. I curled up in a corner on the floor, wrapping my arms around my legs, burying my face against my knees.

Not that it would stop the visions. Nothing would. I couldn't control them, couldn't understand them— months could go by without anything, and then they would hit, and I'd be on my knees, sobbing, hiding my weakness away from the others.

I never said anything. Life in a world of fallen angels was never easy for a mortal, particularly one who'd lost her mate. If they had any idea of the pain my visions caused me they would want to help, and I couldn't bear the thought of it. Whether I embraced them or not, the visions came, and the best way to get through them was to keep them private. Otherwise there were too many questions, too many demands for a clarity that was maddeningly out of reach. I needed quiet to make sense of the bits and pieces that came to me like shards of glass, piercing my battered heart.

I huddled in the darkness like a miserable coward, despising myself, trying to calm my thundering heart. I was covered with a cold sweat, even though the room was warm, and I forced myself to take slow, steadying breaths. Letting the vision take form.

He was coming. The dark man, who brought disruption and destruction. The name had been clear in my mind for months now, but I had said nothing to the others. I knew nothing. Only his name.

Cain.

And he was coming for me.

I should get up. I had no idea whether it was this day, or the next, but soon. Soon he would come, and everything would be chaos. It was little wonder I hadn't told Raziel. As leader of the Fallen, he had more than enough to deal with, and now, with the astounding miracle of his wife's pregnancy, he had no time to worry about obscure visions that might mean nothing. No one trusted my dreams, unreliable as they were, and I hadn't wanted to make another mistake, giving everyone half-formed fears that could simply distract them. I'd chosen to wait until later, until I knew more about the prophecy that hovered around me like an angry bird of prey.

Later was now.

My fears were absurd, of course. I knew it, but my heart still pounded. What disaster awaited the Fallen? What disaster awaited me?

In the hierarchy of the Fallen I was a vestigial organ, neither angel nor mate. Thomas had plucked me from the chaos of my human life. He'd been watching over me, he'd said. I'd once told him he had been a pretty ineffective guardian angel, considering the first seventeen years of my life, and he'd been offended. Thomas hadn't had much of a sense of humor. I'd been so young when he'd brought me here, but he had given me love and safety and a peace I had craved and never known, and for five years I had been happy.

And then the monstrous Nephilim had broken through, and he had died, and the visions had begun.

At first I'd welcomed those visions. They gave me a purpose, a role in the world of the Fallen. While the angels had varying abilities to see the future, none were nearly as good as my own imperfect dreams. As incomplete and frustrating as they were, they gave me a reason to stay in Sheol, one I welcomed despite the pain.

So why should the dark man be coming for me?

The next vision hit me like a knife, and I jerked, moaning, horrified by it. It was raw, embarrassing, a vision of sexual intimacy that made me close my eyes, trying to shut it out, but it wouldn't stop. I didn't want to see this, didn't want the sensual reaction that spread beneath my skin like the fire that poisoned the Fallen.

But the visions never listened. Closing my eyes only brought the pictures into clearer focus; running didn't help. I curled in on myself and endured as the couple moved on the bed, and I could see the man's face, angelically beautiful, devilishly wicked, as he slowly thrust into the woman beneath him. She was looking up into his face, and it was my body he was pleasuring. The dream Martha tried to move, but her hands were tied above her head. There was no coercion—this was sex play—and I watched it in fascination. I wanted to say something, to weaken the power of the dream, but all I could hear was a moan coming from my throat. The sound I made as the visions sliced through me, the pain ripping at me. A pain that was mixed with deep, forbidden pleasure.

It vanished. One moment I was reaching for sexual ecstasy beneath the dark angel; the next I was alone in my room, huddled and shaking on the hard floor, the early-morning sunlight streaking into the room from the garden beyond.

I took a deep breath. The mist was gone with the vision, leaving me incomplete, my body still tingling with arousal. I had learned nothing new, nothing helpful. Only that the dark angel was coming.

For me.

Which was absurd. I was the least important of the inhabitants of Sheol—I was no use to anyone. I pushed to my feet, using the wall to steady myself, and straightened my bedding before heading into the small, utilitarian bathroom. The hot shower helped, easing some of the tension from my muscles, beating against my oddly sensitized skin. I shook my head, wiping the moisture from the mirror, and looked at myself dispassionately.

The bonded mates of the Fallen aged differently than they would have in the human world they'd left. I was thirty, and because of Sheol's strange laws I looked ten years younger. I would live to the century mark and well beyond, if the violence inherent in the lives of the Fallen didn't kill me first. I looked normal, calm, my annoyingly curly brown hair around my narrow face, my changeable hazel eyes a cool sea green today. Others said I looked slightly fey, called me gamine. Meant kindly, but I hated it. I wanted to look calm and solid, not naughty. I had bit my lip during the vision, though I couldn't remember when, and my mouth looked bee-stung. As if I'd been thoroughly, relentlessly kissed. If anyone looked at me, they would never know I'd spent the last hour wrapped in pain. Wrapped in sex.

Then again, no one tended to look at me too closely. In Sheol, as in the human world, widows were invisible. My dubious gifts were valued, if not trusted, and I was welcomed and cared for. But in the end I was allied to no one.

The ominous rumble of thunder broke through my thoughts, a welcome distraction. I shoved my fingers through my hair, then went to dress, as the thunder grew louder.

I heard the sizzle of lightning, followed by a crash that seemed to shake the earth, and an eerie blue light speared into my room. I froze, sudden panic filling me. I had waited too long. He was coming now, and I had to warn them.

I didn't bother with shoes, racing along the corridor, dodging the sleepy inhabitants who'd emerged from their rooms to observe the storm. I had to get to Raziel as fast as I could.

I rushed around a corner, almost slamming into the archangel Michael; one look from his dark eyes and I slowed to a brisk walk. Panic wouldn't help anyone.

"Where is Raziel?" I resisted the impulse to grab his shirt and force an answer as another bolt of lightning slammed down, followed by a roar of thunder.

"On the beach," he said shortly. "It's dangerous out there—you should wait until it's safer. Unless . . . do you know anything about this?"

Suspicion and annoyance tinged his voice, and I couldn't blame him. He had already been a victim of my half-assed visions, and though they had brought him his wife, Tory, he still held a grudge.

"I don't," I said, semitruthfully. Because I didn't know. I could only guess.

People were heading out onto the beach now, in the midst of the lightning storm—an act of utter insanity. Few things could kill fallen angels, usually only other unearthly creatures or the open flames that poisoned them. But what about the fierce power of lightning? And what would it do to the human wives who moved out into the storm with them?

"It can't wait," I said. If it brought an end to my existence, then so be it. I pushed past him, moving through the open doors and down the slope onto the beach, searching for Raziel's tall form among so many tall, beautiful creatures.

The moment I set foot on the sand all hell broke loose, as if the storm had been waiting for me to unleash its final restraint. The sky turned black, roiling with angry clouds, the only light the almost constant bolts of lightning slamming into the ground, into the sea, shaking the very pillars of the earth. The roar of the wind battled with the constant, deafening thunder, and the gale plastered my loose clothes against my body. It felt like the end of the world.

Raziel loomed up out of the chaos, vibrating with fury. "Do you know anything about this?" he demanded, somehow being heard over the noise.

Time to face the music, I thought uneasily. Raziel needed any information I had, as insubstantial as it was. "Someone's coming."

The wind caught my voice and whipped it away, but he heard anyway. "Who?" he shouted.

I shook my head. "I don't know. I'm not sure."

"Who?" he repeated.

I heard the sizzle; my ears popped and my face burned with sudden heat, and in the midst of the beach something burst into flames. Flames that could consume the Fallen, destroy them.

People scattered in panic, some plunging into the healing safety of the furious sea, some running toward the house. I stood transfixed, staring at the column of flame, Raziel motionless by my side as the form of a man appeared in the midst of the blaze.

Not a man. An angel—I could see the wings outlined against the orange-red glow, and I stifled my horrified cry. I had seen the agonizing devastation fire could wreak on the angels, even a spark, and this angel was consumed by it.

I watched, unable to turn away, expecting him to disintegrate into ash. No one moved to help him—no one could. They all stared at the culmination of their worst nightmares come to fruition.

He didn't scream. Didn't thrash or struggle. Instead he stepped forward, out of the flame, and it dissolved behind him, leaving him standing still, untouched, his deep-hued wings spread out behind him as he surveyed the people around him.

And then the angel smiled, the most devilish, charming, diabolical smile, as he snapped his fingers. The fire vanished. The sky cleared; instantly the wind dropped, the thunder and lightning gone as if they had never consumed the universe. He looked around at the shocked faces almost benevolently.

"I always did know how to make an entrance," he said.

I could feel hatred pierce Raziel, so fierce and powerful it reached into me as well. "Cain," he said in tones of utter loathing. "I should have known it was you."

CHAPTER
TWO

EVERYONE WAS TOO BUSY STARING at the newcomer to notice the shock on my face. I don't know why I was surprised. I had already known exactly what he would look like. Hadn't I seen him, time after time, as he made love to my dreaming self?

The Fallen were beautiful. All angels were beautiful, including, I gathered, the sumptuously evil archangel Uriel. But this one, this Cain, was different.

The Fallen were austere, powerful. But Cain surveyed us all with clear amusement, something I seldom saw in the men who surrounded me. He had long, sun-streaked hair, high cheekbones, and a strong, elegant nose. He stood too far away to tell, but I already knew his eyes were a clear gray, almost silver, and they were laughing.

I knew his mouth as well, curved and sensual.

I had seen that mouth on my body, doing things Thomas had never done. Too many times I'd reacted to those visions with restless longing, and they'd never brought me any closer to understanding. Why should I be tormented by such intense, erotic dreams?

Dreams that had taken on a disturbing reality as the dark man suddenly appeared in a pyre that should have killed him.

He pulled his wings into his body, and they vanished in that astonishing way of all angels, so I hadn't time to ascertain their color. Color made a difference. The darker the shade, the more powerful, the older the angel. His wings had been very dark.

He moved then, almost gliding toward the angels awaiting him, so graceful I had to fight back a gasp. "And where is Azazel to greet me?" he murmured, not even glancing at me.

It gave me a chance to observe him even more closely. He seemed to hum with energy, with a sexual heat that I could feel vibrating in my own body. Perhaps they all could feel it.

He was here, he was now. He would destroy us all.

"Azazel no longer leads the Fallen. I do," Raziel said in deceptively calm tones. He nodded toward the small burned patch on the beach. "What was that?"

Cain laughed, and the sound was shocking. Charming, almost musical, after the violence of his arrival. "Smoke and mirrors, old friend."

"I'm not your friend," Raziel said.

And then Cain glanced at me. I kept myself very still, waiting for the power of his gaze to hit me, but it simply danced across my face. "Who's the little mouse hiding behind you?"

That was enough to move me. I met his eyes calmly. "Not a mouse," I said. "I'm Martha, wife of Thomas." I don't know why I made it sound as if he were still alive.

"The seer," Raziel said briefly.

If I expected that to elicit any more attention from the newcomer, I was disappointed. "And how is that working out?" he said smoothly, more to Raziel than to me.

"She didn't tell me you were coming," Raziel grumbled, and I kept myself from flinching. There'd been nothing to tell. Indeed, this time my visions had been turned upside down, clearly mixed up with my own pent-up sexual frustration. I'd had the vision of his arrival, and transposed him into my unwanted fantasies.

Which explained why, when he looked at me, it was with only distant curiosity. That odd, heated connection had nothing to do with him. He was looking at me now, and it took all my self-control not to squirm. "But you knew I was coming, didn't you?" he murmured. "I can see it in those secretive eyes of yours."

I was far from transparent—I'd spent my human life hiding my emotions, and there was no way he could read me. He must already know of my premonition, and lying would do no good.

But I could slide around a bit. "I knew someone was coming," I allowed. "But that was all."

Again that smile, but there was a knowing quality to it that I found distinctly unsettling. "Indeed?" he murmured. He turned back to Raziel. "You should get yourself a better seer. This one seems to have fallen down on the job."

I didn't even blink. I had learned in my human life not to respond to a blow, and it served me well now. Inside I wanted to blast the charming, arrogant prick who'd just arrived, but Raziel had already come to my defense.

"Prophecy has always been an imprecise art," he said. "Why have you returned, Cain?"

This gilded, seductive creature had been here before? Then why had I never heard of him? Surely someone of his magnetic charm and obvious age and power should have been well-known. And yet I'd never heard his name until my dreams, or I might have been better warned.

Cain's mouth curved in another secretive smile.

"Why, I've come back to help you in your hour of need, brother."

"Don't call me brother," Raziel snapped.

Before Cain could respond there was a sudden roar from the wide doors to the big house. Azazel stood there, bristling with fury, Rachel beside him, a restraining hand on his arm. A hand he shook off before he plowed toward Cain, barreling into him, knocking him onto the sand with the force of his assault. I leapt out of the way, expecting the other angels to break up the vicious fight that erupted, but no one moved as the two of them pummeled each other.

Finally Raziel spoke, but only after Azazel had managed to land several punishing blows. "I suppose we'd best break them up, Michael," he said in a languid voice.

"Must we?" the archangel replied. "Azazel is winning. He could solve the problem for us."

By this time Rachel had reached us, and she glared at the angels on the sidelines before turning to the fighting men. "Stop it!" she shouted. They were so lost in rage they didn't seem to hear her.

I was the only one to see her do it, and I wasn't surprised. I already knew of her powers, perhaps more than she did. A rogue gust of wind hit them like a tiny sirocco, rolling and tumbling their battling bodies toward the now calm sea.

A moment later they were immersed in the icy water, the shock of it pulling them apart. Azazel went under, then arose, sputtering, to glare at his wife, while Cain emerged grinning, shoving his wet hair away from his face.

There was blood on his face as well as Azazel's. Azazel made no move to lunge at him again, frowning instead at his wife, but Rachel had only the most innocently concerned expression on her face.

"If the two of you are finished measuring your dicks," Raziel said dryly, "then I suggest you both get cleaned up before we find out exactly why Cain has chosen to grace us with his presence."

"Good idea," Rachel said in a deceptively serene voice. "Martha, why don't you take care of Cain while I see what I can do with my idiot husband?"

Her idiot husband didn't look any more pleased than I felt, but after my first start of protest I didn't dare say anything. Cain hadn't even glanced at me. Dreams, I reminded myself. Not visions.

"Excellent idea. We'll meet in the gathering room in, say, half an hour." There wasn't a question in Raziel's rich voice.

I wasn't sure if I was pleased or disappointed. Half an hour wouldn't give me much time to discover what this man's clearly unwanted appearance meant for me, but it would mean less time in his troubling presence.

"Go with Martha, Cain," Raziel said impatiently, when neither man moved from the gentle surf.

I felt the full force of his eyes on me now, an unsettling reminder of the erotic dreams that had plagued me. Dreams that had nothing to do with this particular newcomer, but instead were simply a coincidence. I was convinced of it.

He walked out of the surf then, his already tight black clothes now plastered against him, clinging to his lean, muscled body, and I had to keep myself from staring. I should have been used to masculine beauty by now, taken it as the norm, and in fact, I had. What I wasn't used to was the pure sexuality of the man who was now looking at me with his entire concentration, and I could feel my own body heat in response.

Cain strolled up the beach toward me, apparently undisturbed by the biting autumn wind. He already knew who I was in this pack of twenty or so men and women. He stopped too close to me, raising an eyebrow inquiringly, and for the first time I felt the full force of his mesmerizing attention. His smile was facile, charming, never reaching those amazing silver-gray eyes.

"Shall we go play doctor?" he purred.

I nodded, all business, and turned toward the infirmary. He could follow me or not. The healing powers of the seawater would have taken care of any significant damage, such as cracked ribs—my help would be more along the lines of cleanup, and he could take it or leave it.

Unfortunately, he chose to take it. I could feel him behind me, and I quickened my pace into the cool hallway of the big house, hoping to force him to hurry. I wasn't very tall, much to my chagrin, surrounded as I was by the towering Fallen and their long-limbed, willowy wives, and it required no particular effort on his part to keep up with me as I hurried down the corridors.

By the time we reached the infirmary, I'd schooled myself into calm, practical concern. I even held the door for him, waiting for him to precede me.

He didn't. He caught the door above my grip, pulled it gently out of my hand, and gestured me ahead of him. "Indulge me," he said in that voice of liquid gold. "I come from a different time."

I could hardly get into a wrestling match over the door. *Choose your battles,* someone had once said to me. There would be far more important reasons to fight with Cain.

The infirmary was off to one side of the main building, a series of small rooms surrounding a central gathering place. It was seldom used; the wives of the Fallen, though all too human, lived long and healthy lives in the sheltered world of Sheol. There were no colds or illnesses, no cancer or heart disease, no arthritis or diabetes. Apart from the occasional broken bone, the women of Sheol were a healthy bunch.

I gestured toward the examination table and turned to wash my hands. I heard the click of the door latch over the sound of running water, and felt him near as he walked into the room.

"Why do you wash your hands? There's no chance of infection around here. Or are you one of those people who spend far too much time trying to wash everything away?"

I turned to face him, my eyes not quite meeting his, cool and businesslike. "It's automatic," I said. "And a courtesy. If you prefer, I'll go out and grub in the mud before I tend to you."

"Is there mud in Sheol? I would have thought everything was too clean and perfect here." He hopped up on the examination table, relaxed, casual, and I realized that to get close enough to clean the cut over his eye and the bleeding lip, I'd have to move between his legs.

But I would be damned if I'd ask him to change position. I wetted a cloth with hydrogen peroxide and advanced on him, reaching out to dab at his forehead.

At the last moment his hand snaked out and caught my wrist, and I jerked, startled at the touch of his skin against mine. It was as if a small electric current sparked between us. But he'd tightened his hold—automatically, I guessed—and my efforts to pull free were useless. "Is it going to hurt?"

I made an exasperated noise. "You're immortal. Don't be such a baby."

He released my wrist and sat back, relaxed. "That's better. Go ahead, do your worst. I can take it."

I suppressed my instinctive growl and dabbed at the oozing blood. He could have done with a couple of stitches, but the last thing I was going to do was put a needle and thread through that warm golden skin, so close to his observant eyes. "You're lucky you're an angel," I said. "Otherwise you'd have a scar."

His laugh was totally mirthless. "If I weren't an angel, I'd be dead," he said. "So . . . what's your name again? Mary?"

Despite his proximity, some of my tension drained away. He couldn't even remember my name. More proof that those dreams had been an aberration, a mishmash of my own useless longing.

"Martha," I corrected.

"Martha," he repeated, as if it would take a serious effort to commit it to memory. "I should have known. You're much more of a Martha than a Mary, aren't you?"

I didn't answer. I hated the biblical stereotypes of Martha, the hardworking martyr, and Mary, the soulful free spirit.

He was wise enough not to wait for me to respond. "So tell me, Martha. When did Raziel take over as leader of the Fallen, and why?"

I eyed him warily. "Sarah was killed in an attack by the Nephilim, and Azazel . . . decided to leave."

"But he's back. With a new mate? Why?"

I considered whether to answer him. "Shouldn't you ask Raziel about all this?"

"I prefer to go into battle with all the information I can get."

"Battle?" I echoed, disturbed. "What if I don't care to arm you?"

He ignored my question. "Who's Azazel's new wife? Is she the Source?"

It was too much trouble trying to put him off. "Allie is the Source. She's Raziel's wife, and when Sarah died she took over. As for Azazel, he was prophesied to marry the demon Lilith."

"Knowing Azazel, he probably decided to kill her instead."

I wasn't about to tell him he was right. "He's married to her," I said dryly.

Cain didn't look surprised. "You mean that sweet-looking woman? Well, he was always fairly adaptable. Do you know why everyone's so fucking happy to see me?"

It wasn't as if the Fallen didn't use those words, frequently and with force. Even I used them. But for some reason the word *fucking* coming from his mouth now summoned far too literal thoughts.

"You'd know better than I," I replied in a businesslike manner, not hesitating in my ministrations. "I'd never heard of you before today."

"Liar," he said softly, and my eyes jerked up, startled, meeting his directly for the first time. A mistake. His were much too knowing, and meeting his gaze was uncomfortably intimate. I stared at him, long and hard. I wanted to look away, but that would be showing cowardice, and I didn't dare. Not with this man.

"I assure you, we don't sit around discussing you," I said in a suitably icy voice. "I've only been here ten years, but in all that time I've never heard your name mentioned. What did you do to make everyone hate you?"

"It's my winning personality." He tilted his head, surveying me. His mouth was swollen, his lower lip split, and I dabbed at that as well, ignoring the grin beneath my hand. "I'm not saying people were talking about me. I'd think everyone here was happy to think I was gone forever. I'm just saying you knew my name, didn't you, Mary?"

"Martha," I snapped, goaded. And then realized he'd done it on purpose, just to annoy me. "And unless you rose up and slew your brother and went to dwell in the land east of Eden, there's no way I would have heard your name." As I dabbed at his lip, he caught my hand again, wrapping his long fingers around mine, his thumb in the center of my palm. Pressing. Massaging.

"Such a liar. No, I haven't killed my brother. Humans don't become angels, it's the other way around—and even if they did, I wouldn't earn the honor by committing fratricide. You're the seer. You knew I was coming."

"My visions aren't very . . . reliable. I knew *some-one* was coming," I corrected, pulling my hand. He wasn't letting go. "That doesn't mean I knew it was you." I didn't lie. I had grown up lying in order to survive, and I had promised myself that I would never lie again once I entered the safety of Sheol. But I had become an expert at avoiding an honest answer.

The man holding my hand was more than a match for my semantics. "No, it doesn't mean you knew. But you did. Didn't you?"

I was having a hard time concentrating. The combination of his thumb pressing against my palm and his silver-bright eyes looking into mine seemed to have sent my brain on a road trip. I blinked, trying to break the insidious spell he was casting over me, and managed to summon a counterattack rather than an answer.

"I'm not used to being manhandled," I said icily. "Let go of me."

"Not used to being manhandled?" he scoffed lightly. "More's the pity. Some man needs to handle you well and often. What's up with old Thomas that he can't take proper care of his wife's needs? Not that he ever was a ball of fire, but I don't remember his previous wives complaining. Mind you, they were all a fairly stolid, boring bunch, not a live wire among them. I think you might have more fire."

If he thought the mention of Thomas's previous wives would wound me, he was mistaken. I hadn't a jealous bone in my body. "What's wrong with Thomas is that he's dead. He was killed in a battle with the Nephilim."

I'd hoped to shame him, but he didn't even blink. "How long?"

If he'd released my hand, I would have punched him in the mouth myself. "Seven years. Would you please let go of me?"

"And have you punch me in the mouth? I don't think so."

His words shocked me, and I froze. How could he possibly know what I was thinking? I was adept at keeping my face a polite mask, and I'd been wary of this man from the start. Even Thomas hadn't been able to penetrate all my defenses—I'd always kept a part of me locked away. In Sheol, bonded mates could sense each other's thoughts with varying degrees of accuracy, but I had always resisted that particular intimacy. And now this dangerous stranger was sensing what I most wanted to keep hidden.

"Why do you say that?" I asked carefully.

"Because most people want to punch me in the mouth after being in my company."

I could feel my shoulders relax. "True enough. However, I'm here to heal you, not to make things worse. If you'll let go of me, I'll find you an ice bag to bring the swelling down and some dry clothes."

His thumb still rubbed against the softness of my palm, slowly, mesmerizing me. "My mouth will heal on its own, and my clothes are almost dry already. I think I'd rather hold your hand."

That was enough. I yanked myself free, and this time he let me go with a soft laugh. "You are far too transparent, Mary."

"Martha." This cheered me. If he thought I was transparent, then he was underestimating me, always a good thing. I summoned a deceptively calm smile. "What you see is what you get."

"Not exactly." He smelled of sun and salt water and warm male skin, the scent potent and arousing, bringing all sorts of strange feelings alive inside me. Ones I was more than capable of ignoring. "How long do we have until we're supposed to meet Raziel and the others?"

"We should be there now."

He cocked his head. "Too bad. I was thinking I

might like to take you to bed, just to see if I could rattle that alarming self-control of yours."

He'd meant to shock me, and he had, but I didn't show it. I laughed, sounding genuinely amused. After all, it was simply an empty bluff. "Don't be absurd. If you're in need of a woman, Raziel can make arrangements for you. You don't even have to leave Sheol."

"I have no intention of leaving Sheol, at least not right now. And I can find my own woman." His eyes slid over me like a cool, wicked caress. "You'd do for starters." And before I realized what was happening he'd moved, faster than my eyes could follow, and I was backed up against a wall, his body pressing against mine.

CHAPTER
THREE

I T WAS SO EASY IT SHOULD HAVE BEEN boring, Cain thought. He'd always liked a challenge, and the seer, Martha, was reacting just as he'd intended. He crowded her up against the wall, his body barely brushing hers, just to see what she'd do. Whether she'd put her hands on him in an effort to push him away. And whether he'd pretend to let her, or not.

She was nothing special, particularly compared to the kind of woman he usually had. She was small and curvy, with a cap of short brown curls, big hazel eyes trying to look fearless, smooth skin, and a soft, vulnerable mouth that belied all her attempts to appear unmoved. She was a fighter, though. He had to grant her that. She kept her hands at her sides.

"We're due in the assembly room." Her voice was com~~ ~~ely calm, and he bit back a smile.

"And if we're late?"

She looked at him. She'd avoided meeting his gaze at first, and he wondered why. Maybe she simply had good sense in recognizing a predator when one homed in on her. Or maybe she actually had had a premonition about him. But now she was looking at him full-on, as if in doing so she could prove he had no effect on her.

Poor baby. He was just beginning.

He hadn't decided whether she'd be his partner in crime or not. He'd yet to see what else Sheol provided nowadays. He'd been thrown a curve—he'd had no idea that Azazel had stepped down from his place as leader of the Fallen. He would have to adjust, but he was good at that. The best plans were fluid, responding to change, and Martha the seer might be just the right sort of change. If he took someone's bonded mate, the shit would really hit the fan in a most satisfactory manner, but he wasn't convinced that was his best approach. Not that he believed in either the sanctity or even the existence of those bonds. But the Fallen and their mates did, which lay at the core of the chaos he intended to bring down on their heads.

He smiled down at the girl, at his most charming, but she surveyed him stonily, and he stepped back without letting the full length of his body touch hers. He couldn't afford to waste time, but he would be smart not to rush a decision this important. Thomas's widow seemed soft and quiet and malleable. She might easily bore him.

"You'll need to lead the way, Mary," he said, and waited for her to correct him again.

She didn't, and he silently applauded her. *That's it, my girl. Fight back. There's only so much the Fallen can protect you from. Sooner or later you're going to need to grow up and protect yourself.*

She pushed away from the wall, carefully avoiding him. The loose white clothes matched what most of the others in Sheol wore, cult uniforms for the original cult, and it amused him. She moved past him, and she smelled like lilies of the valley. Of course she did—something sweet and innocent and untouched—and right then he decided that even if he ended up choosing someone else as his unwitting accomplice, he was still going to strip those baggy white clothes off Martha and fuck her the way she needed to be fucked.

Because he remembered Thomas. Thomas had been created an old man, gentle and unassuming. If that was all Martha had ever had in bed, she was in for a happy surprise. He wouldn't leave without giving it to her.

He heard the rumble of anxious conversations the moment they reached the hallway, and he smiled to himself. The Fallen were in an uproar at his unexpected return, as they should be. He fell back, letting Martha lead him into the large chamber that held a goodly portion of the Fallen and a select few of their wives, presumably including the new Source. Azazel was glaring at him, and Cain assessed the woman at his side. High-and-mighty Azazel had married the Lilith of ancient lore, part demon, part patron saint of womankind. She regarded Cain stonily, and he decided a demon would be a good match for a tight-ass like Azazel. He turned to face the new Alpha.

Raziel sat at the head of the massive table, as befitted the new leader, with a soft, pretty woman by his side. And then Cain froze, though he knew he gave nothing away.

The woman next to Raziel, presumably his wife and the Source for the current batch of mateless Fallen, was noticeably pregnant. Which was flat-out impossible.

He wondered whether she'd simply carried a healthy plumpness to an extreme. But that, while not as surprising, was just as unlikely. Once the Fallen brought their wives to Sheol, the women stayed relatively the same shape and size, aging very slowly. But no one, *no one,* could possibly be pregnant.

Again, this changed the situation. He needed the Fallen to believe in the impossible, to throw out their preconceptions. A pregnant Source was the first step.

Everyone else was the same, though many were missing. He let his eyes drift over each of them, enjoying their discomfort, and then Raziel distracted him. "I see you haven't been informed of my wife's pregnancy."

Cain grinned easily, to annoy them and to keep any further reaction hidden. "May I offer congratulations to both of you? How many goats did you have to sacrifice to achieve such a miracle?"

"No goats," the red-haired woman beside Azazel said. "And I don't reveal trade secrets."

"May I at least congratulate the demon Lilith on her ability to twist the laws of nature?"

Azazel stiffened, and Cain saw the sudden fire that lit the woman's eyes at his gentle slam. Cain smiled with infinite sweetness, just waiting for Azazel to launch himself at him again, but the demon put a hand on his arm. Cain wanted to laugh. Azazel, restrained by a demon.

"I realize you've come here to cause trouble, Cain," Raziel broke in before things could escalate, "but there's nothing new in that. I presume you have another reason for gracing us with your presence after all this time? And where have you been?"

"Most recently? In Australia, clearing up the mess the rest of you left behind. The Nephilim are now gone from Down Under."

"I am gratified to hear it," Raziel said. "Did you

want a parade in your honor or will a simple thank-you suffice?"

"You always were a sarcastic son of a bitch," Cain said pleasantly. "I want to come back."

Raziel froze. In fact, the entire room went motionless, with the possible exception of the pregnant woman. Obviously no one had told her about the notorious Cain. "Impossible," Raziel snapped. "Had it not been for your lies, Ezekiel would still be alive."

Really, this was child's play. "How can you say that, old friend? That was simply a misunderstanding, and I grieve for his loss as much as any of you. Sheol is for the Fallen, of whom I am clearly one. I might remind you that you didn't kick me out—I left of my own accord after that tragic misunderstanding. Therefore I should be able to return whenever I wish to."

"In theory. You left before Azazel could banish you. You've been gone a long time. Why come back now?"

"Perhaps I am lonely," he said gently.

"You aren't capable of such tender feelings, Cain. You've come back to cause trouble. That's all you do."

"You wound me, Raziel. I came back because I miss my own kind. It's difficult to live among humans—they fuss about the most ridiculous things. No doubt due to their foreshortened life spans." He considered going for a winning smile, but Raziel would never believe it, so he aimed instead for polite sincerity.

Raziel surveyed him stonily, but Cain already knew what he was thinking. There was no way he could deny Cain reentry into the sacred haunts of the Fallen, not unless he had proof that Cain meant them harm. Ezekiel's death could be considered an accident, though Cain, of course, had been blamed. As for whether or not Cain meant them any harm— they would find out far too late.

"You would have to abide by our rules," Raziel said finally.

"Of course."

"You realize that we are in the midst of all-out war with Uriel and the Armies of Heaven? There is no guarantee that we will succeed."

"There never is. And I am, if you'll remember, a very good fighter."

"True enough. You have no bonded mate?"

"No." Cain hoped his sudden monosyllable would put them off, but he wasn't counting on it.

"And how long have you been without a mate? How soon do you need to partake of the Source? Because I must warn you, Allie has been called upon to serve far more often than usual, and she needs all her strength. I am not certain another Fallen taking from her might not be too much."

"And on that off chance, you'd banish me?" he returned lightly. "How cold-blooded of you, Raziel. I'd expect as much from Azazel, but you, I thought, would be more concerned with following the letter of the law."

"The letter of the law is that I protect Sheol and the Fallen first, and I would not endanger them for the sake of one rogue angel. Besides, the only way you can find another bonded mate is out in the world of the humans."

"Oh, I wouldn't say I'm a rogue," Cain shot back. "Maybe a bit of a rebel, but any society needs its rebels. In fact, I am in no immediate need of the services of the Source. My wife just died, and I am . . . unready . . . to embark on another relationship." He planned that little break purposefully, to express his manful grief at the loss of his mythical wife. In truth, he had had no mate for hundreds of years, but that was one reality he wasn't ready to share with the rest of the Fallen. Not yet.

Raziel glared at him, and Cain could sense the uneasiness of the gathered Fallen. He glanced over them; for some reason his gaze stopped for a moment on Martha's troubled expression, and his quick mind leapt ahead.

"Ask your seer," he suggested. "I imagine she'll tell you I'm meant to be here, and I'll bring no harm." It was a gamble, but he had always been luckiest when he took extravagant chances. If she had any clear knowledge of the danger he presented, she would already have warned them; therefore he could reasonably assume that she was either a piss-poor seer, as even Raziel had suggested, or that the art of prophecy was as much a fiction as fairness or compassion or the sanctity of the blood-bond.

But he was in no hurry to enlighten them about all the dirty little secrets you could discover when you believed in nothing and questioned everything. That time would come.

All eyes turned to Martha. Calm Martha, with her soft mouth and her big eyes and her determination that would avail her absolutely nothing in the end. If he decided he wanted her, he would take her, body and blood.

She nodded reluctantly, and for some reason he wanted to rumple her soft brown curls as if she were an obedient puppy. "I have seen no danger to the Fallen from his presence," she said carefully, and he wondered what she was leaving out. He'd known almost instantly that there something she wasn't telling, and his curiosity, always insatiable, rose up. He filed that thought away, to be explored later, and turned back to Raziel with a limpid smile.

"You see?" he said in a dulcet tone. "Absolutely harmless. The seer verifies it."

"I didn't say that," she said sharply.

"Then what do you see?" he countered.

He wondered if the others would notice the faint wash of color on her cheekbones. So Miss Martha had been having naughty thoughts about him? How very interesting. Still not enough to push him into making a premature decision, but it looked as if Thomas's quiet widow was a front-runner in his search for the woman to help him bring down the entire organization of the Fallen.

"You may stay," Raziel said abruptly. "On a trial basis, at least. As Michael will tell you, we can use all the warriors we can find. Your former rooms have been reassigned, but you have a choice. You can have a small room on the third floor, or a larger room in the annex near the gardens."

All he needed was Martha's almost imperceptible jerk to know the answer. "The larger one in the annex. If I remember correctly, that area is relatively private. I find, after so many years of being away from communal living, that I value my solitude."

"No one's back there but—"

"We're done, aren't we?" Martha interrupted Raziel just as he was about to say something interesting. She didn't realize Cain had already surmised that she was the sole resident back there. He should be distrustful of things happening too easily, but one look at Martha's mouth and he was more than happy to take the easy way out this time. He wasn't normally a being who believed in signs, but when circumstance aligned with appetite, it was foolish to resist.

Raziel cast the woman an enigmatic look. "We're done," he said. "Martha, you may show Cain his rooms, since you're the only one who sleeps back there, and we'll expect you both for dinner. We need to celebrate the return of our lost lamb."

In wolf's clothing. It required no magic spells or ESP to know that that was exactly what had entered Martha's mind while she was trying not to gnash her teeth over Raziel's lack of discretion. Cain glanced at her, but she was back to refusing to look at him, and he wanted to laugh. Life wasn't about to get any easier for Thomas's widow, and if he were a kinder man, he'd regret the necessity of using her.

But he wasn't a kind man.

Regret was a waste of time. If there was someone so surprisingly tempting to keep him busy, then he was more than happy to take her. She was going to serve him very well indeed.

If only all decisions could be this easy, he thought, smiling at them all agreeably.

CHAPTER
FOUR

FOR A DAY THAT HADN'T STARTED out particularly well, things had gone downhill in a truly spectacular fashion, and the very last thing I wanted to do was show how unnerved I was. This was my home, these were my people, and the dark angel who'd arrived in tongues of flame this morning was a threat to everyone and everything I cared about. I wasn't going to let him hurt them.

Absurd, of course. As if I could protect mighty warriors like Michael and Raziel from one man, one being, when they were far more capable of protecting themselves. I strode down the hallways as quickly as I dared, wanting to dump him in his room and escape.

"Is this a race?" Cain's liquid voice purred from behind me. "Because my legs are longer, and if things really get bad I can fly, so you'll never outrun me."

I slowed down reluctantly and glanced over my shoulder, then jumped. He was much closer than I'd realized, watching me with amusement, as if he knew exactly what I was thinking. "Sorry," I said briefly. "I have things to do."

"Of course you do, little one. I'm certain the Alpha's request ranks far down on your list of priorities."

I slammed to a stop. I was surrounded by tall, graceful people, and my lack of height had always been a sore point with me. "Do not call me little one," I said in a dangerous voice.

His long lashes drooped over his intense eyes. "You *are* little," he pointed out unnecessarily. "Why should the truth distress you?"

I considered all the things I could possibly say and rejected every one of them. "I have things to do," I said again, turning back. I could get past this. I could get past anything.

The main house was a rabbit warren of rooms and balconies, a strange, cantilevered building that looked oddly like a bureau with its drawers left open. When Thomas had died I'd wanted nothing more than to hide away, and I'd left the rooms I'd shared with him for the annex, a section tucked between the main house and the cliff face behind it, well out of the mainstream of Fallen life. I'd been happily, peacefully alone there, content to grow old and die in blessed solitude. There were two more apartments back there, but I had foolishly assumed no one would ever want to stay so far away from the open camaraderie of the Fallen.

I was unpleasantly aware that we hadn't passed anyone at all in the last few minutes. By the time I reached the first of the apartment doors, I was almost running again, and I forced myself to an abrupt stop. "Here you go," I said hurriedly, turning to leave.

He blocked me. Easy enough to do—the halls were much narrower back here, and he was much bigger than I was. "Why the hurry? Didn't Raziel tell you to get me settled, make me comfortable? Don't you think you ought to make sure that I'm pleased with my rooms? I may need something."

"I don't think Raziel cares whether you're pleased with your rooms or not," I said shortly. "Besides, you've lived here before, and you chose."

"So I did." In any other man I would have thought his voice even and pleasant. Not this one. There was just the faintest undertone beneath it, one I couldn't identify. "Nevertheless, I think you need to show me my new quarters, don't you?"

Before I realized what he was doing, he'd reached past me to push the door open, and a moment later he'd crowded my body into the apartment simply by using his size, closing the door behind us, shutting us in.

I skittered away from him with what I hoped was composure, looking around me. This apartment was more than three times the size of my own small room, with a bedroom off to one side and French doors leading out to our shared courtyard. The plain furniture was white, overstuffed, and comfortable-looking, and I could see past the open door to the huge bed.

"I see the Fallen still think they live in the clouds," he drawled, moving past me to survey his surroundings. I wondered if I'd be able to slip away before he could stop me.

"Did they ever?" I was surprised at myself for asking. The origins of the Fallen were as shrouded as Sheol within its mists. To be sure, we all knew the stories: how the original, Lucifer, had been driven out of paradise by the archangel Michael himself, how the next had fallen because of their love for human women. Still later Michael himself had come, and others as well, exiled by the archangel Uriel, who now ruled in the place of the Supreme Being, who had simply granted humankind free will and then disappeared, leaving a sadist in charge. I'd heard stories of strange, unhappy places like the Dark City where souls lived in torment, but never had I heard of what humans thought of as heaven, a place of angels and harps and fluffy clouds.

Thomas had never wanted to answer my questions, and eventually I'd stopped asking. He'd been one of the first to fall, and he'd told me that world was long gone. Only the world of Sheol remained, and we should live in the present, not the past.

We'd done so, until Thomas had been eviscerated and murdered in front of my eyes, and I had gone down in a welter of blood, barely managing to survive. Even now my loose white clothes hid scars that I showed no one.

Cain didn't answer my question either—not that I'd expected him to. He seemed to have forgotten about me, looking around him with an odd expression on his face, and I began to edge toward the door. "I don't know how long it's been since you were here," I continued briskly, "but things run relatively smoothly. If you're hungry you need only think about food, and it will be provided. The Source . . . well, you know what the Source provides."

"Blood," he said absently. And then his gaze focused on me, and his easy smile was back. "I have no need of blood at the moment. On the other hand, it's been a while since I've gotten laid."

The word startled me, as it was doubtless meant to. "I'm afraid everyone here is already bonded. Most widows choose to return to their homes with no memory of their years with the Fallen. Raziel says it's easier that way."

"But not you, sweet Mary," he murmured. "Why didn't you go back home?"

Because I had no home to go to, I thought mutinously, but I wasn't about to admit that to *him.* "I never liked the idea of having my memory wiped clean." I wasn't going to bother correcting him about my name. I couldn't rid myself of the feeling that this was just part of some complicated game he was playing, and that the only way to win was to refuse to play in the first place.

"So clearly you're the only game in town. And how long has it been since you were widowed?"

I froze. "Why do you ask?"

Out in the ordinary world, people talked about angelic smiles. Cain's was the very opposite—charming and devilish. "I simply wondered how long it's been since you've enjoyed the pleasures of the flesh. I'd be more than happy to oblige."

I knew he was trying to shock me. "I don't think so." I sounded calmer than I felt, turning away from him.

I should have been able to reach the door before he did—I was much closer. But he was there ahead of me, smiling down at me, genuinely amused. "Don't look so shocked, sweet Mary. I was only asking. I'm certain I'll find someone else who's interested if you're not."

"Martha!" I snapped, giving in to his goading. "And you're not going to find anyone in Sheol. I told you, everyone here is bonded."

"And you think that would stop me?" His voice was very gentle.

I didn't move. I understood instinctively that he would let me pass if I simply asked him. I looked up at him, into his wicked, beautiful face, and wondered if this was what sin truly was. Seductive, almost irresistible, calling an otherwise sane woman to do things she'd never, ever consider doing, simply by smiling at her. I had no doubt at all that he could manage to seduce whomever he wanted if he set his mind to it. Who could say no to such a soft, sensual lure?

I let the feelings suffuse me for no more than a nanosecond, and then I stepped back. "You never answered Raziel's question," I said, and if my voice sounded tense, I didn't care. "Why are you here?"

He stared at me for a long, speculative moment. "I'm not sure. It could be to seduce you, sweet one."

"Then you may as well leave now, because you're doomed to failure."

"Why?"

His simple question surprised me. "I beg your pardon?"

"I asked you why. Why am I doomed to failure, when I can feel the heat from your body, hear the blood rushing beneath your skin, can practically smell your arousal? Why?"

I had never hit anyone in my life outside of battle. I hated violence, yet I wanted to slap that taunting smile from his mouth, slap him so hard my hand ached from it.

"I think you're deluded." My voice was glacial. "But in the end, I don't really care why you're here. If you don't want to tell anyone the truth, that's your business, as long as you leave me alone. Now, if you'll get out of my way, I have things to do."

"So you keep saying." With that he moved, no longer standing between me and the door, and I hid my relief. "Feel free to change your mind."

I admit it. I gave in to temptation for the first time in what felt like years. "When hell freezes over."

He glanced around him, a faint, distant expression in his eyes. "Darling girl, it already has."

CHAPTER
FIVE

CAIN STARED AT THE DOOR AND realized he was smiling. Sweet, pretty Martha the seer was a firecracker underneath her demure exterior. He'd sensed it almost immediately, and it hadn't taken much prodding to get her to lash out. She'd be more guarded in the future, but he had absolutely no doubt he'd be able to break her down. He never failed when he put his mind to something.

He turned, surveyed the bland room, and sighed. He hated it here, and always had. This was a world of penance for those cursed, and he had never been one to wallow in regret. Life was a banquet of riches to be tasted and even squandered, yet the Fallen locked themselves away in a kind of purgatory.

Not he. He would have thought nothing could possibly make him return, but he was back, all right.

And when he left, if Sheol was still standing, it would never be the same.

He felt the shadow pass by the French doors off the main room, but he didn't turn to look. Only one man would come after him this quickly, only one man that big, and it increased his reputation as being eerily prescient if he greeted him without turning.

The door opened and his visitor stepped inside, surprisingly quiet for such a large man. "Metatron," Cain said in a cool voice. "You're quicker than I expected." He turned to face the big man. "I hope no one saw you come."

The angel Metatron, the most recent of the Fallen, was huge, with arms of granite and legs the size of tree trunks. "What do you think?" he rumbled, looking at Cain with his usual disdain. "We're going to have to be careful of Martha. She may seem quiet, but I don't trust her. She knows things. And I don't mean just her visions."

"I'll be taking care of Martha," Cain said, dropping down on the white sofa. It was surprisingly comfortable—at least the Fallen weren't entirely intent on living like penitents. He'd half expected a monk's cell with a narrow cot. That had been his allotment last time he'd been forced to live here. But then, as usual, they hadn't wanted him. He reminded them of things they wanted to forget.

Metatron simply grunted. Cain liked that about

the man. He seldom spoke, and when he did, he was usually worth listening to. Cain had no illusions about himself—he'd rather listen to his own voice than someone else's droning on and on. In this, at least, they made excellent coconspirators.

"Do you think they suspect anything?" He stretched out his legs in front of him, propping his booted feet on the white coffee table with its fragrant cluster of gardenias floating in a white bowl. Damn, he hated white. His own black clothes were a bit singed from his little magic trick, and he would probably leave scorch marks on the spotless linen. Too fucking bad.

"Raziel and the others?" Metatron gave a derisive snort. "Not a bit. They're so busy getting ready for the next big battle that they haven't time to worry about the likes of you."

Cain didn't particularly care for the "likes of you" slur, but he didn't argue. "Any idea when this next great battle is coming up?"

"You'd have to ask the seer about that one."

Cain smiled reminiscently. "Oh, I intend to. Though I gather her prognostications are a bit . . . uneven."

Metatron shrugged. "Sometimes she's right on. Other times it would be better if she just kept her mouth shut—it only confuses things."

"But Raziel trusts her?"

"Sometimes."

Cain leaned back, crossing his arms behind his head as he considered it. "That could be extremely helpful. I shouldn't have any trouble manipulating her visions to our advantage."

"She's stronger than she appears," Metatron said.

"I always did like a challenge. Then again, I like when things are dead easy as well. What about the Alpha and his Source? A heads-up about Azazel abdicating his post might have been helpful. And how the hell did the new Source get pregnant?"

Once more Metatron shrugged his massive shoulders. "I didn't think it mattered."

Cain controlled his instinctive snarl. "Why don't you let me decide what matters?" He looked out the window into the garden, shrouded in the soft light of Sheol. It was a glorious patchwork of color, unlike everything else here. Life in Sheol was bleached of color. He wanted red splashed across everything, the rich, deep, garnet red of the blood he loved. Blood on his tongue, blood on his skin.

He turned back to Metatron with an easy, deceptive grin. "Anyone you need to warn me about?"

"Michael's suspicious, but he's newly bonded, and what with training the Fallen for battle and bedding his wife, he's easily distracted. Particularly since his wife is Victoria Bellona, the Roman goddess of war."

Cain cocked an eyebrow. "How did he manage to pull that off?"

"The seer. She had a vision, and he fought like hell, but in the end she was right."

"Interesting," Cain murmured. "Who else?"

"Azazel hates you."

"Azazel has always hated me. With good reason. Ezekiel was one of his closest friends. My reasons for hating him are stronger. I'll be taking care of Azazel. You said both Sammael and Asbel are dead?"

Metatron nodded. "As we will be if they realize what we're doing."

"Then the trick, dear friend, is not to get caught."

"I'm not your friend."

Cain laughed. "That's right. As you've often told me, I have no friends."

Metatron said nothing, and Cain grinned. "Point taken," he said. "If you've changed your mind, I can do this on my own. It might take longer—"

"I haven't changed my mind." Ah yes, taciturn Metatron.

"Good," Cain said. "Then let's get busy. I need to look over the wives and see if one of them will be of use. They're all pretty, aren't they?"

"If you like that sort of thing."

"Oh, I do. I like pretty and plain, plump and thin, old and young. Women are delightful, Metatron. You really ought to indulge. It would help you relax."

Metatron just looked at him. "There haven't been

any available women here. They're either bonded or mourning, like Martha."

"I'm not about to let that stop me. You shouldn't either."

"Why do you need to look at the wives? I thought you'd decided the seer would be the most useful."

"Probably. But I haven't seen the others, have I? I'll definitely have the seer on the side—I find her much too tempting. But it's always useful to set the cat among the pigeons, and an unfaithful mate would shake things up quite nicely. Besides, I'll need a second female eventually."

Metatron grunted, though whether in approval or not, Cain couldn't tell. At least he didn't bother to ask why, since Cain had no intention of telling him.

"In any case," he continued, "you'd better get out of here before someone decides to come and see how I'm settling in. We don't want anyone to get the wrong idea." He grinned then. "Come to think of it, maybe we *should* give them the wrong idea. We could always pretend that you and I are romantically involved, unless the Fallen have some edict against that, and—"

"No!" Metatron said in a stifled roar.

Cain looked at him out of limpid eyes. "No, they don't have an edict, or no, we shouldn't pose as lovers?"

Metatron headed for the door, and this time Cain kept his smile to himself. Now that he knew the fastest way to get Metatron out of his rooms, it could come in handy.

"Don't push me, Cain," Metatron snarled, pausing.

"Push you? Me? Never, old friend." He waited for Metatron to remind him that they were far closer to mortal enemies, even if they were reluctant coconspirators, but Metatron simply glared at him and left, closing the French doors silently behind him when Cain knew he wanted to slam them so hard the glass would break.

Two people wanting to slam doors and smash his face in before he'd been in his room for half an hour. He was right on track. By the time he got through with them, the Fallen would be such a mass of anger and upheaval they wouldn't know what hit them.

He expected to find it all extremely entertaining.

CHAPTER SIX

I'D BEEN TRYING TO NAP, WITHOUT much success, when I heard the muffled sound. Someone, a man, had said "No!" so strongly the power of it reached through the thick walls of the annex. I sat up, listening. Who could be visiting Cain? The Alpha, most likely. Certainly not Azazel, who had looked at the newcomer as if he were shark bait and Azazel was a great white. Michael hadn't looked much happier.

I glanced toward the narrow glass-paned door that led from my small room to the courtyard I shared with Cain. The courtyard I would never use again, at least not until he left or moved to more central quarters. It was going to be difficult enough trying to avoid him in the narrow hallways back here. No longer would I lie naked beneath the blissful rays of a sun that never burned, never tanned, just soothed me with warm, radiant heat.

It was a price I was willing to pay. If things got bad enough, I could always ask Raziel and Allie to move me to a room up in the big house. I'd feel safer there, surrounded by the people who were more family to me than anybody I'd grown up with. I wasn't sure why I thought safety was an issue. There was no reason to think that Cain was any particular danger to me. Why should he be?

Anyway, I had no intention of giving him the satisfaction of driving me away. I was an inventive woman—I could tell him I'd had a vision requiring me to move. That I was supposed to be close to Allie as her time grew nearer.

I hated the thought of using my visions, of lying to get out of an uncomfortable situation. The prophecies were already extremely dodgy—if I started manufacturing them whenever things got difficult, I would destroy what little credibility I had.

I pulled myself into a sitting position, listening, but there was no more sound from the rooms next to mine. Maybe I'd be better off if everyone ignored my dreams and portents. They were a curse, nothing but trouble, and I'd be much happier slipping back into my role as quiet little Martha, Thomas's widow.

I'd even considered lying about my confusing bona fide visions. I didn't dare risk it—knowing Allie was pregnant before she did enabled her to take better care of herself. Knowing the ancient Roman goddess of war, Victoria Bellona, needed to come to Sheol before the first battle with Uriel meant we had a chance of surviving. Knowing Tory was going to die in that battle gave Allie a chance to save her, bring her back.

No, I couldn't turn my back on my responsibilities, no matter how difficult. And I couldn't run away simply because I found our newly returned fallen angel unsettling. I wasn't used to all that charm and intensity directed at me. I didn't like it. But I could put up with it.

Besides, sooner or later he'd go off hunting for a mate—in my experience, the Fallen didn't remain single for long. And once he did, he'd probably settle down and become like all the others.

Or not. I couldn't quite see it. Cain was too different from the rest of them, with that wicked, taunting smile. The Fallen had never been much for smiling. More likely he'd simply leave once more and not return until long after my mortal life had ended. One could only hope.

Pushing myself out of bed, I paced my room. Sleep was evading me—maybe tonight would be better. Now that the dark man of my vision had arrived, I didn't have to fear dreaming so much. Another prophecy was unlikely to come for weeks or even months. I could throw myself into the preparations for the baby, the first baby ever to appear in the endless time since angels had first tumbled to earth. After all, in my mortal life I had mostly raised the children around me, siblings or not, and I knew about babies. I had even helped my mother deliver one of them in our dismal apartment with no electricity or heat, only running water. Allie's delivery would be a piece of cake compared to that, and Rachel would be in charge.

A hot shower went a ways toward making me feel human. For some reason, it took me much longer than usual to dress—everything seemed to fit strangely and feel uncomfortable. I finally ended up in a dress, something simple, with ankle-length skirts flowing around me and a high-enough neckline to cover my scars. I seldom bothered with makeup, but my face was pale, my eyes looked a little hollow, and I didn't like my reflection. Brushing on some blush and mascara, I stared at the new and improved Martha in dismay before wiping it all off.

I took off the discreet gold hoop earrings that Thomas had given me when we were mated, earrings that I never wore. I would have gone back and changed my dress to an enveloping shroud if I'd had time, but the dinner chime had already rung, and Raziel would grumble if I was late. Even worse, Tory and Allie would wonder why, and quiz me until I came up with a believable answer. Or, worst of all, they might make a totally absurd guess that I was reacting to the appearance of the new man in our midst, which was obviously ridiculous.

I hurried along the hallways, keeping an eye out for Cain. The last thing I wanted was to march in at the same moment he did, like a bonded couple. With any luck he'd forget how to get there and spend dinner wandering the labyrinthine passageways. Not charitable of me, but I was desperate for any kind of reprieve from his mercurial presence. It disturbed me in ways I couldn't begin to fathom.

People were already seating themselves when I skidded into the assembly hall. This had been Allie's idea, that the Fallen and their mates should share a daily meal. It fostered their skills when working together, fighting together, and only those newly bonded were excused. I dashed to my seat beside Tory, keeping my head down.

It was then I noticed how damnably low-cut my dress was, even if the scarring was hidden, and I moaned in despair. I couldn't very well drape a napkin over my front, much as I wanted to.

"What's wrong?" Tory whispered.

"I left the room in my underwear," I muttered.

"I can fix that," she said cheerfully, pulling the shawl from around her own shoulders and draping it over me. It was soft wool, fine as silk, and I covered myself gratefully.

"Now, that's a crying shame," came an all-too-familiar voice on my left, and I turned to watch Cain slip into the seat that had once been Asbel's.

Before I realized what I was doing I groaned out loud, then at least had the presence of mind to keep from clapping my hands over my traitorous mouth. Averting my gaze didn't help—I could feel him, the heat of his body; I could smell him, the scent of leather and sea air and indefinable male like no other. "Are you feeling sick, Miss Mary?" he inquired solicitously. "I heard you groan—are you in need of a healer?"

I had no choice but to look up at him, and I wanted to bang my forehead on the table in front of me in frustration. I met his strange silver-gray gaze, keeping my emotions hidden.

"I'm perfectly fine," I said politely. "Thanks for asking."

His mobile mouth curved in a smile. *"De nada,"* he murmured. "Though I take it you have a chill."

"A chill?" I echoed, momentarily confused.

He nodded toward my shoulders draped in Tory's shawl. "You're swathed like a mummy. Maybe I should see about getting the heat turned up in our rooms."

I managed to hide my reaction to that one. He made it sound like we were sharing a room, and for some reason I felt my body warm. Presumably in embarrassment. "The heat in my separate room will be just fine for me," I said. Bad phrasing, but it was too late.

I should have known he wouldn't let it slide. "The heat in your *separate room*?" he echoed, amused. "Did you think we were going to share?"

"Don't be ridiculous," I snapped, turning my back on him, by now thoroughly irritated, still gripping the shawl around me. It was too hot, but I was damned if I was going to let go.

Tory was watching all this with great interest in her green eyes. She was the newest addition to Sheol, not counting the albatross on my left, and after a rough beginning we had become good friends. It had been my stupid vision that had thrown her entire life into upheaval, and the half-assed nature of my prophecy hadn't helped, but Tory wasn't one to blame me for something that was out of my control. Besides, she'd managed to pluck a ridiculously happy ending out of death and disaster, and her happiness washed over everyone.

"Interesting," she murmured in an undertone as the conversation around the table rose and Cain forgot about taunting me, caught up in a conversation with Tamlel. "I've never seen you so rattled."

"Wouldn't you be?" I said, equally quiet. "He's trying to get my goat and I don't know why."

Her grin was sly. "I don't think it's your goat he's interested in."

I felt color suffuse my face. "Don't be ridiculous. He strikes me as the sort who wants to cause trouble wherever he can, and he sees me as a likely victim. With luck he'll find someone else to torment. That, or he'll go away. Soon."

"Oh, I don't know. I think he's an interesting addition. He'll shake things up a bit."

"I don't like things shaken up. I like stability."

"I know you do, sweetness," Tory said soothingly. "But we're at war. That's hardly stable."

"All the more reason for the Fallen to remain constant. Having an outsider come in and disturb everyone—"

"Who's disturbing everyone?" A silken voice was at my ear, and I could have kicked myself. I angled my body just slightly toward him, giving him as little of my attention as possible.

"We were having a private discussion," I said in what I hoped was a suitably chilling voice.

"Then you shouldn't be having it at the dinner table." He was too close to me. The tables in the assembly hall were massive—there was plenty of room for all of us. Tory wasn't practically in my lap, and when Tam had been on my left side, he hadn't pushed his energy all over me like a blanket of nettles. Not like this man.

"Point taken," I said, turning back to the watchful Tory. He'd chosen that moment to move as well, and my shoulder brushed against him. It was as if I'd been hit by the mother of all static-electric shocks—I jumped back with a muffled curse, almost landing on Tory.

He'd done it on purpose, I knew it, and I was about to give in to temptation and snap at him when I saw his eyes. He was looking as startled as I felt. A moment later that expression was gone, and he was smiling down at me. "You're a dangerous woman, Martha."

Enough was enough. I needed time to compose myself. This man had disrupted my life in a few short hours, with nothing more than a wicked smile and an accidental touch, and I needed to put it in perspective.

I started to push back from the table, searching for an excuse to leave, when Tory put a restraining hand on my arm. The shake of her head was almost imperceptible, and as she leaned forward to help herself to the mounds of buttery mashed potatoes in front of us, she whispered, "Don't let him get away with it. You're tougher than that. Grow a pair."

I froze. She was right—I was being a coward. Then again, I had no delusions that I was a warrior like most of the Fallen and their mates. I had been trained to fight—everyone in Sheol had—but I'd spent the first battle with Uriel's armies in the infirmary, tending to the wounded. I had already barely survived one horrific skirmish with the Nephilim, and even if my wounds were now scars, the ones inside had never quite healed. I could fight if I had to. But I would rather run and cower, much as it shamed me.

Cain couldn't hurt me, I reminded myself. He was an arrogant little boy tugging on my braids to make me react, wanting to cause mischief wherever he could. I had no idea why—maybe it was simply his nature, which would explain why Raziel and Azazel had welcomed his reappearance with a singular lack of enthusiasm.

"You're right," I said to Tory. "Pass me the potatoes." There was nothing like buttery carbs to make a girl feel better.

Somehow I made it through dinner, with Tory's help and plenty of comfort food. Cain must have decided he'd had enough fun tormenting me; for the rest of the meal, his attention was elsewhere. I held myself stiffly, making certain I didn't accidentally brush against him, but he was turned partly away, talking with Tam, and instinctively I knew I was safe. For now.

WHAT THE HELL had happened? If there'd been a carpet beneath the banquet tables, Cain would have thought she'd been rubbing her shoes against it simply to give him the mother of all shocks. But they were by the ocean, the air was moist and light, and static electricity was unlikely.

His plan had been simple—start to move in on her. All that had gone sideways with a spark that zapped him so hard he'd almost cursed out loud. He had no idea how she'd done it or why, but he'd be a fool if he didn't respect her power. She'd wanted to keep him away, and she didn't mind using magic to do so.

It surprised him. Magic existed in this world as well as the ordinary one, but most people avoided any outward use of it. Of course, he'd used it to herald his arrival, and she was probably fighting back on his terms. He was impressed.

Impressed enough to change tacks. Advance and retreat was the best way to stalk a victim, which was how he saw her. He was a predator, and he had decided she was just what he needed, particularly after checking out the other choices during the endless dinner. He would have her, but right now she was too wary, just about ready to jump out of her skin.

He would give her a little time to lull her fears. And then, when she least expected it, he would pounce.

But first he had to figure out how the hell she'd done that.

CHAPTER
SEVEN

RAZIEL SLID INTO BED BESIDE HIS wife, pulling her into his arms and absently stroking her rounded belly. The babe inside leapt at his touch, a fact that always shocked him, but he continued the caress, for her, for him, for whatever lay inside her.

It was a fear he'd shared with no one. He didn't trust fate, didn't trust Uriel. This miracle had been granted them, due in no small part to the demon patron of women and fertility, Lilith—who was now the perfectly normal Rachel—but he was waiting for the other shoe to drop. He was deeply, secretly afraid that Allie would die, that the babe would be some kind of horror, or, if it was normal, that it too would die. No way would Uriel allow a child of the Fallen to be born. No way he'd allow any part of their curse to be broken.

Even the seer's insistence that all would be well meant nothing. Martha's visions were imperfect at best, infuriating and disruptive at worst. She'd never been precisely wrong, but the realization of those prophecies could be tangled indeed. She insisted that Allie would be delivered of a healthy baby, and that mother and child would be well.

He didn't believe it.

"Is everything all right?" Allie said sleepily.

"Everything's perfect," he said, kissing the side of her neck, breathing in her sweet scent. It was different in pregnancy, and it had taken him a while to recognize the new note in her own unique fragrance. It was the sweetness of milk.

He shut his eyes, a silent prayer suffusing him. He, who never prayed, because he knew more than anyone the uselessness of it.

"Now, that's a lie," Allie said, and for a he moment he froze. Had she guessed his misgivings? The worst thing he could do would be to pass on his fears. She had enough of her own, the natural uncertainties of a first-time mother, Martha had told him.

And then she continued, "You've never told me about Cain, but I saw the way you all acted around him. You don't like that he's returned to Sheol. Why?"

He didn't show his relief, simply pulled her against him, spoonlike. "He's up to something. He's tricky, deceitful, and troublemaking. Always has been."

"Doesn't sound very angelic to me," she said, curling into him contentedly. "Why is he so different? When did he fall?"

Raziel hesitated, but only for a moment. She was the Source to his Alpha, and her insights and wisdom had been invaluable over the years. But Cain was a legacy he would have preferred to forget.

He no longer had that choice. "Cain fell when we did. There were two hundred of us, sent to earth to teach the children of men."

"That's right," she murmured sleepily. "You taught them makeup." She giggled.

"Disrespectful wench," he said, giving her a tiny bite on the back of her neck. "Just because some deranged translation of a semideranged prophet got passed around here a few years ago . . ."

"I know, I know, the Book of Enoch is a tissue of lies." She chuckled softly. "You taught them astrology, Azazel taught them warfare and armaments. What did Cain teach them?"

He hesitated. "He was sent to teach humans about sex."

Allie laughed. "I thought that's what all of you did."

"That was an accident."

"Having sex with a woman was an accident?" she scoffed.

"Falling in love with them was." He always had to tread carefully with this. In his limitless existence he had loved many women. He knew, deep inside, that Allie was different, a soul mate whose bond would never break. When she ceased to exist, so would he, but he didn't tell her that. She would argue with him, and she would still suffer from irrational jealousy.

"I can believe that," she said in a deceptively steady voice. "You certainly did your best not to fall in love with me."

"And I was a lot stronger by the time you came around. Back when we were first sent to earth, we were new, unused to temptation. We didn't even realize what we were feeling for the human women was lust—no such thing had existed. But Cain knew. He was the first to give in. He fell in love with a young girl named Tamarr, and he broke the cardinal rule. He bedded her, and got her pregnant."

"And then *après moi le déluge*?"

He could almost laugh. Almost. "Not quite. No mass capitulation by the rest of the angels. The Supreme Power discovered what had happened. And he sent Uriel to deal with the situation." He felt her body tense, her warm, pliant skin grown suddenly cold, and he pulled her tighter against him.

"What happened?"

"He killed her. Gutted her, then burned her while she still lived, while Cain screamed and fought and was forced to watch. She was pregnant at the time."

There was a long silence in his bed, and his lovely,

warm, pregnant wife slowly pulled out of his arms, turning over with difficulty to look at him in the moonlight. "And what were the rest of you doing while this was going on?"

It wasn't as if lying was even an option. They knew each other's minds, and she already knew the answer. She was just waiting for his admission. "We did nothing. We couldn't. Even if we had been able to move, we might not have. We thought it was God's law. We didn't know he'd already abandoned us to free will."

She was silent for a long moment, and made no effort to move closer. "And then what happened? Was Cain then the first to fall after Lucifer?"

He shook his head. "Cain was taken back with Uriel. I don't know what happened to him, what torture he went through. But once he'd given in, everything changed. You know the old myth about Adam and Eve?"

"Now you're telling me they didn't exist either? Then how does Rachel fit in? You can't have Lilith without Adam and Eve."

"It's part history, part mythology, part magic, all mixed up into such a complicated tangle that no one can unravel it. People simply believe the parts that resonate. The part about the snake . . ." He hesitated.

She waited.

"The snake was Cain, bringing sinful knowledge to the holy. Once he bedded Tamarr, we all started noticing. It was as if our hormones and, even worse, our emotions had finally begun working."

"'They looked upon the daughters of men and knew them,'" she quoted, somewhat inaccurately. "And what did this mean for Cain?"

"We were thrown to earth, fallen, cursed, never to return. And Cain was sent down to join us."

"That must have been a happy reunion. Did he try to kill you? I would have."

He shook his head. "He had always been the sunniest of us. Charming, sweet, a boy filled with limitless joy and affection. When he returned, he was like the dark shadow of that boy. Still charming, but twisted, manipulative, dangerous. He stayed with us for a time, then vanished who knows where, and it's been his habit ever since. He comes and goes, not tethered to Sheol. You needn't worry he'll drink from you—he seems to have little need."

"I wasn't worried," she said. "But isn't he a blood-eater?"

"He is. His curse is the same as ours. But apparently he can survive longer periods of time without it. Either that, or he's never gone more than a few weeks without a bonded mate."

"I could believe that. Cain is . . . like catnip. Or chocolate. Or ice cream. Or single-malt whiskey. You know he's bad for you, but he looks so tasty."

He was aware of the unpleasant tightness to his

jaw. Jealousy had never been part of his makeup, and he had yet to accept it. Allie was as bonded to him as he was to her. But even the thought of her looking at another man sent fury through him. When others fed from her, he wanted to hit them. This was worse. He'd be damned if he let Cain feed from her. He'd kill him first. "He's dangerous," he said flatly. "Every time he's come back here, disaster has followed, and he always has a hidden agenda. The last time he came, our brother Ezekiel died."

"Did he murder him?"

"No. It's complicated. But Ezekiel would still be alive if he hadn't listened to Cain."

She nodded, accepting it for the moment. Then she said, "Well, I would think you could rule out that he's working for Uriel. If he hates all of you, then he would have even more reason to hate Uriel."

"Maybe," he said. "But we were his friends, his brothers. We betrayed him, and then followed in his footsteps. Those are things that can't be forgiven."

She thought about it for a long moment, and he wanted to pull her back against him, feel her smooth, sleek, warm body against his. Warmer now in her pregnancy, deliciously warm. "Did you ever tell him you were sorry?"

He made a sound of disgust. "Don't be such a human. You think saying 'I'm sorry' is worth anything after such a betrayal?"

Not a good move on his part. "I *am* human," she said icily. "And it's a start." She managed to edge even farther away from him—no mean feat, considering her pregnant belly.

"I don't think he'd listen," he said in a more conciliatory tone. "But you can see why I view his sudden arrival with less than complete enthusiasm. I don't know what he could do to harm us, short of betraying us to Uriel, but I wouldn't put it past him to try."

"So what does he want with Martha?"

"Martha? What makes you think he wants anything to do with her?" he said, mystified.

Allie sighed, and he knew she was rolling her eyes at his cluelessness. "It's plain as day to anyone who pays attention. He's zeroing in on Martha, and she's like a butterfly in a spider's web. She doesn't know how to deal with him. I don't remember much about Thomas, but I've been told he was one of the sweetest, kindest of men, and he brought her here when she was only seventeen. She wouldn't know how to deal with someone like Cain."

"No, she wouldn't," he agreed. "But I think you're wrong. Oh, you might have seen Cain teasing her. All he'd have to do was guess that he made her nervous, and he wouldn't have been able to resist taunting her."

"Nice guy," Allie muttered.

"That's what I've been trying to tell you. But I doubt he has any real interest in Martha. He's much more likely to go after someone's bonded mate—he's done that in the past."

"How is that even possible? I thought the bond was unbreakable," she said, shocked.

"It is. Unless, apparently, you've got someone as ancient and powerful as Cain doing his best to disrupt things."

"I don't think that's going to happen. I think he wants Martha."

"You're wrong," he said flatly. "There's nothing to be gained by taking Martha. He's only interested in causing chaos. There's no reason for him to be interested in someone like her."

She moved even farther away, more displeased than ever. He'd shot himself in the foot again. "You're an asshole," she snapped. "Martha's beautiful!"

"I didn't say she wasn't." His voice was placating. At this rate, he was never going to get any sleep. "But she's beautiful in a very quiet way, and Cain isn't into subtlety. If you're worried about Martha, you can take my word for it—she's the last woman Cain would go after."

"I doubt it. A pregnant Source is even less appealing."

Ah, the night was saved, he thought with relief. "No," he said, with complete honesty. "I can't imagine any man being able to keep his hands off you, and you're even more beautiful pregnant. He knows if he comes near you he'd die a slow, horrible death, and he's too smart to try. But he would in the blink of an eye if he had the chance."

He heard her release her breath, felt her tense body soften. "Humph," she said, but he'd reached her. "I think you're prejudiced."

"I'm the Alpha. I'm too old and wise to be subjective."

She laughed, the last of the tension leaving their bed, and he felt her move marginally closer again. He crossed the rest of the distance, pulling her against him, burying his face in her shoulder.

"Indulge me," she said finally. "Keep an eye out for Martha."

"I'll be watching Cain like a hawk anyway. If he goes near Martha, I'll know it, and I can put a stop to it. I promise."

She covered his hand with hers, moving it over her belly, and he could feel the fetus move beneath their combined touch. Cain was forgotten as another irrational prayer fought its way past his defenses.

Please let everything be all right. Let Martha be right this time. Let all things be well.

CHAPTER
EIGHT

I DIDN'T THINK I'D BE ABLE TO SLEEP. Despite my scars, I liked to sleep naked, the door and windows of my small room open to the soft night air. I loved listening to the sound of the surf in the distance, the gentle breezes through the trees, the scent of flowers and growing things mixed with the salt tang of the ocean.

He was in the room next door. Or he would be—I knew after I made my way surreptitiously down our shared hallway that he wasn't there at the moment. And as long as he was so close, there was no way I was going to leave the door open to our shared garden. I didn't even want to crack my window, but I would suffocate with it shut. Not literally—the rooms in Sheol, despite Cain's suggestion that he could adjust the thermostat, were all a perfectly controlled temperature, a necessity in a society that couldn't tolerate flame. But I needed at least a trace of fresh air, psychologically if not physically.

For the first time I locked both doors, then gave myself a figurative shake. What was wrong with me? He was hardly going to loom up and try to break in to get to my thoroughly unremarkable self.

Still, there was no way I was stripping. Instead of taking clothes off, I put more on—an oversize shirt over the dress, then a sweater over that before I climbed into bed. Five minutes later I climbed out, took off the smothering sweater, and climbed back in. Another ten minutes and I stripped off my clothes and replaced them with the loose pants and shirt I usually wore during the daytime. I climbed back into bed, suitably armored, and lay still, listening for him. Waiting for him.

Until I fell into a deep, exhausted sleep.

I knew it was a dream before it started, and even smothered in deep sleep I tried to shake it off. I never knew whether the things I saw and felt were actual dreams or visions of a possible future, and the weight of those visions was too much. I tried to sink deeper into slumber, to shut off my thoughts, but the voice floated on the gentle breeze, slipped into my room, under my skin, inside me, a soft, insistent voice.

Come to me.

I didn't recognize it. It wasn't Thomas—his voice had been higher pitched, softer. There was an insistent roughness to the silent voice that called to me, and I kicked out, shoving my covers away from me, onto the floor.

I could feel his hands on me, sliding up my arms, cupping my face, and my eyelids fluttered open for a second. No one. This was a dream, nothing more, a sweet, lovely dream. I closed my eyes as his lips feathered softly against mine, a sweet, gentle kiss from a tender, tentative lover, and it felt so real I sighed. Not Thomas. He had never been demanding, but this was unlike his kisses. This was unlike any kiss I had ever felt, and I smiled against his lips.

His tongue was against my closed mouth, tracing the line between my lips, and for a moment tension filled me. I didn't like that kind of kissing, and neither had Thomas. We had kissed chastely, even when he was moving inside me. Why was this dream changing things?

Don't fight it, the soft voice whispered against my lips. *It's just a dream.*

So it was. I relaxed my tense muscles as he covered my mouth with his, and he coaxed my lips open so easily, so gently; the feel of his tongue in my mouth was different from anything I had ever felt, erotic, arousing, and I let him kiss me, his tongue tasting me, so thoroughly that I forgot to breathe, lost in the strange, seductive sensation that wasn't real.

He lifted his head and with a note of laughter

whispered, *Breathe, Martha*. I let out my pent-up breath and wondered if I could I feel him, my phantom lover. I lifted my hands tentatively and felt them caught in his; he brought them to rest on his warm, bare shoulders.

I jerked, startled by the heat of his flesh, and almost opened my eyes again, but I remembered this was a dream. If it were real I would have heard him, known he was here. If I opened my eyes all this would stop, and I didn't want to let go. Just for once I could do as he said. Stop fighting it.

He was leaning over me, and I felt the silken wash of his long hair. I turned my face into it, and it smelled like the sea, like leather, like sex itself. I racked my brain, trying to remember who smelled like that. Who was I fantasizing about in this erotic dream that had come out of nowhere?

His hands slid down, and I realized I was naked. It didn't matter—in a fantasy world, I had no scars crisscrossing my body. In a fantasy world, I was perfect, beautiful, irresistible, and when his hands covered my breasts I arched up against him. I could feel my nipples bud and tighten beneath his practiced fingers, and I heard my moan in the stillness. For a moment I froze, afraid it would break the spell, but then his lips closed around my nipple, pulling at it, sucking, and I could feel it down my body and between my legs, and it was suddenly becoming too real. Real, as his hand slid over my stomach, between my legs, cupping me, and I jerked, frightened, about to open my eyes and dispel the powerful dream.

His other hand closed over my eyes, a benediction, and his voice was soft in my ear. *Just a dream, sweetness. Let go.*

Yes, just a dream. Nothing to be frightened of, nothing to be ashamed of. No one could see, no one could hear, no one would know. His tongue touched my other breast, and I felt the soft bite of his teeth as his fingers slid against me, knowing just where to touch, how hard, how soft. Of course he knew. He was me, he was my imagination, he would know what I liked. When he slid his fingers inside me, I bit my lip rather than cry out again and risk waking up. I needed to finish this, needed to desperately, and I arched my hips up against his hand as his fingers moved inside me, the heel of his hand pressed against my clitoris, and his mouth was at my breast, sucking, pulling, pressing, rubbing, pushing, thrusting—

The orgasm took me by surprise, more powerful than anything I had ever felt. I screamed, the sound sharp in the silent room, and fell off the bed onto the hard marble floor. I lay still for a moment, completely awake, wrapped in a welter of sheets and blankets, and I clutched at my clothes. Of course I still wore them. I was alone, as I had always been. As I always would be.

I sat up, pushing the covers away in disgust. I touched myself, finding my nipples hard against the loose shirt, and I didn't need to check to know I was wet between my legs. I was thoroughly and completely aroused, my body that of a woman well satisfied.

It wasn't the truth, of course. It wasn't a portent, a sign of the future, a vision. It was simply the female equivalent of a wet dream. Nothing to be ashamed of, though shame was hovering. No one knew but me. And I liked it. Shameful or not, I wanted more.

I climbed back onto the bed, too hot for covers now, and felt the soft breeze blow over my heated flesh. I glanced over at the door to the courtyard, but it was still locked, and I was safe. I didn't know what had caused the dream, and I didn't care. It was nobody else's business. I stripped off my clothes, leaving them where they fell, and lay back against the cool sheet, gloriously naked. And this time my sleep was dreamless.

WAKING LATE THE next morning, I scrambled out of bed in sudden guilt and worry. A strange sense of oppression and anticipation rippled through me—until I remembered what had caused it. The sun was already up in the sky, some of the overnight mist had burned off, and the man next door wasn't in residence. I wasn't sure how I knew that, but I did. Maybe he'd never come back last night. Either way, it was none of my business. He had nothing to do with my dreams last night, nothing at all. Those were mine.

Even sleeping late, I was still an earlier riser than many in Sheol. As I walked down to the sea, I could hear the sounds of people training under the archangel Michael's stern tutelage, the noise drifting from the open doors of the huge room where they worked, but the beach was empty. I kicked off my sandals at the edge of the water and walked through the ripples of surf, feeling the sun beat down on me, drying my freshly washed hair into a mass of annoying curls around my face. I'd hoped cutting it short would give me some kind of gravitas, despite my height. Instead I had ended up looking like a waif, and there was no room for waifs in a world of oversize, too-beautiful fallen angels.

I gazed out at the dark blue water as I waded along the shore. It was another illusion that I couldn't get rid of. The ocean was a healing world for the Fallen—its waters could mend even a mortal blow in an angel—but for their human counterparts it was simply water. There was no reason I should feel strengthened and healed when I went into the sea that lay at our doorstep, but I did, and Michael had taught us that perception was half the battle. If we believed we would triumph, we would. If I believed the ocean strengthened and healed me, then emotionally, at least, it would.

It wouldn't heal me physically. I'd already tried that surreptitiously, hoping the cool, cleansing water would wash away the scars. It hadn't, but when I'd emerged that first time, I could feel their importance slipping away.

In fact, I hadn't thought about the ugly scars marring my flesh for a long time, months, perhaps years. Not until Cain had arrived in a shower of flame.

I was annoyed with myself. I had things to do today, yet the erotic dream lingered. I could still *feel* it. Whether I wanted to fight or not, everyone was required to spend at least two hours a day in combat training, and nothing would exempt me. It was hard, exhausting work, but I liked how strong it made me feel, the pleasant sense of tiredness that suffused my body. I would train twice as hard today, I promised myself. Work my body so hard that I was too tired to pay attention to anyone, so hard that my sleep would be dreamless.

I turned, ready to head back—and saw him perched on the cliffs overhead, the very same bluff where Raziel flew when he needed to think. Raziel hadn't been bred to run this unruly bunch of fallen ones. It had always been Azazel's task, through untold millennia, to guide the Fallen in their ongoing battle against Uriel and his viciously cruel decrees. There had been centuries of détente, and then the war would flare up again, as it had when Allie first came to Sheol.

But something had snapped inside Azazel when his beloved wife Sarah fell in the same battle that took Thomas, and he'd disappeared, leaving everything to Raziel. It wasn't until he'd returned, bringing with him the embodiment of what had once been the most powerful female entity in the universe, that it became clear everything was about to change.

But it wasn't Raziel up there, overseeing his people. It was Cain, the dark angel. Watching us.

I glanced up at him. What was he looking at, so far out to sea?

I could feel his gaze slide over me, and I jerked my eyes away and started walking. He was probably looking right through me, not realizing or caring who the lone woman on the beach was.

Allie was on temporary bed rest after some minor cramping had paralyzed her with fear. She shouldn't have gotten up yesterday, but the curiosity had been too much for her to withstand.

I wasn't the slightest bit worried about her. At least in this one matter, my vision was completely clear. Allie would deliver a strong, healthy baby, and she would be fine.

There wasn't much I could do to calm Raziel's

fears. It was his choice to believe in the best or the worst, and I couldn't help him. I would work in my garden, visit with Allie, put in my time training. I would follow my usual peaceful routine and forget all about the dark angel who watched me.

Work in Sheol was optional—there was no need for me to tend the patch of earth filled with healing plants and flowers, but putting my hands in the rich, warm earth grounded me, calmed me, just as the ocean did. One of my mother's friends had been obsessed with astrology, and I still remembered her words from when I was seven years old. She'd insisted on doing my chart, and after much prodding it turned out my mother actually remembered what time I'd been born. The beginning of the end of her freedom, she'd said, so she'd paid attention, but this time her apathy brought results. According to Latierra, I was Taurus with Cancer rising and too much Scorpio in my chart. Being told I was sensuous was an unsettling concept when I was seven, and in a high-rise tenement in a concrete jungle, I couldn't understand what she meant by a connection to the earth. In the ugly Midwestern city, there was no ocean to call to me, and I'd ignored Latierra's insistence that I was destined for great and wonderful things.

I liked to think I'd had no visions back then, trapped in that dark, chaotic life, but that wasn't true. I had known I'd be rescued. I knew someone would come for me, and in fact, I'd known it would be an angel. When I was younger I thought that simply meant I would die, and I viewed that future with the calm acceptance of a morbidly romantic adolescent. I read everything I could find, escaping into the world of novels, and I pictured myself as Beth from *Little Women*, calm and sweet and doomed.

So when my angel had appeared, I'd gone willingly, not even questioning. I'd left my siblings behind, secure in the knowledge that the latest man in my mother's life was clean and sober and responsible. He would look after them and love them as best he could, protect them from the worst of our mother's choices. I could go live my life now, with my dark angel.

But he hadn't been a dark angel. I'd been wrong about that part. Thomas had been angelically fair, sweet and open, generous and loving, and he'd gone a long way in the task of healing my heart and soul. I'd been like a tightly curled bud, hiding from the world, and I flowered under Thomas's gentle coaxing. I'd given him everything I could, moving closer and closer to the kind of bond others took for granted and I longed for.

And then the Nephilim had attacked.

It had taken me so long to heal I'd barely had time to mourn him. I'd been delirious with pain and drugs, and I'd accepted his loss with grief, despair, and guilt. I had never truly given him what he deserved. Not my complete trust. And not my blood.

Something had always kept me from that final connection, and he'd calmly made do with the Source until I was ready. I understood the curse, the reluctant need, but I wasn't ready to offer my blood to my husband's mouth. That night, after the Nephilim were driven from our world forever, I was planning to give him that final trust.

Instead he'd been torn apart, screaming, as I'd tried to get to him, and my own body had been slashed open, my blood spilling on the beach among all the others, and I had reached out my hand, willing to join him in death.

But I had lived. Eventually I had healed. The only signs of that horrible day were the lines across my body, the parallel scars from the claws of the Nephilim. And the guilt and emptiness in my heart.

The garden had gone a long way toward healing me. There had been no medicinal plants in Sheol, since there was little illness, but flowers abounded everywhere except in the courtyard beyond my room. The patch of land outside the annex had been ready and fertile, and it had embraced the transplantings and the seeds I had found with enthusiasm. I had grown flowers and plants with riotous abandon, letting the brilliant color wash over me, purples and pinks, blues and yellows and every shade of red; and the feel of the rich loam on my hands, the scent and taste and delight of it all, were my rescue and my solace. Until Cain had invaded my serenity.

I was a fool to let him affect me so. Besides, he was still up on the bluff. He appeared to have forgotten about me, thank God. I could safely tend my garden.

The late-morning air was soft and cool, a breeze ruffling my hair and my loose clothes as I knelt in the dirt, carefully pinching back unruly offshoots. I would need to transplant some of the bloodred anemones, perhaps move some to one of the front gardens. I could put a small container garden on the tiny balcony outside of Allie and Raziel's top-floor apartment—the anemones would provide a burst of color for Allie to enjoy during her bed rest.

Latierra had been right. I was a sensual being—I loved tastes and textures and smells; I loved everything about the earth and the sea and life in general. It was full of such wonderful things that one simply needed to notice to enjoy. An older friend of my mother's used to say, "Stop and smell the roses." I'd always wondered about that—there were certainly no roses where we'd lived.

But now I understood. And I had planted a gloriously fragrant rosebush just under my window, so that the scent could drift into my sleep and cushion my dreams.

I sat back on my heels, looking at the barely restrained effusion of color, well satisfied, until I heard a voice behind me.

"This doesn't look like you," Cain said lazily. "It's too wild. You're hardly the type to let gardens sprawl all over the place, full of lush flowers and tangled greenery."

I looked up, not moving, and resisted the urge to scowl. I didn't know what to say. I could hardly defend the haphazard mass of scents and colors that I nurtured so carefully. I didn't understand it myself. "Things grow very rapidly here," I said in a noncommittal voice. "It's hard to keep up with it."

"You forget—I used to live here. Gardens will behave exactly as you want them to. You must like all this chaos, despite your outward appearance, and I wonder why."

I pushed my hair out of my face. "You can draw your own conclusions," I said severely. Because he would, and my only defense was to ignore him. "Now, go away and leave me alone."

His mouth curved in amusement, and of course he stayed put. "You're quite a mess," he said, looking me over. "Your pants are caked with mud, your hands are filthy, and you've got a streak of dirt right"—he reached out toward my cheekbone, then hesitated—

"here." He didn't connect, but I could feel him, feel the warmth of his skin, too close. The odd buzz of power between us.

I didn't jerk back as I wanted to, and I was proud of myself. "Please don't touch me," I said in a controlled voice, and scrambled to my feet.

"Why not?"

"You're like a three-year-old, you know?" I snapped, goaded. I never showed annoyance or discomfiture. I was calm, nurturing Martha, efficient in all things but my visions. But Cain managed to get under my skin like a rash. Last night's absurd dream flashed through my mind, and I felt myself blush. "I've never heard so many questions in my life," I continued, trying to sound more amenable and failing. "Sometimes there is no answer, it simply is."

"And your not wanting to be touched 'simply is'? Or is it that you're afraid after what happened last night?"

I panicked. How did he know about my dream? And then I realized he was talking about that strange electric shock that had sparked between us, and I took a deep breath.

"Nothing happened last night," I said. Two lies in four words.

He moved closer, and I would have given anything to be six inches taller. My eyes were level with his beautiful, enticing mouth, and I wanted to look at anything but that.

"Nothing happened?" he echoed. "You're telling me you didn't feel it?"

"Feel what?" I said stubbornly.

"Should I touch you again, just to see what happens?"

So close. If I just swayed slightly, I could brush against him. I could smell his clean, masculine scent above the perfume of the rich soil and the roses, and it called to me. The sea. And leather. And sex. Tempting me.

"I asked you not to touch me," I heard my voice say, stiff, prudish, not at all like me.

For a moment he didn't move, and then the slow grin appeared on his face. A second later he stepped back, releasing the odd hold he had over me. "Not now," he said. "I'll give you a little more time to wonder what will happen when I do."

I fought down the sudden alarm. "What do you mean?"

"Now who's asking too many questions? You know as well as I do what I mean. When I really touch you. When I get you into bed."

He was trying to shock me again. The calm tone of those last words had belied the meaning, and he expected me to run away, to panic.

Not likely. Yesterday he'd thrown me into turmoil. Today he was simply one more annoyance, one more distraction that I could easily deal with. "Get over yourself." I managed a disinterested drawl. "I'm sure there are other people who would be much more fun to annoy. I'm not interested in playing whatever game you've got going."

He tilted his head, surveying me like a judge at a horse show, teeth to withers. "Maybe you're not." His voice was low, and it felt almost physical, wrapping around my skin. "But I plan to change your mind. You can fight it all you want. You can run away, you can tattle to Raziel or whomever. But in the end you're going to come to me. You'll give me your body, you'll let my mouth move over every inch of your skin, you'll give me your sweet, hot blood, and you'll weep with pleasure when I take it."

I stared at him, mesmerized by his voice, until the meaning of his seductive words broke through, and then I backed away, furious. "Are you somehow so delusional that you think I'm your bonded mate? Because that's insane. I've already been bonded, and even though Thomas is dead I will always be his wife. The laws are very clear. A woman cannot bond twice."

"Laws are made to be broken," he said, unmoved by my anger. "But no, you're not my one true love, which I know relieves you." He smiled at me, that charming, devilish smile that was making all the women weak in the knees. Not me.

I gave a derisive snort. "Then you can't take

my blood. It would kill you." *And good riddance,* I thought.

"And good riddance," he said, and I jerked, shocked, then realized it was simply a logical conclusion. He couldn't have heard me. Only mates heard each other, and he'd agreed he most certainly wasn't my mate. "That's presumably what most of Sheol would think. But what the Fallen believe, all their tight, careful little rules and rituals, isn't necessarily the truth of the matter."

"Tell me something new," I shot back. "Both Allie and Tory live today because they drank from their husbands."

He raised an eyebrow. "And now all of the Fallen share blood with their spouses?"

"Of course not. Both those cases were emergencies. They were dying. It's forbidden, for good reason. The potential for harm is enormous."

"The potential for everything is enormous," he murmured, "if you don't let rules and traditions shackle you."

I rolled my eyes at that. "Go away," I said, sounding bored. "Just go away and bother someone else."

"But it's you I'm interested in bothering." His voice was low, seductive, and it was a good thing I was immune to it. Completely untouched by it. And denial was more than a river in Egypt.

I stared at him for a long, considering moment.

Would it be so terrible? What would happen if I called his bluff? Would he laugh and say he was only kidding?

Or would he take me to bed and put all that sexual promise into delicious action? He wouldn't take my blood—that was an empty threat. He and I both knew I was only a temporary distraction, and if he tried to drink from me it would kill him. I was forever safe from that kind of intimacy.

Yet here he was, threatening me with a world of sensuality I had never experienced. Thomas had been a tender and careful lover, just what I had needed. Danger held no interest for me. Unless I left Sheol, I would not take another lover, and I had no intention of leaving.

"No," I said. No to all the dangerous, seductive things he offered.

"Perhaps I'll have to . . ." He was moving toward me, and I held my ground, trembling slightly, waiting to see what would happen next, when he stopped. I heard it then too, the noise from the room behind us. His room, not mine.

"We'll continue this game later," he said, turning away and dismissing me. He was gone, the French doors to his rooms closed tightly behind him, and a moment later his curtains were drawn, so that I had no opportunity of seeing who was visiting him so unexpectedly.

A woman. There was no other reason to be so secretive. Which meant if I stayed in my room, I'd have to listen to bumps and knocks and moans and sighs.

I paused only long enough to scrub the dirt from my hands and face and to throw on fresh clothes. Before I left, I stared at the adjoining wall.

And then I gave in to one moment of sheer pettiness.

I slammed my door when I left.

CHAPTER
NINE

METATRON GAVE CAIN A DIS-approving glower. Any other man would have grinned at him, Cain thought, sharing amusement over Martha's huff. But Metatron had no sense of humor.

"Can't you leave the women alone?"

Cain smiled lazily. "Why should I want to?"

"And why are you bothering with her? There are prettier women here. She doesn't seem your type at all."

Cain felt an unexpected trace of annoyance at Metatron's condescending tone. "What would you know of my type? We've been enemies for countless millennia."

Metatron shrugged his massive shoulders. "The seer's a mouse and you're a panther. You need bigger prey."

Cain hooted with laughter. "I never thought you

were so fanciful. What does that make you, a mastodon?"

As usual, Metatron didn't even crack a smile. "I'm the man who's helping you bring down the Fallen."

Cain considered him. "So you are. In which case, why are you worried about whether I'm going after a mouse, a juicy rabbit, or a fox? As long as we get the job done, that's all that counts. Unless you had your eye on Martha yourself."

Metatron made a dismissive sound, annoying Cain further. "I have no need for such diversions. Clearly you do."

"Clearly I do," Cain agreed amiably. "So why don't you keep your nose out of my business, and we'll concentrate on what we do have in common."

Metatron nodded, too humorless to be offended. "Have we decided whom we take down first? The archangel Michael is the obvious choice—if he is not leading them, the Fallen will have a hard time defeating the Armies of Heaven. He is also the most difficult to wound. Uriel already tried to kill him, and Michael is hypervigilant. Now he has the goddess of war at his side to further complicate matters. He is close to untouchable right now. If we get rid of him, we'll be in a better position."

"Not Michael. Raziel is so wrapped up in his pregnant wife that he'll be easy enough to distract, so we can rule him out as well. He'd be child's play."

"You think so?" Metatron said doubtfully.

Cain ignored him. "Azazel is our target. He may no longer be the Alpha, but he holds tremendous power and influence." He kept his voice light. It wouldn't do for Metatron to know how deep his hatred lay—it was a weakness he couldn't afford to share.

"Not to mention that he was in charge of the angels when your woman and her unborn child were executed, and he did nothing," Metatron said, cutting to the heart of the matter. "Though you may have forgotten about that."

"No," Cain said. "I haven't forgotten."

"I believe his wife still has powers. She won't admit to them, but if it weren't for her I would have killed Azazel in combat. I don't trust her."

Cain laughed. "Don't trust the Lilith? Imagine that. Do you trust any woman, Metatron?" He looked out over the sprawling, passionate garden, giving the big man only half his attention.

"No. I don't like women."

Cain pulled his gaze back, amused. "You prefer men? And Uriel countenanced that? You astonish me."

Metatron's solid jaw tightened. "It pleases you to mock me. I have no need for sexual congress. It is a distraction, a weakness, and it doesn't interest me. None of this would have happened if you hadn't started everything by lusting after the human woman. And now you probably cannot even remember her name or what she looked like."

He let the silence between them grow. "Tamarr," he said finally. "Her name was Tamarr."

But Metatron was paying no attention. "You cannot jeopardize our plans just to get between the legs of Thomas's widow. You came back to help me destroy the Fallen from within and bring them back to Uriel. I knew when I sought you out I was taking a chance on whom you'd hate more—the Fallen or the archangel Uriel—but in the end, you chose wisely. Uriel was only doing his duty. You trusted the other angels to side with you, and yet they watched your woman burn and did nothing. And then, once you'd been driven out, they turned around and committed the same foul crime."

"Sleeping with a woman is hardly a foul crime."

"It was forbidden!" Metatron's voice rose, and Cain would have silenced him had Martha not been out of earshot. "And yet not one of you has learned. Your lustful natures still drive you, all of you! If they did not, you would leave the seer alone and concentrate on what is important."

"Ancient history," Cain said in a deceptively light tone. "So I find the seer a delectable challenge. What makes you think it's lust and not love? Even you must recognize the bond between Raziel and his mate. Between Azazel and Rachel."

"And you are in love with someone like Martha?"

Again he felt that surge of annoyance, and it startled him. Why should he feel protective of his chosen prey? "Hardly," he drawled. "I don't believe in the whole sacred-bond thing that seems to drive the Fallen. But I'll allow that it's more than lust that drives them. At least I remember that much from when I fell."

Metatron glowered at him. "It matters not why the Fallen do what they do. It only matters that you are not distracted from our prime directive. We must weaken and destroy the Fallen from within, so that when Uriel comes, resistance will be futile."

Cain cocked his head. "You're starting to sound like a space opera."

Confusion wiped out the malice on Metatron's heavy features. "What is a space opera?"

He didn't bother answering him. "Why have you never gone out into the world of mankind? Watched television, gone to the movies, gotten drunk, gotten laid?"

"Weaknesses," Metatron said, dismissing life itself. "Why are you bothering with the seer? She means nothing to you, I know that. You cannot resist trying to annoy me, and I expect she is simply a tool."

"That's exactly what she is, Metatron, old friend," he said, letting just a trace of malice through. "She's a means to an end. If I can feed her visions, we can convince the Fallen they're safe, making them more vulnerable to Uriel's attack. The fact that I find her . . . pleasing is simply icing on the cake."

Metatron looked confused at his reference. "But—"

"I've given this some thought, and you must admit, thinking is more my strength than yours." Cain glanced at him for a moment, and gave in to temptation. "Look at it this way: you're Pinky and I'm the Brain."

Once more Metatron looked lost. "Pinky?" he echoed, horrified. "What kind of name is Pinky for a warrior?"

Cain schooled his face into an expression of solemnity. "It was probably shortened from something else. Just be assured I have this all well in hand. To be successful, one must be flexible, and my original plans have changed. Easier and quicker to start with the seer and work that way."

"You're overlooking one problem. The seer's prophecies are so erratic they can be an example of what won't happen, rather than a reliable warning."

"I've taken that into account."

Metatron gave a grudging nod. "Good."

"I'm so glad you approve," Cain purred.

"I did not say I approved," Metatron snapped. "Killing them off one by one would be faster."

Cain sighed. "If any of them die, I'll be the first

one they suspect. As they said in *The Wizard of Oz,* these things must be handled delicately."

"Who is the wizard of Oz? Can he help us?"

Cain didn't roll his eyes. He had an abiding affection for movies, television, rock and roll, all the glories of modern life. It was typical of Metatron that he would refuse even to taste such treasures. "No, Metatron, we're on our own. At least until we can assure Uriel that it's safe to lead his armies into battle. And to do that, we need to destroy the Fallen from within, which is what I'm doing."

Metatron glared at him. "And what do you expect me to do while we're waiting for you to accomplish your little plan? Sit quietly?"

"Do what you always do, Metatron. Train, keep an eye on Michael and his wife, and watch the others, watch the Lilith. Report to me if something happens."

Metatron didn't look pleased. "I have some ideas of my own."

"Do they involve killing anyone?"

"No."

Cain considered him for a moment, then nodded. "Just be discreet. If they toss you out of Sheol, it will take me that much longer to get the job done."

Metatron shook his head. "No one will suspect me." He turned to go. He never sat when he checked in with Cain, and Cain had stopped offering him a seat. Absently he wondered whether Metatron even bent at the waist.

"Then go ahead."

"I intend to," Metatron said. He closed the door silently behind him.

HE TRULY DESPISED Cain, Metatron thought. He hadn't been around him for millennia, not since Cain had been one of the chosen, the angels who sat on the right hand of the Supreme Power. Even back then, Cain had been annoying. Now that they were working together to bring down the Fallen, he was even worse. Back then Cain had been irrepressible, filled with obnoxious charm that everyone else found delightful.

He preferred the new, cynical, manipulative Cain, but he could have done without either. Unfortunately, Metatron needed help if he was going to defeat the Fallen and earn his way back into Uriel's good graces, and he'd turned to the only original fallen angel living outside the safety of Sheol. It hadn't taken long to find him, once he'd figured out where to look. The largest remaining pack of Nephilim was on the vast subcontinent of Australia, and that was where Cain would be. Hunting. Because the Cain he had known, the charming, sweet seducer, had become a most efficient killer.

Metatron wasn't quite certain how things had shifted. How Cain, whom he'd recruited as his coconspirator, had ended up in charge. But then, that was part of Cain's gift. Cain knew how to manipulate people to get what he wanted—and he'd manipulated the hell out of him.

At least Metatron could now concentrate on what he did best and leave the scheming up to that devious bastard. He had promised he wouldn't kill anyone, and Cain's reasons made sense. If he killed someone, there'd be an investigation.

But what grew in the womb of the Source wasn't someone. Wasn't a human being, at least not for his purposes. Who knew what grew inside the Source? This would be simply a means to an end. Nothing would demoralize the entire community more, and he was surprised Cain hadn't thought of it. Cain, the trickster, the liar, the charmer, hadn't even noticed the most obvious form of attack.

Of course Metatron hadn't mentioned it. Cain would either come up with some ridiculous reason to leave the spawn of the Source in place, or he'd take over and do it himself, depriving Metatron of the victory.

No, he would take care of it on his own, and present Cain with the ensuing chaos that would result from it. And then they could decide who was . . . Pinky? He shuddered at the name. And who was the Brain.

CHAPTER
TEN

THE BEST PLACE FOR ME TO BE was with Allie, and I headed up to her apartment at the very top of the main house, secure in the fact that Cain was otherwise occupied. The Source and I shared a mostly unspoken bond. Her childhood had been unpleasant, though she didn't say much about it. I kept my own past locked tight inside, afraid to let it out into the sunlight, but somehow I'd said enough to tell her that my mother had been a horror of her own, and it was something we'd bonded over.

Tory was sitting cross-legged at the end of the bed, the most appalling mess of yarn in her hands.

"Are you knitting or playing cat's cradle?" I asked with a singular lack of tact.

Tory stuck out her tongue at me. "It's not like you're any better. I needed something to do with my hands. I'm nervous."

"Why?" Allie asked from her spot at the head of the bed, like a Gypsy queen with her subjects. Her belly was a nice, healthy bulge beneath the covers, and her color was good. Not that I was worried. I knew she and the child were safe. Were blessed.

"We keep training and training." Tory dropped the tangle of yarn into her lap. "And nothing happens. We haven't seen or heard from Uriel and his armies since the attack months ago. I keep waiting for the other shoe to drop."

"I would think Michael could help you work off that tension," Allie said with a wicked grin.

Tory grinned back. "He does his best. But even an archangel doesn't have that much energy twenty-four hours a day, and there are two hundred and sixty-five souls to train."

"I'm not sure we have souls," I said. "Not to be depressing about it."

But Allie just laughed. "Probably not. I'm dead, Tory's a goddess, and you're a human who turned herself over to the unholy, if Uriel is to be believed. And I gather the Supreme Being stripped the Fallen of any chance of an afterlife, so I would expect they're soulless as well."

"Don't be pedantic. You sound like Metatron," Tory muttered.

Allie sighed. "Yes, he is a bit literal, isn't he? He's been here long enough—I'd have thought he would have lightened up by now."

"I don't think 'lighten up' is in Metatron's vocabulary," I said. I didn't like Metatron. His granite features were incapable of smiling, and he seemed to consider the women of Sheol a subspecies unworthy of conversation. I had trained with him—everyone in Sheol eventually sparred with everybody else—and he had beaten me quickly and efficiently. I hadn't even been able to get in one sharp blow before he'd slammed me to the floor pad, my breath and my pride knocked out of me. We needed his strength, his ruthlessness. Didn't mean I had to like him.

But Allie was thinking about something else. "Are there really only two hundred and sixty-five of us? Counting Cain?"

"I'm not sure that we should count Cain," I said darkly, "but yes, I think that's the number. When you give birth, that will make two hundred and sixty-six."

"Yeah, and he's going to pop out and pick up a sword first thing," Allie scoffed. "In fact, when it comes to our fighting force, we're a man—or more precisely a woman—down. I can't do much to defend myself, much less Sheol."

"You'll be fine," I said with a reassuring smile.

"Yeah, yeah." Allie waved her hand dismissively. "What do you know?"

"Everything," I replied with a serene smile.

Tory hooted with laughter, and I couldn't blame her. My incomplete visions had almost killed her.

"Sorry," Tory said. "It's not your fault your gift is . . . imperfect."

"My gift is a disaster," I said, truthful as always. "Unfortunately, it's the closest thing we have to a glimpse into the future, and we just have to interpret it the best we can."

Tory nodded. "The ancient Romans and Greeks had to interpret signs. Reading the future has never been easy."

"At least I don't have to poke through the entrails of a slaughtered goat."

"Please!" Allie suddenly looked green, and I resisted the impulse to smile. Even at this late point, Allie was still having morning sickness, another thing to worry her. I rejoiced in it. The stronger and more long-lasting the morning sickness, the stronger the baby. It was an old wives' tale, but who should know better than old wives?

I turned back to Tory. "If you want to lure your mate from the training floor and work off some of that energy, I'll stay here. I have nothing better to do."

"Gee, thanks," Allie said wryly.

Tory jumped up. "It's not that I don't love you, Allie," she said, "but when it comes to a contest between you and Michael's delicious, er, arms, Michael wins every time."

"Yeah, it's his arms you're enamored of," I drawled. "Go away, and we'll talk behind your back."

It didn't take any more encouragement. Tory was gone in a flash. Allie sighed gustily. "I hate to say it," she said, "but there's one really bad thing about pregnancy. Oh, it's still completely worth it, and I'm not complaining. But . . ."

"You're allowed to complain. You can bitch about the morning sickness and the hemorrhoids—"

"I don't have hemorrhoids!" she protested, shuddering. "And it's not the physical stuff. That's kind of cool. Watching the changes, feeling them. Did you know I have a third more blood moving through my body than normal?"

"Raziel must like that."

Her face fell. "That's the problem," she said in a low voice. "We don't have sex, and he barely touches my blood. When he feeds, he does it like one of the other Fallen, from my wrist, chastely." She looked woeful, pathetic, and very beautiful. Pregnancy had given her a glow that was almost Madonna-like. All those Renaissance masters had probably used their pregnant mistresses as models for their Virgin Mary paintings, to capture that glow.

"Well, you know there's no reason you can't have sex. You're only on bed rest because you're nervous and need to be coddled, not because you require it. If you're worried, try out something less . . . traditional to help you get over the dry spell," I said judiciously. "And Raziel is being ridiculous not to take your blood. I don't know how many times I've told you, but you and the baby are going to be fine. I doubt there's anything either of you could do to hurt the little one."

"You want to take Raziel aside and talk to him?" She laughed. "I can tell by your horrified expression that you don't. And there's no obstetrician to reason with him—we have to make do with your visions combined with Rachel's healing expertise and power. It's not black-and-white, and Raziel is . . ." Her voice trailed off.

"He's afraid," I said. "For the first time in his endless existence, he's afraid of something, and he doesn't know how to deal with it."

"So what am I going to do?" Allie demanded in what was close to a wail.

"Do about what?" Raziel said from the doorway.

I kept my face slightly averted, afraid my expression would give it away.

Trust Allie. "Do about our lack of a sex life," she said bluntly.

Silence, and now I didn't dare look at him. After a moment, he spoke. "And did the seer come up with any solution?"

I didn't move. I wanted to disappear, crawl into a corner. But Allie was looking at me expectantly, her eyes a mix of misery and hope, and I couldn't let her down.

So I turned and met his fulminating gaze squarely. "I know a lot about pregnancy and babies," I said. "I helped my mother through three, I delivered one, and I helped her friends as well. I've seen a lot of children born into the world, and I know what I'm doing. And I know, I *know,* that the Source is strong and healthy. And . . . er . . . marital relations are part of a healthy pregnancy."

"And did your father have sex with your mother when she was pregnant?" he countered.

Okay, I was definitely blushing, but I couldn't back down now. "I read everything I could on pregnancy and delivery, because my mother and her friends didn't have obstetricians or midwives either. You can have . . . er . . . traditional sex up until the eighth month, as long as the mother is comfortable. After that, you should indulge in . . . in noninvasive alternatives."

To my embarrassment and relief, Raziel choked with laughter. "'Noninvasive'? You make it sound like cancer."

I met his gaze fully, irritation winning over my discomfort. "You know what I'm talking about."

"*No penetration* is the term I think you wanted," he said coolly.

"Yes."

"But you never answered my question."

"What question?" I demanded, harassed. I'd already

answered far more questions than I was comfortable with.

"Did your father have sex with your mother while she was pregnant?"

The pain-filled memories pushed at me, the misery and deep, bleeding shame that I kept as well hidden as the scars on my body. I was tempted to tell him it was none of his damned business, but even in my distress I knew you didn't say that to the Alpha. And suddenly I was tired of it all.

"My mother was a whore, and I have no idea who my father was. We lived in a tenement apartment with a bunch of petty criminals and drug dealers and prostitutes, and when the women didn't abort the babies, I helped them give birth. I would help them through pregnancy, make sure the babies were taken safely to a hospital rather than be abandoned by the mothers, and try to keep the mothers off drugs while they were pregnant, but I couldn't keep them from earning a living. So trust me, those unborn babies were subjected to a steady battering, and they all survived, without a doctor's care or a midwife to help. In the last month or two, most of the women were too uncomfortable to sell more than a blow job, and of course their sexual pleasure was immaterial. I doubt any of them knew what sexual pleasure was like by then. But the point is, they survived, and

when . . . penetration"—I said the word defiantly—
"was uncomfortable, they practiced alternatives.
And your wife needs to get laid!"

The two of them stared at me in shocked disbelief. Allie reached out her hand to touch mine,
but I snatched it away. I rose, stalking to the door,
and Raziel—big, scary Raziel, ultimate leader of all
the Fallen—wisely moved out of my way. "So get
over yourselves," I said as a parting shot, "and get
fucked."

I made it down the first flight of stairs, out of
sight, before I began to run. Allie and Raziel lived at
the very top of the huge, ungainly, beautiful house,
and there were flights and flights of stairs to get to
the ground floor.

"What's the hurry?" Tory was heading back upstairs.

I made the mistake of pausing. "If you're going
to visit Allie, Raziel is up there. I think we can leave
them alone for a while."

"Raziel's getting over his fear of touching her?"
Tory inquired. "We've all tried to tell him she's fine,
but he's a stubborn bastard. Like most men."

"Yes."

"So what did you say that made him listen? I
thought you were afraid of him."

I shrugged. "I managed to convince him, at least
for now, that Allie isn't made of glass. She's going to
have delicious sex."

Suddenly it washed over me again, the pleasure of that too-real erotic dream, reminding me of something I could never have, except in dreams. I was a woman without a mate in a world of mated people. I had no man, no sex, and the Fallen were innately sexual. I was a widow, a figure of loss, and an oracle with broken powers.

"I have to go," I said in an unexpectedly rough voice, turning away. I was the calm, unruffled one as far as anyone else knew. I wasn't about to demonstrate just how thin that veneer actually was.

But Tory knew me too well, and she was having none of it. She took my arm in an unbreakable grip. "No you don't," she said. "I think it's time we have a talk."

"I'm tired of talking!" I wailed. I needed to go hide long enough to pull myself together.

"Too bad. You're too wound up, and you're going to talk to me whether you like it or not. Come on."

She wasn't giving me much choice. She and I could have a fight in the middle of the winding stairs that led to the upper reaches of the big house, but she was six inches taller and presumably stronger, and I didn't think the two of us rolling down the stairs would help anyone, though it could provide a certain level of amusement.

To my surprise she pulled me into a room one flight down, and I realized this was the other empty apartment at Sheol. It was even more cell-like than mine—a small window looking out over the horizon, the sea barely visible, a narrow bed, and a dresser. "Sit," she said sternly, pushing me toward the bed.

I sat. Not that I had much choice.

CHAPTER
ELEVEN

TORY TOOK THE CHAIR, SPINNING it around and straddling it like a man, resting her arms on the back as she watched me. "So you decided to come clean about your childhood," she said abruptly. "Why now?"

I was sitting cross-legged on the sagging bed. I wasn't really in the mood for this. My momentary weakness had abated. "They were both miserable, afraid to touch each other and about to explode from sexual frustration, and neither of them would really believe it was safe. My word wasn't good enough, so I told them of the pregnancies I had seen, the abuse they'd taken. Allie's baby is strong and healthy and the delivery will be fine for both of them, but they won't believe it."

Tory nodded. "So you decided the things you witnessed would shock them into doing the deed? And it worked?"

I closed my eyes, listening to my unreliable senses, and then I smiled. "It worked."

"That was pretty nice of you," Tory said.

I shrugged again. "No need to make such a big secret out of it. It was a rotten childhood. Thomas rescued me, and I lived happily ever after. Until he died."

"He died," Tory said gently. "You didn't."

I didn't move, but I felt frozen inside. "I don't want to leave here."

"You're afraid to leave here," she corrected me. "That's a different thing. You need a husband, a mate, sweetie. Someone to care for you and love you and push you when you try to hide."

"No," I said stubbornly. "Thomas was the love of my life. I don't want anyone else."

"From what I've heard, Thomas was a gentle, sweet angel who was more of a father to you than a lover. I know he never took your blood. Did he even take your body?"

"Of course he did," I said sharply, regretting how much I'd told her. "And it was very nice."

"*Very nice?*" she echoed with a sharp laugh. "Honey, you need to get laid. Even more than Allie, and that's saying a lot."

"I told you, I don't want anyone else."

She wasn't convinced. "And have you ever looked into your own future? Do you know what life holds for you? Are you going to spend the rest of your life as a ghost?"

She knew me too well, knew that I was an empty shell wandering through the world I had once inhabited. "I tried," I said. "My gift doesn't work that way."

She looked at me, then nodded, accepting. "I want you to find someone," she said. "That's no secret. But that someone isn't Cain."

I laughed. "Are you crazy? No one needs to warn me about Cain. I can see just how dangerous he is, and I'm not going anywhere near him."

"You may not have any choice in the matter. He's far too interested in you, and from what I've heard, that's not like him. His interest makes no sense. Not that you aren't gorgeous, but Cain arrives only to disrupt things, create havoc. Taking you to bed wouldn't further whatever agenda he has."

"Don't!" I protested. I was growing unnaturally warm at the vision her words were drawing for me, and last night's dream came back to me in blazing detail, and my skin warmed. I took a deep breath. "I promise you, Tory, that I am keeping my distance from Cain. I don't want to have anything to do with him, and I can recognize a danger when I see one. He isn't some dream lover come to save me." He wasn't a dream lover at all.

Tory looked at me long and hard. "Maybe. I still

think you're underestimating just how dangerous he could be."

"I'm not. He's just not that dangerous to me."

"You're wrong." She sighed. "Whatever. We need him to leave, but right now I don't know how or even *if* Raziel can kick him out." She rose, striding across the tiny room to look out the window. "Michael told me what happened to Cain. He saw his wife and unborn child butchered by Uriel for his transgressions, and the other angels stood by and did nothing. Let's just say he has a reason to hold a serious grudge."

"Oh God," I said, feeling sick. "No wonder they're afraid of him. He has a huge score to settle."

She shrugged. "If that's why he's here. It's not the first time he's been back, so maybe the time for revenge has passed. Whatever his reasons, the Fallen are watching him, prepared to counteract whatever he might do. I don't want you caught in the middle."

I laughed. "I'm hardly likely to be. I think you're wrong. Oh, not about his malice. But I'm in no particular danger. I'm just someone he's practicing on. He likes to see me squirm, but there's nothing more than that. Believe me, I'd know."

"I thought you weren't able to look into your own future."

I made a frustrated sound. "I can't look into anybody's future. It either comes to me or it doesn't. But no vision has ever come to me about myself."

My dream last night meant nothing, I told myself. Just a confluence of circumstances. "You don't have to worry about me, Tory," I continued. I needed to convince her, almost as badly as I needed to convince myself. "I'm just a toy for Cain to play with when he happens to see me. Whatever his scheme is, I have absolutely nothing to do with it."

"I don't—" Tory began.

"Trust me," I interrupted. "But, just to make you feel better, I'm going to move my things up here temporarily. I know there's nothing to worry about—he'll never even notice I'm not next door. It will be easy enough to avoid him."

"You know you're a pain in the ass, don't you?" she grumbled.

"Yes," I said, shooing her out the door. "But you love me anyway."

I closed the door behind her, then turned to look at the small room. I slid down on the narrow bed, letting the cheery smile vanish from my face, letting the tension drain from my body in the cocooning half-light of blessed solitude. None of this made sense. I didn't bother to look for a mirror—I knew exactly what I looked like. Cute, rather than gorgeous. Hair too curly, eyes an ordinary, changeable hazel, body too short, too curvy, too ordinary. I had no interest in drawing men to me, particularly not someone like Cain. I was happy, damn it.

Sitting up, I looked around the room. It was late afternoon and the sun was setting, sending long shadows up the walls, but I didn't bother turning on the lights. I would be safe here. I had spoken nothing but the truth—Cain rattled me, deliberately, when he saw me, but he would never seek me out. I was safe here.

"There you are," said Cain. He'd opened the door so silently I hadn't even noticed. He slid inside and closed the door behind him, while I sat frozen, staring up at him. "You're a hard woman to track down. Are you hiding from me?"

CHAPTER
TWELVE

CAIN WANTED TO LAUGH AT THE expression on her face. She was so shocked, her usual defenses weren't in place, and her dismay was clear. He wasn't used to having such a negative effect on someone he was trying to seduce—and, oh yes, he was trying to seduce her. She looked at him as if he'd stolen her favorite doll.

Maybe he'd gone too far last night, letting those erotic images loose, but even in sleep she had a choice. Either she opened her mind, her heart, her legs, or she rejected the wickedly insidious mind-play he'd initiated. And last night she'd welcomed him.

The tiny, cell-like room was faintly stuffy, and he moved to the window, pushing it open, letting the soft sea breeze into the room. He kept his body loose and relaxed, deceptively at ease. If she made one move toward the door, he would be there ahead of her.

Fortunately, she was still frozen to the bed, which was exactly how he liked it. He turned to look at her, leaning against the windowsill.

"I need you to explain something to me, Miss Mary." He deliberately misused her name, just to see the fleeting reaction in her changeable eyes. They looked more blue than green today, even though she still wore the boring white clothes. "You don't seem to like me very much, and I wonder why. Did I kill your dog or something? Or is it because I've made no secret of the fact that I want you? Is it me you're afraid of, or sex?"

He caught the nearly imperceptible jerk of her body, and he nodded. "Ah, so it's sex. I wonder why. It can't be Thomas's fault—he was about as predatory as a rabbit. He certainly couldn't have traumatized you in bed."

He could sense her struggle to remain polite. "My relationship with my husband is none of your business. I loved him very much, and we were very happy. In *every* way."

If it was none of his business, why had she told him that? He smiled, a slow, wicked smile. "Then you've probably had a vision about me and it's a disastrous one. No, wait, that's not possible, because I gather your visions are about as reliable as those of a carnival fortune-teller. Or are you seeing different visions? Perhaps more personal ones?"

The expression on her face was priceless.

"You know, you really ought to learn to hide your reactions," he continued, pushing away from the window and approaching the bed before she could scramble off it. "You practically telegraph them. Or no, people don't use telegraphs anymore, do they? You practically e-mail them? Either way, they're very clear." He sat down on the bed, and she simply looked at him out of her big eyes, unable or unwilling to move away.

"Please," she said in her small, determined voice. "Leave me alone. I have no idea why you've taken it into your mind to torment me, but I would think you'd find more suitable prey."

He smiled at her lazily. "What an interesting turn of phrase. You think I'm a predator?"

"Aren't you?"

"Yes."

She was practically vibrating with emotion. It wasn't pure fear, he could sense that much. Fascinating. He leaned forward, resting his hands on either side of her, trapping her there, still not touching her. The bed was too narrow, and it was too soon, but she was so tempting, and their shared dream from last night had only added to his arousal. That soft mouth, those rampant curls, the uneasiness in her eyes that he could soften and turn to heat and desire . . . He wondered how long it would take. He might time himself, just to see. Two days? Two hours?

"I don't suppose I could convince you that I'm absolutely harmless?" he asked softly.

"No."

"What exactly do you think I'm going to do with you, Miss Mary? I'm not the big bad wolf, you know."

"And I'm no Little Red Riding Hood," she shot back, starting to regain her fire.

"Then what are you so afraid of?"

For a moment he thought she was going to deny it. And then she blindsided him. "I'm afraid you're going to hurt the Fallen, and you're somehow going to use me to do it. I don't know where I come into things, but I don't trust anything about you."

The pretty little mouse was more observant than he'd given her credit for. He smiled at her, all innocence. "You're paranoid, you know that? Why would I want to hurt the Fallen? Oh, I expect you've heard rumors of my tragic past." He put a light, ironic twist on the word *tragic*. "Each and every one of the Fallen has the same kind of tragedy in his history. And it *is* history—so long ago that time can't even record it. It's a little late to be holding a grudge. And why"—he leaned closer—"do you think I wouldn't simply want to take you to bed for the sheer pleasure of it? Or are you afraid I'm going to shake up your safe little world?"

He could read truth in the sudden darkening of her eyes, and he wanted to laugh. She was almost too easy. It was too soon—he'd only been here thirty-six hours—but he couldn't resist. "Look at me," he said softly. "I'm going to kiss you. It won't hurt, I promise. Just a sweet, safe little kiss, nothing more." Her face was averted, as if staring at the wall would make him disappear. "Look at me, Martha," he said again, forcing her to turn by sheer will. And then he covered her mouth with his.

He slammed back, off the bed, halfway across the room before he realized it and stopped himself. He stood there, staring at her in shocked disbelief.

She was looking even more shaken than he felt. She'd scrambled back into the farthest corner of the bed, her eyes so big they practically filled her gamine face, her body curled into a tight little ball.

"What the hell was that?" he demanded in a rough voice.

She said nothing, and that pissed him off even more. "Answer me."

She flinched as if his voice were a blow, and he took a deep breath, giving her a moment as well. The moment his mouth touched hers, he'd seen it, felt it—power, pure and dangerous, tied up with an almost physical vision. The two of them, limbs entwining, mouths and hands on heated skin, sweat and sex, rolling on the bed. He'd been aroused since he'd come into the room, but now he was so damned hard it hurt, and he could still feel it in his gut, the complete, raw sexuality of it, the bruising force of it, defying even his usual iron control.

Finally she spoke. "I'm a seer," she said in a steady voice. "I get occasional flashes of the future, and they feel very real and physical. One might have been coming when you . . . you touched me."

"When I kissed you." And two were coming, he thought with dark humor. "I saw it too, and I'm not a seer. And it was more than the sex, delightful as it was. We both know that's going to happen, and it's not important enough to hold that kind of power."

When he kissed a woman, he knew her soul. Knew her needs and fears and longings. It had served him well in the past, an immediate key to their bodies and beds. All he had to do was say the right thing, make the right gesture, and they would be his, body and blood. It had been almost too easy, and that was what he'd expected from the woman staring at him as if he were Uriel himself.

But he'd never felt anything like the bolt of power that had almost blown him off his feet when he'd kissed her.

"So did you see anything specific?" She sounded uneasy. So she'd seen the same thing, and didn't want to admit to it.

He grinned at her. "Apart from you writhing

beneath me, me inside you as you were about to explode with pleasure? No, nothing at all."

Her cheekbones were stained with color. "Wishful thinking on your part," she dismissed it bravely, and he was momentarily impressed. She kept surprising him.

But then, that was part of the attraction. Every time he thought he had her figured out, she ended up startling him, charming him. And that wasn't a good thing. "I don't think so," he drawled. "I think that you saw the same thing I did, felt the same thing I did. I think that if you weren't wearing that loose top, I'd see that your nipples are hard in this warm room, and I'd find out you're wet." She squirmed just a little, confirming that suspicion.

"It wasn't a vision," she snapped. "That's not how they happen."

"Then what was it? And why did I feel it too? Why did it feel like I was blown off my feet?"

She stared at him, biting her lower lip, and he felt that in his cock as well. It should be his mouth biting her in all her soft places, ending with her sweet neck. "I don't know."

But she did. Or at least she suspected—he could see it in her eyes, sense it in the emotions that came off her body in waves. Fear and longing and rich, dark sensuality. And he needed to taste it again, to see if he could harness it, ride it out.

He started toward her, but this time she was fast, off the bed and to the door by the time he got there. He slammed it shut with the flat of his hand just as she managed to pull it partly open, and she leaned against it, her forehead pressed against the wood, trembling, as his arms trapped her there.

"I'm not going to hurt you, Martha," he said softly. Because he wasn't, at least not physically. He was good to his lovers, generous and inventive, and he would give her the kind of pleasure she clearly had never experienced. "Turn around."

She didn't move. A kind man would step back, let her escape, leave her alone. He'd never been kind, and he wasn't a man. He was an avenging angel, heartless in his pursuit of justice. If Martha was collateral damage, so be it. At least he could give her exquisite pleasure before all hell broke loose.

He pulled his hands away from the door and put them on her shoulders gingerly. He could feel the tension vibrating through her, feel her barely banked emotion. He turned her, keeping his hands on her at all times, almost as if he feared static electricity. That would have been an easy explanation for what had happened—if static electricity felt like a lightning bolt.

He pushed her back against the door gently. "Let's try this again," he whispered. He took her stubborn chin in his hand, tilted her downturned face up to his, and kissed her again.

She tasted so damned sweet, he thought with a groan. Her lips were soft, vulnerable, and she didn't think to tighten them before he managed to part them with the pressure of his mouth. He slid his other hand around her back, cradling her as he pushed his tongue into her mouth and tasted her more fully. The visions were back, but he managed to withstand them as they danced and swirled through her body into his and back again. He pulled her tight against him, and his infallible instincts told him he was right. Her nipples were hard, she was wet, and her hands had come up to his arms. Maybe she'd wanted to push him away, but instead she was clutching him, her fingers digging into his biceps, a tiny bit of pain that added to his arousal.

He moved his tongue in her mouth, and he knew she wasn't used to kissing like this. He knew how to kiss—God, he'd had enough practice—and women liked to be kissed, to be held. He liked to kiss them and hold them. And fuck them. He'd get around to that. Right now he was enjoying Martha's slow capitulation, a nerve cell at a time, and when her tongue moved against his he wanted to crow in triumph, to shove her back against the door and bury himself inside her as he drank from her. Drank deeply.

He could lose himself so easily, his body, his clever, calculating mind, in the sheer pleasure of her.

He didn't want to think, to plan, to scheme. He simply wanted.

Wanted what he couldn't have. He was almost at the point of no return, and he sensed she was already there, the erotic visions tumbling through her mind in a kaleidoscope of images, and he knew if he saw them as well he'd climax there against her, fully clothed.

It took everything he had to slowly bring her down. To soften his kiss, let his hands move over her back in a steady, soothing gesture, calming her as he tried to calm himself. He finally broke the kiss, and she gasped for breath, and he wanted to laugh. He really would need to teach her how to breathe when he kissed her.

He pressed her face against his chest, letting her rest there as she slowly came back from that exquisite, almost painful state of arousal, and he stroked the cap of dark curls. He wanted her blood so badly he could already taste it; it would be thick and sweet, filling his body with the kind of power few knew. But he had to hold back. Couldn't rush her. No matter how badly he needed to.

He heard the faint sigh as the last bit of tension left her body, and for a moment she was quiescent, limp, leaning against him. As her muscles tightened again, as if she realized where she was and what she was doing, he released her, stepping back.

"You know," he said in a conversational tone, "when we actually fuck, we'll probably blow the roof off this place." He used the term deliberately, just to see her reaction.

He expected her to turn and run. He was very dangerous to her, and she knew it. A cautious woman would have run as far and as fast as she could, and Martha struck him as a cautious woman. But instead she stood her ground, facing him, small and stern. "How many times must I tell you? I want you to leave me alone."

"Do you? You could have fooled me. Whose tongue was in my mouth, then? I thought it was yours."

He saw her hand twitch, and he knew she wanted to hit him. He was used to bringing that out in women. At least he never hit back.

"Don't worry, little rabbit," he said with a laugh. "Go ahead and run away. For now."

She ran.

CHAPTER
THIRTEEN

METATRON DID NOT CON-
sider himself a man made for
stealth. He had a warrior's bru-
tal acceptance of the price that must be paid, and
he climbed the stairs to Raziel's apartment with a
solemn, heavy tread. He didn't worry about people
seeing him. Cain would get the blame for this, which
was fine with Metatron. They wouldn't be able to
prove anything, because Cain would have no knowledge of it. The deed would be done swiftly and efficiently, distracting everyone.

It had taken him long hours of deliberation to
decide how best to accomplish his mission. He had
promised not to kill, so the Source would stay alive.
Besides, he relied on her blood to survive, at least
until his curse was lifted as he brought Sheol under
Uriel's power. It would have been so simple to throw

her off the balcony outside her window. He knew she liked to perch up there—he'd seen her often enough as she looked out over Sheol. Easy enough to slip. But that would kill her as well, and he had promised.

He took his promises very seriously. Besides, he didn't want her dead. She had been kind to him, and her blood had kept him alive. He honored his obligations, and he owed her.

He'd finally decided to use poison. He didn't like the thought—poison was a woman's weapon, and he was a man of action. But in Uriel's service he had learned to be devious, to do what needed to be done. As he would do now.

Sheol had no poisons, he'd learned with disgust, and hadn't that knowledge taken a great deal of cunning to discern? Nothing to rid her of the spawn from a distance. The best he could come up with was a powerful but essentially harmless sleeping draft, and it had taken him a while to work out the details. He could drug the Source, get rid of her friends, and then kick her in the stomach. No more foul offspring of the unholy. Not only would Raziel be useless, the entire community would be grief-stricken. And those who depended on the blood of the Source would be deprived at first and then victim to the sorrow that suffused her. During the years she'd moped about because she couldn't have children by her accursed husband, her blood had become more and more depressing. The few unbonded went into an empathic decline when they fed, and several of them had gone in desperate search of a mate rather than endure that constant grieving.

They would be prey to even deeper despair once the thing growing inside her was gone, and this time Uriel would be able to march in and take over with little difficulty. In fact, Metatron hadn't even needed Cain. He could take care of all this himself.

Perhaps Cain might be the one to fall from a balcony, if something could be done to his wings. It was hard to kill one of the Fallen, particularly one strangely impervious to fire, but Metatron had little doubt he could do it. He was, after all, an expert at death.

The demon Lilith sat in a chair by the Source's bed, some kind of needlework in her hands. Her fingers moved swiftly, efficiently, but he had no interest in such frivolity. He bowed, low and respectfully, as he'd learned with Uriel. Raziel kept insisting it was unnecessary. Metatron still bowed.

"Metatron," the Source greeted him in soft surprise. Everything about her was soft, her brown hair and eyes, the dreamy expression on her face, the smile that lingered around her mouth. He frowned. There was sex in the air, and he glanced at the Source. Surely that was impossible.

"Is something wrong?" Rachel asked sharply. She worried, did the demon. He liked that.

"No," he said. "I've simply come to offer my respects to the Source. I haven't seen her in several weeks and I wished to reassure myself that all was well." That had sounded like a reasonable excuse to him. There had been no ritual bloodings in the past few months. Rachel had unexpected talents, and she'd removed blood from the Source by means of some strange, ungodly combination of needles and tubing, and the blood had been delivered in a tiny bottle, enough to sustain him. Indeed, he preferred it that way. The drinking of blood was shameful enough; to put his mouth to a woman's body had been anathema. This way no one had to witness his degradation, and he could keep himself away from her decadent female flesh.

She lay in bed, ripe, fecund, the roundness of her belly a reproach to the Supreme Power who had made them and cursed them, and a danger to everything Uriel ruled. It was wrong, and he would end it.

"That's very sweet of you, Metatron," she said, taking him at face value. That was another failing of the Source—she trusted too easily. She didn't see danger until it was too late.

He hoped Uriel wouldn't destroy her as he'd destroyed Tamarr. Even though she was the unholiest of the unholies and deserved to be ripped apart, he liked to watch her. Asbel had told him he had an unfortunate fascination with the woman, and Metatron had almost killed him for that. He'd resisted, sensing Asbel would be an easy one to turn, unaware that Uriel had already taken care of it. But now Asbel was dead, and Metatron had been forced to turn to Cain, with his snakelike charm and his annoying manners, bringing him back to Sheol to help him complete his mission.

"I wondered if there was anything I could do for you, my lady," he said respectfully.

"How very kind of you, Metatron. But I'm fine. Well taken care of, in fact."

"She's fine," Rachel echoed with just the slightest edge to her voice. They'd never liked each other, not since she'd interfered with his intended execution of Azazel. In the end Metatron had been the one to die, and only the healing power of the ocean had saved him, leaving him no choice but to cast his lot with the Fallen. He wondered why it hadn't saved the first wave of Uriel's armies in the battle that followed a few months later. They'd drowned in the water, their wings weighted down by it, pulled underneath to vanish into the darkness.

He'd killed his share of Uriel's followers that day. After all, he needed to convince everyone he hated Uriel as much as they did. The only way Uriel would lift his banishment and allow him back in was if Metatron brought with him a substantial boon. The death of the threat growing in the Source's belly would go a long way toward achieving that, and the destruction of Sheol should ensure it.

"Then I will take my leave." He began to back toward the door, when Rachel grew suddenly alert. She rose as well, setting her knitting down, clearly expecting to return to it today.

"Azazel needs me," she said to the Source in an undertone, obviously hoping he wouldn't hear her. "I won't be long. Unless you need me to stay?"

He didn't need to hear. He'd arranged this, quite neatly, if he chose to compliment himself. A note delivered to Azazel at just the right moment ensured Rachel would be called away on a perfectly reasonable pretext, and with any luck the Source would be unguarded. Though others visited, there was usually only one person keeping her company on a steady basis, and he'd simply waited until it was Rachel's turn.

"I'll be perfectly fine," the Source said. "Metatron can stay and talk to me."

He'd anticipated this as well. "I wish I could, my lady, but I am late for a meeting with the archangel Michael. I promised I would train with him. If you prefer, I can stay, but I hate to disappoint him."

He could sense Rachel's relief. The demon truly didn't trust him, long after everyone else in Sheol had accepted him. He was going to have to do something about that, and soon. But first things first.

"Of course not, Metatron. You go along with Rachel. I only have company because I get bored, and boredom is not a fatal condition." She smiled at him, and Metatron felt that familiar, uncomfortable feeling inside him. If Uriel gave orders to kill her, he would follow them without question. But for some complicated reason, he was pleased those orders hadn't come.

Metatron descended the stairs with Rachel in a hostile silence. He supposed he could make an effort to charm her out of her suspicions, except that he had no charm, unlike Cain, with his glittering, devious smile. This way Rachel could never suspect him when they found the Source on the floor, bleeding. He had an alibi, an excuse. He just had to hope the Source would drink the tea he'd dosed.

It had been a simple matter of distracting the women while he dropped the powder into the omnipresent mug of greenish tea the Source drank by the gallon. According to Rachel, who mixed the concoction herself, it helped nausea and strengthened the creature inside her, and she'd been religious in her intake. He calculated she'd be unconscious in thirty-three minutes. He was very good at numbers.

He followed his plan, showing up at the workout room to meet with Michael, who'd forgotten an appointment that had never existed in the first place. "Do not bestir yourself, Archangel," Metatron said with unusual magnanimity. "I will run on the beach for an hour or so." Thereby setting up his final alibi.

He did run, a light, effortless jog, until he reached the second cove formed by the uneven coastline, well out of sight of everyone. And then he took off, soaring upward, keeping out of sight as best he could, until he landed lightly on the small ledge outside the rooms that housed the Alpha and his mate.

She was still awake, and he wanted to curse. He watched as she took the mug and drained it, making a face as she did so, and he waited, pleased with his plans, patient. Uriel would call him home when this came to pass, and Metatron would once more take his place at his right hand.

The Source reached over to set the empty mug on the table beside the bed, but she fumbled; it fell on the floor as she collapsed back against the pillows, unconscious at last.

It didn't even matter if she was still slightly awake. The draft had an amnesiac side effect—she wouldn't remember anything of the hour or so before she took the drug. He could walk in there and take care of this at any time now.

But he didn't want to see her eyes when he did it. Even if she forgot, he wanted her to be asleep. She deserved punishment, but that would be for Uriel to decide. This was the best he could offer his erstwhile master.

The window was unlatched, as always. No one in Sheol worried about security among themselves. He pushed it open and stepped inside.

I HAD NOWHERE to go that felt secure. My rooms were too isolated, which had been a blessing before Cain showed up. Not any longer. He seemed to have a preternatural awareness of my presence—he found me wherever I went to ground.

I went to the one place that always calmed me. I went down to the water.

I slipped off my sandals and wiggled my toes in the sand. I could still feel his mouth on mine. Still taste him. Thomas had never kissed me like that. Oh, I knew what it was like—or I'd thought I did. The men, my mother's friends, had tried to do that to me when they thought no one was looking. I hadn't let them, keeping my jaw clamped and my mouth tight.

I had let Cain.

The vision hit me so hard I sank to my knees with a cry of pain. It was cruel and bloody: the Source lying on the ground, clutching her stomach, screaming, screaming, in a pool of blood, as the dark figure watched and her baby died within her.

I didn't pause to catch my breath, to recover. There was no time. I surged to my feet and began screaming for Raziel, shrieking his name as I ran toward the house. It took me only a moment to find him.

"Calm down," Raziel ordered, dictatorial as always. "What's wrong?"

"Allie!" I cried. "She's in danger. Someone's trying to hurt her! We have to get to her. Now!"

Thank God he didn't hesitate. People often took my visions with a grain of salt, questioning me, trying to find a different interpretation. But Raziel didn't take chances with his beloved, and he tore up the main flights of stairs like a madman, with me on his heels.

Others joined us as we raced up those endless stairs—Rachel, Tamlel, and . . . goddamn it, Cain—but I couldn't slow down or even think about them. We had to get to Allie before the unthinkable happened.

Why did they have to live at the very top of the great house? It seemed to be taking us forever to reach their rooms, but Raziel never slowed, and neither did I, and in truth, it would have taken just as long for him to run outside and fly up there. When we reached the landing I wanted to collapse in breathless exhaustion, but instead I followed Raziel as he slammed open the doors and strode in.

I heard his cry of agony a moment before I got there. Allie was lying on the floor, unconscious, one arm protectively around her belly even in sleep. But it wasn't sleep, and Raziel was scooping her up, cradling her against him, and the second vision hit, harder than the first one, a slice of pain so deep I cried out.

She was safe. The baby was safe. The dark presence was gone, scared off. But not gone far.

And then it left me, as everything else abandoned me, strength and muscles and will. I couldn't breathe—all my air had been expended on the mad dash up countless flights of stairs—but I managed something.

"They're all right," I gasped. "We got here in time." And then I gave in to the blackness, falling.

I WAS SAFE. Warm. Protected. I hadn't felt that way since Thomas had died, and in the lush darkness I reached out for him. But it was different, more encompassing, somehow more intimate, and I sank deeper, letting myself be soothed and pampered, no need to run and fight and hide. Safe. I could stay there forever, I thought dreamily.

"Is Martha all right?" I recognized that voice, even through the heavy mists that swirled around me. Raziel. What had been so important? It didn't matter now—all was well, the danger had passed.

My face was pressed against a warm shoulder; hard arms were holding me with unexpected gentleness. Not Thomas. Thomas was dead. I needed to wake up.

But I didn't want to. Visions often did this to me, and I had had two of them in quick succession. It was as if I were covered in a dark, viscous cloud, something to keep me still and safe while I recovered. But this time I wasn't alone. This time I was cradled safely, and I could let the cloud in, to heal me. I didn't have to fight it.

It felt strange, the ripples dancing through my body, chasing out the danger, and the heat of the one cradling me was like a warm blanket. The heat between my legs, the sensitivity in my skin, the longing . . .

And then I knew who held me so tenderly, so at odds with his teasing, taunting nature. It was Cain. But why him? Why now?

I struggled toward the light, toward consciousness. I couldn't let this happen. I couldn't let him hold me while I healed. I couldn't—

"Be still," his voice whispered in my ear.

For some reason, my body obeyed, wiser than my troubled mind, and I let the darkness close in once more.

IT WAS DARK outside my window, only the faint glow of the one lantern illuminating my perfect garden, and I was alone.

I managed to sit up. The small light by my bed

was enough for now, and I shoved my curls out of my face. My hair was growing more and more out of control, and no matter how I tried I couldn't flatten it into obedience.

I had a mild headache, not nearly as bad as the usual aftermath of two such clear visions, and I pushed the covers aside, swinging my legs over the side of the bed. So far, so good. Allie and her baby were safe. We had gotten there in time, and that was what mattered.

Who would want to hurt Allie? Who would want to rip away the first sign of hope for the Fallen?

Cain was the obvious answer, one I resisted. It wasn't him. Cain was capable of all sorts of under-handed behavior, but I instinctively knew this was one thing that would cross his own particular, twisted sense of honor.

I wanted to laugh. The thought of *Cain* and *honor* in the same sentence was absurd. But I could only go with my gut instinct. He wouldn't hurt Allie. He wouldn't make war on women. Except, perhaps, me.

I pushed myself to my feet, standing for a moment on weak, shaky legs. I knew who had held me when I'd fallen in Allie's room. I knew who had brought me here, tucked me into bed. I could still feel him, feel his hot, smooth skin all around me, and I needed to wash away the sensation before I did something stupid. I needed the cold, bracing waters of the ocean to bring me to my senses, to restore and strengthen me.

I was wearing a long, loose nightgown that covered me from neck to ankle. I didn't want to consider who'd dressed me in it—the possibilities were too disturbing. I took a robe from my closet and moved slowly to my door. Cain wouldn't hear me—my less-than-perfect instincts told me that much. I was alone in the annex.

Forced to hold on to the wall as I made my way down the endless corridors that eventually led toward the sea, I paced myself, stopping to rest every now and then. Sheol was asleep for the night. I could move about with no fear of being seen.

I stepped out into the night air and paused, taking it in. A warm breeze danced across my skin, bringing with it the smell of the ocean in all its wildness, something that couldn't be controlled or tamed. It felt like a caress, one I wasn't going to compare to any other caresses—this was feather light and soothing. Oddly enough, it started the same ache inside me, the same tension and yearning that had been haunting me since I'd first dreamed of Cain, the same ache that had intensified with his presence, with each time I'd seen him. I wanted him, I might as well admit it, and it was never going to happen. I walked down to the water, then glanced around me, considering. On rare occasions I would swim naked, if I could be absolutely sure no one would see me. My luck hadn't been good of late, and I dropped the robe on the sand and walked straight into the water in my nightgown, its skirts flowing around me as I dove beneath an oncoming swell.

The icy ocean closed over my head, and suddenly I felt alive again, my whole body jump-started like a car with a sluggish battery. I shot up into the air, and I could breathe for the first time since I'd been in Raziel's top-floor apartment. I flipped backward, moving through the water, letting it cradle me, and I wanted to laugh out loud. At times like this I was a goddess, and anything was possible. I was all-powerful, and I would live forever. I looked up into the scattering of bright stars overhead, and the vastness of everything soothed me. I turned and dove beneath an approaching wave, moving deeper into the water's embrace, a goddess of the sea, a mermaid. I lived in a world of demons and fallen angels and blood-eaters, monsters like the Nephilim, and yet mermaids and fairies were nothing but stories. It wasn't fair.

The water was too cold to stay in for long, and I started toward the shore in long, clean strokes, standing when I was close enough. I was walking out of the water, my gown plastered against me, before I realized someone was standing on the beach, watching me. And I knew who it was.

CHAPTER
FOURTEEN

CAIN STOOD STILL, DECEPTIVELY relaxed and loose-limbed as she moved closer, her eyes meeting his before skittering away. "You certainly pick odd times for a swim," he said, deliberately casual. "I was about to come in after you."

"Why?"

"I was afraid you were going to drown yourself."

She laughed. He wasn't sure if he'd heard her laugh before. He found the sound surprising. Enchanting. Damn it. "The only bad thing in my life is you, and you're hardly worth dying for. I simply happen to love the water. I find it healing."

That startled him for a moment. "It can't be. You're not one of the Fallen."

"I realize that. It doesn't heal me in a physical way, but it soothes my soul and centers me."

"I see." It wasn't all he saw. She had gone swimming in her long nightgown, and now it was plastered against her body, outlining everything. Her dark, cold nipples pressed against the wet cloth, and if he put his mouth on her he would taste cool salt water before he warmed them with his breath. He could see her lovely legs, the lines of her body, the enticing shadow between her thighs.

"Seen enough?" she said pleasantly. He was holding her robe, just in case she felt like stripping off the dress, but she simply took it from him.

"Not nearly." She wouldn't know it, but he could see the scars. Something had ripped across her belly, and if the claws had gone deeper they would have gutted her. Another tear across her shoulder, across the plump curve of one breast before sliding beneath the other. The Nephilim. He knew without having to see them that there were scars on her back as well, and he wondered what she would do if he asked her about them. They were cruel and terrible, for all that they had healed, and he understood her well enough to know they haunted her.

He wasn't such a fool as to break their sudden accord. "So I gather you're feeling better?"

"Why shouldn't I be?"

"You were pretty well wrung-out this afternoon. Do visions always take that much out of you?"

She cast a suspicious glance at him. He was being

careful—at this point he was looking for information, not a shag.

"Not always. They're usually even worse."

He considered that, then filed it away for future use. "Did you eat anything?"

"I'm not hungry."

"Don't bother lying. I know you're starving."

"Then don't bother asking," she shot back. "I'll survive."

"Won't the magic vending machine of the Sheol kitchens make whatever you want suddenly appear? They've always been twenty-four/seven, though I'm damned if I can figure out how they work."

"I hate to point out to you that you're already damned," she said sweetly.

He gave a bark of laughter. "So I am. How tactful of you."

"You don't respond to tact. You don't respond to threats. You don't respond to anything," she said. "I can't get rid of you."

I respond to you, little girl, he thought, keeping his expression bland. "And why should you want to? I'm handsome, charming, and available. Why not enjoy yourself for a change?"

She raised an eyebrow. The salt water had made her brown curls even wilder around her face, and he was having a hard time reading her. "If I were looking for something enjoyable, it certainly wouldn't involve men."

He gave her a curious glance. "I thought you weren't interested in women?"

He'd managed to puncture her newfound calm. "I'm not interested, as you put it, in anyone. Why can't you just leave me alone?"

"Maybe because you're so damned cute."

He knew she wanted to hit him, hard. And he knew she didn't want to touch him. Hitting him would lead to sex as surely as a kiss would.

He kept his distance. Hell, he'd nearly been blown off his feet the last time he touched her. Sooner or later they were going to have to finish this, when the time was right. But not now.

"I wanted to talk to you," he said.

If anything, she grew more wary. "What about?"

"About your vision." She had wrapped the robe around her wet gown and started toward the house, and he easily kept pace with her. "What exactly did you see?"

She cast him a suspicious glance. "Why? What are you trying to hide?"

He sighed audibly. "A great deal, but nothing concerning the Source."

"Next thing I know, you'll say you don't prey on helpless women."

She managed to startle a laugh out of him. "Do you really see yourself as helpless?"

She considered it. "No."

"Agreed. The Source, however, is currently bed-ridden with the most unlikely pregnancy since the virgin birth, and someone got to her much too easily. What did you see?"

She paused at the threshold of the great house, looking at him with frustration. "Haven't you heard about me? How worthless and piss-poor my so-called visions are? They're almost never clear, never precise. This time I was simply shot with a sense of overwhelming dread, and I saw Allie lying on the floor, clutching her belly, blood pouring from between her legs."

"But that didn't happen. We got there in time."

"Exactly. The vision wasn't a true vision of the future, it was a warning of one possibility. An imminent possibility, and if I'd been asleep, I might have thought it was simply a nightmare. I have enough of those."

He wondered whether she considered the erotic dream he'd sent her a nightmare. He'd give a lot to know what Martha's nightmares were, and if they had anything to do with the scars that slashed across her pale skin. "But you were awake, and you knew, and you got there in time. No need to bother with what-ifs. This time the vision saved her."

If she was grateful for his encouragement, she didn't show it. "It could have been better! It could have at least given me a hint as to who threatened her, and why."

"Life is seldom that convenient. What about the second vision?"

Now she was really suspicious. "How did you know I had a second one?"

"I have eyes, Martha. I was there. What did you see then?" Too late he realized he'd slipped and called her by her real name. With luck she wouldn't notice.

"Nothing specific. Just the clear knowledge that the baby was healthy, that the vile concoction hadn't touched it. I've known that all along—that the baby and Allie would come through this pregnancy alive and healthy—but Allie's too afraid to believe me. She doesn't even need bed rest, at least not for the sake of the baby. Rachel sent her to bed because Allie was worrying too much, and this forced her to relax."

"It seems to me it would give her even more time to worry."

"We take turns distracting her. Someone is always with her."

"Not today."

Martha frowned. A delightful little moue that he wanted to kiss, but he kept still. "No, not today. Rachel said she felt Azazel call to her. It was something inconsequential, but she was gone long enough for this to happen. Someone knew what they were doing."

"Apparently. You know, Miss Mary, it seems to me we have an interest in common. We both want to find out who's trying to hurt the Source. I have a suggestion."

"I won't like it."

"No, you probably won't. I think we should work together to find out who's endangering Allie."

"No."

He looked at her averted face, trying to gauge her reaction. "Really? I would have thought your concerns were strong enough that you would use any weapon you could."

"Not you. I work best on my own," she said in a tight, defensive voice.

Defensive was good—it meant he was getting to her. But then, he knew that. "So do I, usually. But we'd each bring particular strengths to an investigation if we decided to work together. You should let me help."

"Over my dead body."

The thought startled him. The very possibility of it was both real and deeply disturbing. If her vision had stopped someone from doing harm to the Source and her unborn child, then the next logical step for that someone would be to get rid of whoever or whatever had gotten in his way. Namely, Martha.

"You might be in danger," he said abruptly.

She laughed at that. "Hardly. No one thinks I'm any real threat to their plans. It was sheer luck I happened to stop the attack on Allie. Even a broken clock is right twice a day."

"Stop it." His words were cold and clipped.

She looked up at him, confused, pulling the robe more tightly around her. She smelled of the ocean, a clean smell, and he wanted to lick the salt from her skin. She smelled of flowers, and determination. She smelled of the rich, sweet blood that pumped so fiercely in her veins, and he wanted her badly enough to forget about everything if she gave him even the slightest sign.

It was a good thing she never would. "You and I both know that your visions have saved more than one life," he went on. "No prophet or seer I've known has ever had exact knowledge. Why do you think cards and runes appeared? They weren't for everyday use, as they are now. They were used by genuine oracles to help explain their shadowy dreams."

"So you're telling me I should invest in a pack of tarot cards?" she drawled, daring to mock him. Few ever did—he was usually the one who taunted and mocked. He looked at her with annoyance and admiration.

"I'm telling you not to beat yourself up. No one likes a martyr."

She froze. So much for getting her to help him. "Go fuck yourself."

He didn't come up with the obvious rejoinder. They both knew he wanted to fuck her, and by even using the word she'd brought it out into the open.

"I guess that means you won't be helping me investigate."

"I guess you're right," she said, starting to move away from him.

Although they were headed in the same direction, he decided to give her a break. Give her time to think about it. "If you change your mind, all you have to do is knock on my door."

"Go to hell!"

He thought of the Dark City, the cold, empty grayness of the place, and grimaced. "Been there, done that," he murmured. "Think about it."

She didn't grace him with a backward glance.

CHAPTER
FIFTEEN

I WAS SHIVERING BY THE TIME I reached my room, the sodden nightgown flapping against my legs. I went straight into my small bathroom and stripped everything off, stepping beneath the hot spray of the shower with a sigh of relief. I seemed to take forever to stop shaking, and I leaned my forehead against the tile, letting the water beat down on me, washing away my tension.

Had I been wrong to dismiss his suggestion so quickly? Maybe I should follow the old advice to keep your friends close and your enemies closer. He was the logical suspect in any plot to hurt Allie's baby, and I knew instinctively that the assault had been against the unborn child, not Allie herself. He was the newcomer, the snake in our garden. He was so obvious that he ought to be discounted.

But life wasn't one of Allie's mystery novels.

Sometimes the most obvious answer was the right one.

He wanted to work with me to find the culprit. I could laugh at the very idea. Wanted to trick me, more likely. But knowing that, wouldn't I be in the perfect position to discover exactly what his mysterious agenda was? It would give me access to him that wasn't based on his totally specious attempts to get me into bed.

At least, I assumed they were specious. Thinking about that was a bad idea, but once I started, it was hard to stop it. Once more I could taste his mouth. Feel the unmistakable hardness between his legs.

That meant nothing. He was male, and I remembered what men were like. Even angelic ones. He would gladly take me to bed, and it would mean nothing more to him than eating a sandwich, a way to assuage another hunger.

But if we had something else to concentrate on, he'd leave me alone. Presumably. There was no guarantee, and he seemed to take a particular delight in trying to unsettle me; but if he really wanted something from me, I could make him behave.

I turned off the water, warm at last, and grabbed a fluffy bath sheet, wrapping it around me before I headed back into my bedroom. I was exhausted, but if I lay down with my hair wet, it would turn into a ridiculous mass of curls. I should look for the strip of toweling I wrapped around my head in a mostly useless effort to tame them, but even that seemed too much effort. I dragged myself to the bed and lay down, the towel still wrapped securely around me. A moment later, I slept.

A moment later than that, I dreamed.

Come to me. The sound of his voice on the wind, but I had sense enough not to move. Even as the bed sagged beneath his weight I didn't move, and he was looking down at me now, his eyes moving over my body. I was completely naked beneath his gaze, and I wanted to cover myself. Not my breasts and pubic area, but my scars. I wrapped my arms around myself. His hands were hard as he pulled them away, exposing me to his steady gaze.

He moved then, and his breath was hot against my skin, his long hair drifting against me, his hands on my arms, holding me still. And then his mouth touched my skin, and I wanted to weep.

It was no erotic kiss, no arousing tease of my suddenly tight breasts. It was a soft, sweet kiss against the place where the claws had bitten deep into my flesh, where the scar puckered in such an ugly way. A kiss, a benediction, followed by another, and then another, as his mouth traced the brutal line of scarring, then moved on to the next one, and I was weeping beneath my tightly closed lids.

He said nothing, but I heard his thoughts anyway.

You shouldn't be ashamed of these scars, his voice said in my dream. *They're a badge of honor.*

His hands slid down my arms, catching my hips as he kissed my torn skin, and I didn't even think about what he was doing, so lost in the blessed magic of his mouth. Until he paused at the end of the last trail, and I realized where he was, his face resting against my belly, before he caught my thighs and slowly drew my legs apart.

I knew I shouldn't let him, but his voice in my head was soft and soothing. *Let me,* he whispered. *I'll take care of you. Let me love you.*

Love me? That was impossible. Further proof that this was nothing but a fantasy, and it wasn't even Cain but some wonderful, dreamlike variant. Even in a dream I wasn't sure I wanted to do this, but his coaxing voice soothed me, and I opened for him, for the shock of his mouth between my legs, his tongue, touching me, tasting me, licking me.

His fingers flexed, caressing my thighs as he held me still, and I knew I should reach down and push his head away from me. Grab his long hair in my fist and yank.

I didn't want to. I wanted his mouth on me, his tongue, wanted the strange feelings swirling through my body; and when he released his hold on my thighs I didn't try to close them, simply arched up against him, wanting more.

The touch of his fingers was a cool shock, but nothing compared to the sensation as he slid one inside me, and I heard my soft cry with distant surprise. It was . . . strange. Good. Pushing into me as his tongue slid over me, and I was suddenly filled with the most astonishing need.

"More." I didn't recognize the raw, needy whisper, but I could feel the strange delight of his laugh against my clitoris, and then his teeth, delicately, as he withdrew his long finger and then pushed two inside.

I shattered immediately, my voice hoarse as I cried out. "Don't . . .

"Don't . . . stop."

He didn't, pushing me over that hill and then dragging me up another, higher, steeper, and I knew the plummet into darkness would be terrifying, and I knew I couldn't—wouldn't—fight him. I wanted this. In the private darkness of my dreams, I wanted everything, because nothing was real. There would be nothing in the morning but the faint shiver of remembrance. Remembrance of things that had never happened.

He moved up and breathed in my ear as I lay, sated and languorous in the aftermath. *Do you want me?* he whispered. *Or was that enough for you?*

How in the world could I have said what I did? Except that it was a dream, and I knew that I really said nothing. It wasn't my voice on the dark night air, saying, "I want you. Show me."

He moved over me, lying between my legs, and for the first time I felt him hard against me, the thick swell rubbing up and down my sensitized flesh, and I climaxed again, so fast it shocked me. I wasn't sure whether I wanted to laugh or to cry.

"I'm pathetic," I said in the darkness.

You're irresistible, he said, and lifted his hips, reaching down to position himself against me, and I wanted, needed, to feel him inside me, feel the push and shove and throb and wash of it all over me, and I arched up, waiting for the thick slide.

When it came, it was better than anything I had ever felt in my life, hard and silken, pushing inside me with such slow care that I wanted to scream. Yet I knew I couldn't hurry him—even without touching him, I knew he was far bigger than . . . The very thought was disloyal. A hard thrust would have hurt me, no matter how much I wanted it, and once more I felt tears well in the corners of my eyes.

And then he was inside me, and I was so impossibly full that I couldn't move as warmth wrapped around my breasts, my skin tingling with an absurd, breathless tension that was equal parts discomfort and delight. His mouth was at my neck, licking, and I shivered. This was going to happen this time, and I would let it. This was a dream, and I was safe. I could fly with the fantasy, and no one would know.

He pulled out, carefully, and pushed back in, and I shifted, trying to adjust to his size. I was momentarily annoyed with myself. Why couldn't I arrange my fantasies better than this, at least conjuring a man of more modest proportions? I wanted this done—I wanted my climax and I wanted him to leave.

But the dream Cain wasn't about to leave me alone. He moved too damned slowly as I began to adjust to him, taking him with no more discomfort, and when he finally thrust so deep inside that I knew I could take no more, I felt another small climax consume me. I sank back, ready to let him ride it out. I was finished.

No you don't, he whispered against my skin. He moved, still hard inside me, and I let myself ride on the tide of it, languorous, lazy, undemanding, until the burn began once more, the sweet little tingles of an emerging response. *No,* I thought. *Impossible.*

Yes, he said, putting his mouth against my ear, trailing it down the side of my neck as he thrust, steadily, hard, and I was slick with response, covered with a film of sweat, and I began to tremble as I felt his mouth against me. I closed my eyes, letting him play at my fast-beating pulse, felt his tongue lick me and stab at the base of my neck, and I arched against him, needy all over again, balancing on the edge of something I was afraid to face.

His teeth nipped at me, and I jerked with pleasure. He couldn't take my blood; he wouldn't dare. I wasn't his mate—it would kill him. But we could play at this game in a dream, and it wouldn't matter. I had nothing to fear from an act that had previously frightened me.

It didn't frighten me now. The tension was building so high it was almost pain, and I needed a release that I couldn't understand. I slid my arms around his neck, threading my fingers through his long hair, caressing him. I needed him to explode inside me; I needed him to suck at my throat and drink from me. Him inside me, me inside him. It called to me, demanding. I wanted to feed him, on such a primal level that it made me shake even more. I wanted to give everything to him, let him find his pleasure in my flesh, until there was nothing left of me.

"Take me," I whispered, my voice hoarse. "Take all of me." And I moved, baring my neck to him.

He thrust, so deep and hard that it was a kind of pleasure-pain that had me teetering on the very edge. And when I felt his bite sink deep into my throat, I went over, lost in the pulsing of my blood into his mouth, the pulsing of his semen inside me. Lost, forever, until, as I wanted, there was nothing left.

I sat up, alone in the darkness, sweating, shaking. It had happened again. The towel had come off while I slept and thrashed; my covers were on the floor. My entire body tingled, and I carefully ran my hands over my skin, uncertain whether there had been other, actual hands on me. My fingers skimmed my small breasts, my nipples so hard they hurt. I traced the first scar, almost tenderly, down over my belly, then touched myself between my legs, shivering at the sensation. I was wet, of course. Swollen. But no one else's hands had been there. No one's cock had slid inside. No one had sunk his teeth into the soft base of my neck.

I had learned how to pleasure myself. That was between me and my body, and I could bring myself to climax in a quick and efficient manner. I traced the soft curls, thinking I might wipe out the memory of the dream with my own hands. But no. I was going to empty my mind, think of nothing at all, and go back to sleep.

I rolled onto my stomach, but the feel of the rumpled sheets against my breasts, my flesh, was a stimulation I couldn't bear. I turned onto my side, wrapping myself into a tight ball, willing myself to sleep. And this time there were no dreams.

CHAPTER
SIXTEEN

I WISH I COULD HAVE SAID THE SAME for the next three nights. It should have been easier. I didn't see Cain. He was there— I heard him at times on the other side of the wall, moving around. But he wasn't at dinner; I didn't run into him in the hallways; he didn't appear when I least expected it. I could walk on the beach with equanimity; I could train under Michael's tutelage in a full workout room that never included Cain. I could sit and talk with Allie, keeping her company, knowing Cain wouldn't suddenly appear to pay his respects. I was safe.

I was miserable.

At night I dreamed, and I almost would have preferred the double-edged sword of my visions. Instead I was plagued with dreams of such blatant sexuality that I woke up blushing. I was in a state of constant arousal, my very skin ready to jump in response; I tried to tell myself they were simply erotic dreams that came to taunt me, haunt me, wake me up in a state of shivering completion. It didn't work. It made no sense. My dream climax would wake me, yet when I woke I was aroused and wanting, and even my own experienced hands couldn't bring me ease. After my first attempt I didn't even want to touch myself. I wanted someone else's hands on me. And I knew whose hands they were.

"What's wrong, Martha?" Allie's voice broke through my abstraction, and I realized I hadn't made a move in our cribbage game for the last five minutes.

I looked up guiltily. By now, three days after the attack, things had settled down to a relatively normal pace, although Raziel was prone to charge in at unexpected moments, as if he were afraid all hell would break loose if he didn't pay close attention. Allie now had round-the-clock protection, and I was merely one of those keeping her company.

"Sorry," I muttered. "My brain was elsewhere."

"I know exactly where your brain was," she said, laying down her cards and pushing the cribbage board away.

I called her bluff. "And where was that?"

"In Cain's pants."

I jumped, startled. "Allie!"

"All right, all right, I shouldn't have put it that way," she said easily, not the slightest bit abashed. Allie had never been the shy, retiring type. "But it's true, isn't it?"

"Of course not. I'm not interested in sex."

Allie let out a hoot of derisive laughter. "You can fool yourself, baby, but you can't fool me. I recognize all the signs. I honestly thought you didn't have it in you. I thought you'd put all that in the grave with Thomas, and you stayed with us so you could hide. In fact, I still think that's true. It's just that Cain's arrival hauled you out of that grave, kicking and screaming."

I made a face. "That's a really horrible image."

She grinned. "It is, isn't it? So how does it feel to be human like the rest of us? Prey to animal lust?"

"I'm not! You've misinterpreted my very real dislike for the man. He enjoyed teasing me, probably because he thought I was repressed. Which I am, and I'm perfectly happy to stay that way. Fortunately, he got over it."

"Aha," Allie said.

"Aha, what?"

"That's what's got you in a swivet. I will admit that Cain isn't the best possible choice for a partner. He's manipulative and wicked and totally untrustworthy, according to everyone, and if he says he's turning over a new leaf, there aren't many who believe him."

"So you can see why I have no interest—"

"Don't bother," Allie interrupted me. "You're practically palpitating with interest. I'm not saying he's good for anything but a roll in the hay, but he's legendary for his sexual expertise, and you could do with an expert. Enjoy yourself for the first time in your life, and when he leaves, *if* he leaves, you can consider a more suitable long-term partner."

"You're crazy," I said, wondering what legendary sexual expertise consisted of. "I'm not that self-destructive. Besides, he's not interested in me."

"You didn't see the way he looked after you had your second vision."

"You didn't either. You'd been drugged," I shot back.

"You were out a long time, baby," she said. "Whatever drug they gave me was relatively short-lasting. I woke up to see Cain sitting on the floor, cradling you in his arms, snapping like a pit bull at anyone who tried to take you away. I saw the way he looked at you, the way he stroked your hair. I *saw* him, Martha. Whatever game he's playing, with you, with Azazel, with all of us, there's still something between you."

"And you base this on your observations as you were recovering from doping and a murder attempt?"

Allie shrugged. "I calls 'em as I sees 'em."

"You're a hopeless romantic who wants true love and happy endings for everyone," I said, hating all this. "And life just isn't like that."

"No," she agreed. "Life isn't. But Sheol can be."

I turned on her. "I had my true love and happy ending. He's gone, and now I can live on in a nice, peaceful widowhood. If certain people didn't decide I was fair game to tease and taunt and pretend . . ." I trailed off, realizing I was ranting. If I wanted to show how untouched I was by all this, ranting wasn't the way to do it.

"Pretend what?" Allie picked up on that unfortunate word immediately.

"Pretend he cares about things when I don't think he has any emotions at all," I finished, a little lamely.

"Oh, Cain has emotions, all right," Allie said judiciously. "Most of them aren't pretty. I think he feels hatred, anger, contempt, lust, a powerful need for revenge. I think he longs for justice, even if he doesn't know what that is. And I think he longs for you, even if he won't admit it. He's so wrapped up in the role he's playing that everything real and good is hidden inside."

"Good God, Allie. You need to get back to writing. You're making up novels out of real people. All these things you're telling me about Cain—they're your imagination. He's not a tormented hero. He's just a shallow troublemaker who's manipulating people into reacting to his games."

Allie smiled, unoffended. "Cain would make a lousy hero. He's too complex. Maybe if I wrote inspirational fiction instead of mysteries—"

"Maybe if you wrote fantasy, because what you're talking about doesn't exist," I retorted. I picked up the scattered cards. "I'm sick of cribbage. There are only so many times you can count to fifteen and enjoy it. Let's play gin."

Allie took the cards. "All right, I get the message. We won't talk about it anymore. But I think you need to have an open mind when it comes to Cain. He tries to provoke knee-jerk reactions. You should know better than to dance to his tune."

"I'm not dancing with anybody," I muttered grimly, wishing I had something to do with my nervous hands. I was suffused with tension, so unlike me. I plucked at the loose folds of my lavender dress. I had suddenly grown sick of all my clothes, which I blamed on the restlessness that filled me lately. I'd found a few things with more color than I was used to in the back of my closet, and Tory had descended with an armful of her old dresses. She was taller than I was and a little more voluptuous, and at least one dress, a deep emerald green that I'd always admired on her and secretly coveted, was cut so low it would expose the top part of my scarring, which meant I could never wear it. But I kept it anyway, because I loved it.

"Glad to hear it," Allie said, her eyes soft and knowing. "I'm not saying you should do anything about all this, you know. I still think Cain is a very dangerous man. But admitting you're capable of feeling lust is a good thing, and eventually you'll find someone you want to f—"

"Yes," I said hastily, cutting off Allie's salty language. "Maybe." I couldn't escape Allie's watchful gaze until someone else came, but I couldn't stand thinking about Cain for another moment. "Any chance we could talk about something else? Like what you remember from three days ago?"

"Nothing," she said flatly. "I don't even remember anything from an hour or so beforehand. I gather Rachel and Metatron were visiting, but they left together. Next thing I knew, everyone was crowding around me and I was coming out of a druggy stupor. And you were lying on the floor, cradled in Cain's arms."

"Skip that part," I said hastily. The man was like an albatross, a curse that followed me into every conversation. "Did anyone look suspicious? Curious? Anyone here that surprised you?"

Allie grinned wryly. "You're thinking that criminals return to the scene of the crime? I'm the mystery writer, remember? I've looked at this from every angle and gotten nowhere. I trust everyone here."

"You shouldn't," I said, my voice flat.

"No, that's clear." Allie sighed. "It seems strange, though, accepting that someone wants to hurt me."

"Some people like to hurt." My voice sounded fine to me, but I felt Allie's hand on mine, and I didn't jump as I usually did. I had been trying to school myself to accept another's touch, but it was hard.

"Yes," she said softly. "But the people in Sheol aren't like that."

"Which is why I choose to stay," I said brightly. "And if we could just get rid of Cain, then everything would be perfect."

"The snake in the Garden of Eden," Allie said. "I've read the stories. It's why the angels fell in the first place. The quest for knowledge. Wanting to know *why*. The question is, do you want to continue in ignorance, hiding in the garden? Or do you want the knowledge the snake brings? Think about it, Martha. You've never been a coward."

But, Lord, I wanted to be.

THE SEER HAD to die. Metatron knew it with certainty, accepted it. He felt no regret—he never felt emotion, and lives meant nothing to him. He had been a soldier, Uriel's second-in-command. He enforced the archangel's decrees without a moment's hesitation, and he would again, once he regained his proper place.

He wasn't weak like Michael, his predecessor. Michael was haunted by guilt and regret for all he had done. The number he had slaughtered was impressive, even to Metatron—yet instead of pride, the archangel felt shame and sorrow. Ridiculous.

That weakness would prove to be the Fallen's

defeat. You couldn't win an epic war like the one waged between the inhabitants of Sheol and those of heaven without being inured to loss, to sorrow, to shame. Those were human emotions, petty, useless. The Fallen had become too tainted by humanity, which had always been their fatal flaw.

Michael would never kill a woman, not unless he was forced to. To Metatron, men and women were the same, tools for his master's use. And without that master, Metatron had felt lost, rudderless, until he became determined to earn his way back into Uriel's good graces. After all, it wasn't his fault he'd fallen. After he'd been killed in battle, his army had left him behind to be disposed of, and the sea had brought him back. The same sea that had destroyed the army when it returned.

He'd watched them die, Uriel's soldiers, their wings dragged under by the icy water, and he couldn't understand why the thing that had healed him had destroyed his people. He didn't waste time worrying about it. He had been well trained to ignore questions or doubts.

The way he saw it, there were two problems with killing the seer. First, how to do it. He had been trained to kill, and it was one of the few things that brought pleasure to his highly disciplined life. He didn't get many chances to indulge his expertise, and he planned to let his imagination run free. Nothing quick and painless—there was no challenge in that. He remembered the fear he used to see in people's eyes when Uriel had sent him. He had enjoyed that fear.

He could have it again with Martha, if he planned it carefully.

The other problem, of course, was Cain. He was too interested in the woman, and not in a good way. He wanted to lie with her—but then, the Cain he knew wanted to lie with anyone female. Cain had plans for her, but he hadn't shared those plans with Metatron, so it wasn't his fault if he killed her before Cain could make use of her. It was Cain's, for not telling him what her role would be.

How to kill someone discreetly? It was a weighty problem, and he would think long and hard. For the time being he would make no new move against the Source's spawn. They were watching her too closely for him to do anything now. The thing growing inside her could wait awhile longer. If he thought hard enough, he might be able to come up with the perfect solution, one that involved both Martha and the fetus, discrediting her and any disturbing visions she might have before he disposed of her.

It gave him something pleasant to ponder while he trained, simulating beating someone to death. Before long, when he regained his seat of power, he would do so in fact. Wiping Sheol out of existence.

CHAPTER
SEVENTEEN

CAIN COULD BE A PATIENT MAN when the situation deserved it. Martha required more than her fair share of patience, and his temper was beginning to fray around the edges. Each night he lived the dreams with her, fantasy fucks that were beginning to drive him crazy. He was doing it to arouse her, bring her to a state of helpless acquiescence, and instead he was walking around with a constant boner and a bad attitude. He needed her in the flesh. He needed to smell her, taste her, feel her. Kissing her in that empty room had only made things worse—now he could use memory instead of imagination. He was tired of dreams—he needed the real thing.

He knew just how to touch her. The long, slow, heated kiss they'd shared in that deserted bedroom should have been enough to jump-start her dormant sexuality. The question of who wanted to hurt the Source would occupy her mind. Both would bring her to him.

It was taking too damned long.

Three days, and he was ready to explode. She was the one who was supposed to be so restless, so desperate that she'd come to him. He was supposed to be in his room, like a spider, waiting for her to get up enough nerve. Instead he was pacing the floor, fighting the urge to go through the garden and show up at her door, which would ruin everything. She had to come to him. He'd pursued for long enough—the balance of sexual power would shift if he had to seek her out.

Come to me, he thought. *Martha, come to me.*

In fact, the question that occupied her mind troubled his as well. There should have been no one in Sheol to prove a threat to the Source and her baby. Unless someone was working for Uriel. Uriel alone would have a vested interest in destroying the first sign of hope the Fallen had ever received. Cain had questioned Metatron, who'd answered in a stony tone that could only be honest. He hadn't attempted to kill anyone in Sheol—he swore it on Uriel's head and that of the Supreme Being. And Cain had had no choice but to believe him. He knew for a fact that Metatron had no way to be in touch with Uriel. Those avenues of communication had closed when Metatron had been killed.

He viewed it dispassionately. They had found no

trace of any poison, and there had been no lasting effect for Allie. The Fallen were already relaxing into their usual complacency, doubting Martha's visions, which suited him just fine.

In the past those visions had proved unreliable at best, a fact he had every intention of using. Once he manipulated her prophecies, she could assure the Fallen of anything he wanted her to, and they would end up believing the opposite. It was infallible. Even if she was occasionally right, her reputation was ridiculed. Her only trustworthy vision lately was of Allie in danger—but she had no idea what that danger was. It could have been a simple matter of the pregnant woman passing out and falling from the bed. When it came to the miracle pregnancy, everyone was on edge, and Martha could simply have panicked, embellishing the warning vision into a conspiracy.

It was night, and he was alone, edgy. He'd kept away from Martha just to see her reaction, but the plan had backfired, leaving him sleepless and edgy. He sat back on his sofa and felt raw desire wash through him.

Come to me, Martha, he thought again, his body hot and tense. He was hungry—for sex, for blood, all the appetites he'd kept banked—and he was tired of waiting, tired of parallel fantasies. He'd thought to control them, but Martha had surprised him, opening to him. They were still only dreams, though, and he needed more.

There were others who could assuage his body. He had only to snap his fingers. But he didn't want any of the others. He could sense Martha in the other room, asleep, no doubt. Maybe lying naked in her bed, curled up, her small, perfect breasts soft in sleep. He could see the scars across her body, like ribbons of silk, and he wanted to kiss them, lick them, as he had in her dream. He would, soon enough.

A cold shower didn't help. The beat of the water against his skin echoed the beat of his heart, and the beat of her heart, so close. God, he was like an adolescent boy entranced with his first fuck. He couldn't think about anything but her.

He had brandy in the living room. The Fallen believed in appreciating the gifts of humanity, and fine liquor was a must. His current bottle of cognac was a monks' brew from early in the last century, and it was so good it was sinful. Worth falling from grace for—if he hadn't done so already.

He poured himself a snifter, warming the amber liquid in his hand. And then he reached for another glass and poured some in that one as well. *Come to me, Martha.*

He waited.

THE DREAMS CAME again, but this time I had had enough. As much as I wanted to drift beneath the seductive touch of him, I suddenly couldn't stand it anymore, and I wrenched myself out of sleep, alone in my tumbled bed, blinking into the darkness. I was so tired I wanted to weep. To scream and cry and beat my fists against the pillows. I needed to sleep, and I couldn't. I couldn't go more than a couple hours before the dreams started and my body reacted, my skin dancing in response to the phantom lover's touch, my body twisting in climax.

I was hiding from the truth. He was no phantom and I knew it. I knew who I dreamed was touching me, tasting me. Who made me want what I had always hated. I didn't have to see his face, hear his teasing, drawling voice, to know who had me beneath him, who pushed between my legs, who did such shameful things to me that in the daylight my skin flushed and my heart pounded at the memory. It was the man I was beginning to fear most in the world. It was Cain.

I sat up, shoving my hair out of my face. I could hear movements next door—that must have been what had set off the dreams. I was so freaking tired, but I knew there was no way I could get back to sleep. I wasn't even sure I wanted to.

I crawled out of bed, stumbling slightly in my exhaustion, and went over to the small desk I'd set up, pulling out the lists. I had everyone in Sheol written down. Some, like Metatron, Rachel, and Raziel, were crossed out, already discarded as possibilities. Some had check marks by them, meaning highly unlikely. And that left the rest of them.

I couldn't imagine any of them wanting to hurt the Source. She was central to the running of Sheol, the well-being of the Fallen. Without her, the life we had would be in chaos. Azazel had always been Alpha, and he'd lost his mate before; so many times. Alphas were immortal; Sources were only human. Even if their lives were extended, they still eventually died.

But if something happened to Allie, Raziel would . . . well, I couldn't imagine what Raziel would do. It would be bad enough to lose Allie. If he lost the miracle child as well . . .

And how would the unmated get sustenance? The Fallen could drink blood from their bonded mates or the Source. Anyone else would kill them—we all knew that. If someone wanted to destroy the Fallen, they couldn't find a better way.

I looked at my pages and pages of lists. I needed to start a new one, I decided, grabbing a fresh pad of paper. Just the ones who were left, not those crossed out or even checked. I picked up my pen and wrote the first name.

Cain.

I put the pad down again, staring at it. Staring at his name, in red, the color of blood. I didn't even remember how I got that pen. It must have been one of Allie's, the kind she used to make corrections when she was writing her mysteries. The ink had leaked onto my hand, and it looked like . . .

I got up and rushed into my tiny bathroom, scrubbing at it, but the stain lingered, and my skin crawled. Blood on my hands. I looked up at my reflection in the mirror, and a stranger looked back. I'd gone to sleep right after my shower, and my hair was wilder than ever, thick brown curls all around my face. My eyes looked haunted, too big, with shadows under them. I was gnawing on my lip, and I stopped that immediately, trying to smile. The attempt was pathetic. I looked like a sleep-deprived mess, and it was only getting worse.

"You should face your fears, you stupid coward," I scolded myself. "He's . . ." All the comforting words died. Harmless? Hardly. Just a man? No. Devoid of supernatural powers? Uh-uh. He was trouble, and I had every reason to be wary.

He'd offered to help me find out who had endangered Allie. Considering he was at the top of the list, that could prove very useful. Sooner or later he'd either betray himself or prove his innocence. Keeping close to him, observing him, made good sense.

Yeah, right, Martha, I thought. I was looking for an excuse.

Come to me.

The words danced into my head, and I had no idea where they'd come from. A whisper on the night air, a promise, a sweet taunt. *Come to me, Martha,* the words came again, and I shook my head to clear it, pushing away from the sink and heading back into my room.

I didn't bother looking around me for hidden speakers. I knew the words hadn't been spoken out loud. I'd felt that kind of communication before, the rare mental bond that sometimes existed in this misty world of shadows. *Come to me, Martha.*

Come to me, Martha. He called me.

I went.

CHAPTER
EIGHTEEN

H IS DOOR WAS UNLATCHED, AND the pressure of my knock made it glide open. I stood there, frozen.

Cain was sprawled on his sofa, his long legs propped up on the coffee table. His feet were bare, and he was relaxed, lazy, a book in his hand. He glanced up at me, unsurprised, almost as if he'd been expecting me, and his eyes were devilish. "Strange time of night for a visit, Miss Mary," he drawled. "Unless you've changed your mind about my suggestion."

"I did." I was astonished at how composed my voice was. "May I come in?" I figured studious politeness would keep things on a professional level. Keep the memory of those insidious dreams at bay.

He raised an eyebrow. "Need you ask?" He waited until I closed the door behind me. "So you decided I could show you the wonders of sex after all?"

"No!" All calm vanished momentarily. And then I realized he was teasing me again. "No," I said more evenly. "I decided I would let you help me find out who's trying to hurt Allie."

"I don't believe that was the way I phrased my original offer, but it's close enough," he murmured. "Have a seat and we'll talk." He gestured to a place beside him on the large sofa.

I took the seat opposite him primly enough, folding my long skirts around my legs as I tucked them up under me. I looked at him, then my gaze skittered away. He was shirtless, and the top button of his jeans was unbuttoned. I understood the reason for it—the waistband could dig into your stomach. But Cain had absolutely no excess flesh—he was lean and strong and there was no stomach for that button to dig into. It was merely unfastened as a temptation, I decided. Which was ridiculous—how could he know that I would choose this night to come to him?

Come to him? Hardly. We were joining forces, that was all.

The room was warm, and the French doors were open to the night air. I looked at him and shivered anyway. He made me so damned nervous. "I was thinking . . ." I began, looking past his left shoulder. Unfortunately, that brought my gaze to the bedroom beyond and the huge bed with its rumpled sheets, and for a moment I wondered what it would be like to lie in a man's bed, to lie in a man's arms, after all this time. To feel him all around me, hot and heavy and—

I tore my gaze away. I was going crazy. The dreams were bad enough. If I indulged in the real thing, I'd be in very big trouble, despite Allie's encouragement. I met his amused eyes, and for a moment it seemed as if he knew what I'd been looking at and what I'd been thinking. No. "I made a list," I said.

"Of course you did. More than one, I expect."

I was *so* glad I hadn't brought my multiple lists with me. I'd meant to, but I'd decided to make this move at the last minute, and I hadn't thought things through. If I had, I never would have come. "Of course not," I said self-righteously. "Just one master list, with the names of the obviously innocent people crossed off and check marks against the unlikely."

"And color-coded and cross-referenced for motive and opportunity?"

"Shut up. So I like to be thorough. It's a useful trait."

"You're a control freak, Martha," he said frankly. He used the right name. That was at least the second time he'd done it, revealing that he knew perfectly well what my name was. Getting it wrong was just one more way to annoy me. "Fortunately, I can use a control freak right about now. So tell me, whom have you ruled out?"

"Rachel, Tory, and me, to begin with." Why couldn't he put on a shirt?

His honey-gold skin was smooth—no bristly hair dusting his chest. Funny that it seemed so familiar. I hadn't touched him—only in my dreams—so how could I possibly know? And I wouldn't touch him, not if I could help it.

"What are your reasons for ruling you three out? Just because you're all female isn't good enough. The demon Lilith is famed for bringing about the deaths of infants. The Roman goddess of war is merciless."

He was annoying me. Good. If I was annoyed, I didn't feel that awful pull toward him. "We call the Lilith Rachel," I corrected him. "And if it weren't for her, Allie wouldn't be pregnant in the first place. Besides, the stories about her were lies. She cared for the lost babies, she didn't kill them. So it couldn't be her, and it couldn't be Michael's wife either. Why should Tory want to hurt her?"

"Because she's jealous?" he suggested.

"No. Maybe in a few years she'll start wishing for children—I don't know. It seems to take about that long for the reality to set in, to know that life will be barren."

"Is that how long it took you?"

My hands were hidden from his view as I clenched them. "Thomas didn't live long enough for me to get to that point," I said, hoping to shame him. "I was only twenty-two when he died." Of course, nothing shamed Cain. And it was a lie. Oddly, I didn't lie to anyone else, but I lied to Cain without compunction. I had known when I went with Thomas, when he took me away from that awful place, that I would have no children. The knowledge had grieved me, but I'd told myself it would be a worthwhile trade-off. I hadn't had time to regret it.

"All right, you've managed to convince me. Not Rachel or Tory. What about you?"

"How could it possibly be me?" I demanded. "Don't you think I would have noticed?"

He shrugged, drawing my attention to his sleek, smooth shoulders, distracting me.

"You could have done it in an altered state of consciousness."

"I don't do drugs," I said sharply.

"Of course you don't. There aren't any drugs in this benighted place. At least, not good ones. There are other kinds of altered states, like hypnosis, or psychotic breaks—"

"We can rule all of those out."

"—or visions. People have been known to commit crimes and not know they'd done them," he continued before I could protest.

"Don't you think we'd be better off spending our time looking for more likely suspects? After all, I'm the one who came to you."

"So you did," he said softly, and I was distracted again. Remembering the taste of him. He leaned forward, and I realized there were two brandy snifters on the table. He pushed one toward me.

I looked at it suspiciously. "Were you expecting someone?"

"I was expecting you, my pet. And searching for the perpetrator isn't necessarily a sign of innocence. After all, half the reason you decided to help me was to ascertain whether I'm the actual villain. You figured this would give you a better vantage point, right?"

I hoped the sudden heat in my face wasn't showing up in a blush. "You *are* an actual villain," I said flatly. "Whether you had anything to do with Allie's attack is another question, but I assume the answer will come out as we search through my lists."

"Aha! I knew there was more than one list," he said triumphantly. "Drink your cognac, love."

Love? That was a ridiculous thing to call me. I wasn't about to bring that up, however—it would give him license to say all sorts of distracting things.

I shouldn't accept anything from him. If he actually had been the one to drug Allie, then I was opening myself up to all sorts of possibilities, from being roofied to being dead. He was watching me, a challenge in his silvery eyes, a faint smile on his mouth. If I refused, he would win.

Then again, if he'd put something in the brandy, he'd win as well.

He leaned forward, pushing his own glass toward me. "If you're afraid it's poisoned, you can drink mine instead."

Put my mouth where his had been? Not likely. I gave him a cool smile. "I trust you," I said, reaching for my own glass.

He was looking at me with stern disapproval. "Trusting me is a big mistake, and you know it. Fortunately, you're lying."

"I didn't say I trust you in all matters," I protested, taking a small sip of the brandy and feeling it burn nicely. "I just trust you not to have poisoned me. This time."

He grinned then, and I wanted to moan. His smile was seductive, his grin irresistible—and I remembered that mouth on my breasts. A mouth I had never felt. "Really? What else do you trust me not to do?

I shook myself out of the strange lassitude the brandy and his eyes were lulling me into. I needed to sleep, I thought wearily, not match wits with a fallen angel. "Why don't we talk about something a little more important?"

"Such as?"

"Like why I'm here. Like who is trying to hurt Allie."

His eyes were slow and languorous as he sipped

at his own cognac. "Those are two different issues entirely."

I stared at him, momentarily confused. "I beg your pardon?"

He leaned back, smiling lazily. "The middle of the night is no time to discuss possible perpetrators. We can presume Allie is safely in bed with her husband, and they are pleasantly sated from the sex you talked them into."

How did he know that? How did he seem to know every damned thing? I didn't deny it. "We can presume so. She's safe for now."

"So what made you decide to beard the lion in his den?"

The spider in his parlor, I thought. The snake in his . . . where did snakes live? Not in apple trees, despite mythology. "I couldn't sleep. I heard you moving about and I knew you were awake as well. You've been hard enough to find the last few days, so I figured now was as good a time as any, before you disappeared again."

Damn. I'd said too much. As always.

His eyes gleamed. "Miss me?"

"Hardly."

"If I'd known you were looking for me, I would have presented myself immediately."

"Ha!" I said before I could help myself. "You know everything."

He laughed at that, and the sound danced across my skin like a silver caress. "I'm gratified to know your opinion of me is so high. Trust me, there are a great many things I don't know. Like why you decided to come to me."

Come to me. The words echoed in my head, and I looked at him suspiciously. He was all limpid innocence, meeting my gaze without a trace of guile.

And then he made his first mistake. "Unless you think I have some sort of magic power to draw you to me."

I stared at him, unmoving. He'd done it. He *had* called me, his serpentine, insidious voice luring me into his dangerous presence. His voice, each time those explicit dreams started. *Come to me.*

I had no idea how he'd done it. The only thing that kept me from getting up and walking out was the knowledge that even if he'd instigated my erotic dreams, there was no way he could know what went on in my mind. In my bed. He couldn't know that I'd welcomed my dream lover.

If I ran, he would win.

I leaned back in my chair, uncurling my legs and stretching them out in front of me, seemingly relaxed. "How did you do it?" I said in a conversational tone.

It was only a quick flash in his eyes, but he realized things had shifted. He was very observant, was the snake in our Garden of Eden. "Do what, Miss Mary?" he countered.

I looked at him. He wouldn't admit to it, and I was tired of fighting. "Why don't you stop playing games? You know perfectly well what my name is."

"I do. But you're so much fun to tease."

"Find other ways to enjoy yourself," I said sternly.

His eyes slid over my body, slowly, like a dark, erotic caress, and I could feel myself heat in reaction. Absurd! How could a look do that? I couldn't feel it, couldn't quantify it.

"Oh, I will," he murmured.

CHAPTER
NINETEEN

SHE WAS TOO EASY, CAIN THOUGHT, shifting a little. He was hard, uncomfortably so, which astonished him. Bantering with a woman didn't usually have this effect on him, not after all these years. But then, Martha was not an ordinary woman.

She was too damned smart. He could make her squirm, just by giving her his patented seductive once-over, but it was starting to backfire, making him as aroused as he wanted her to be. Normally that wouldn't be a problem, but with Martha he needed to be in complete control, not at the mercy of his cock.

He'd always had the ability to see, occasionally, into another's thoughts. It usually happened when there was something powerful that tied them together. He could read Azazel, the betrayer, fairly often. The others, occasionally.

Metatron didn't seem to have a thought in his thick, handsome skull, thank God. It was always better when your confederates didn't come up with unhappy surprises. Martha was full of secrets, full of surprises, and he was becoming disturbingly fascinated by her, so that those private, dreaming, shared fantasies were now the most important part of his day.

"You want to talk about who tried to hurt Allie?" she said, attempting to put things back on a polite, impersonal level—but that ship had sailed days ago.

"Anything you say, Miss Mary." He put deliberate emphasis on her name, just as a little twist.

She made a face, and he wanted to laugh. Using her real name in such a deliberate tone would have bothered her too. Everything he did bothered her. He liked that. "Too bad you don't have a last name," he continued. "I can't very well call you Mrs. Thomas. How about the Widow Thomas, if you prefer formality?"

"Bite me." The moment that instinctive response was out of her mouth she froze, and the image was an assault on his senses. He didn't know if it was her thought or his, but he could see it, feel it, taste it. Her skin, the soft swell of her breast, the inside of her thighs, the lush softness between her legs. Gentle nips, licks, tastes. And, oh God, her blood. Pulsing at the base of her neck, throbbing at the juncture of her legs, rich, thick, sweet, pouring down his throat, filling his own veins, strength and life and love throbbing through him—

"Ahem." She cleared her throat, and he was torn from the erotic fantasy. She was blushing. She blushed a lot—blood flooding to her cheeks—and she had no idea how much that fed his inexplicable lust for her. Blood and sex were inextricably combined in his soul, and she was both.

"Sorry." He blinked, feigning absentmindedness. "I was thinking of something else."

She gave him a disapproving glare. "Who do you think attacked Allie?"

"I have no idea. Tell me about your vision—maybe that might spark something."

She knit her forehead, concentrating, and damned if that didn't arouse him as well. "It was a flash, like most of them," she said slowly. "Allie was lying on the floor, and a dark figure was bending over her. He kicked her in the stomach, and—"

"'He'?" Cain interrupted.

"Not necessarily." She shuddered, clearly horrified at the memory. "He . . . he seemed like a huge dark shadow filling the room. It was . . ." She stopped, shivering, wrapping her arms around her body. "It was hideous."

He considered it. "It couldn't be Uriel himself. Uriel can't come to Sheol without his cadre of angels. He could have sent someone, of course, and this was definitely his style—sneak attack with no warning, hurting helpless, pregnant women." Memory flashed, a wound that would never heal. So long ago. No, he couldn't go there. "Do you sense it was an outsider?"

She shook her head. "It was someone from Sheol. There are any number of us who can sense when an outsider is here, and there is no one who doesn't belong. Or . . . only one."

For a moment he didn't realize she was talking about him. Then he grinned at her. "Well, I'm the logical culprit. Why don't you think it's me?"

Her eyes met his. "I'm not sure. Instinct."

He nodded, not examining that particular thought. Did her instincts tell her he meant no harm to the status quo? If so, she was dead wrong. "Anyone you suspect?" he asked her. "Have you ruled out anyone else?"

"Azazel, Raziel, Tamlel, Michael, Metatron, and Melchior," she said without hesitation. "None of them would have any reason."

"Why not Metatron? He seems a good possibility." A little too good, he thought. He and his minion were going to have a heart-to-heart talk later on.

"Honestly, I would have thought so. He's the second-best option, after you. But he was with Rachel when it happened. He was visiting and then left when Rachel did. On top of that, he's a got a crush on the Source. He wouldn't hurt her."

"I didn't know that," he said, startled. "Metatron doesn't strike me as someone who's much interested in sex."

"It's not about sex," she said reprovingly.

"Honey, it's always about sex," he drawled.

She frowned at him. "Metatron's got a crush on her as if she were a goddess and he were a lowly mortal."

"He's got it backward."

Martha glared at him. "Allie *is* a goddess, if not literally. And Metatron's not worthy. Fortunately, he agrees, but he'd defend her with his life."

"He's supposed to defend everyone here with his life."

"I assume he would. He doesn't seem to be interested in anything but duty. Except for the Source. With Allie, it's because he cares. He'd never let anyone hurt her."

And then he knew. He should have seen it right away, except that Metatron had sworn he wouldn't kill anyone. But "anyone" might not apply to Allie's baby. Maybe he considered a small scrap like that not yet human, thereby circumventing his promise. Damn him.

He wasn't going to tell Martha. He still needed Metatron. And if the mystery was solved, she'd have no reason for her midnight visits, and he was planning on there being more. Ones that took place in his bed.

This time she didn't notice his abstraction. "Clearly the attack was against Allie's baby, not Allie. Otherwise it would have been easy to give her enough of the drug to kill her."

"Maybe he thought he *had* given her enough."

"Then why would he or she bother to come back and kick her?" Martha said, pulling her legs up underneath her again. She was beginning to relax around him. Foolish of her, since she was in direct danger from him, but he liked the softening of her prickly exterior. "No, I'm sure the attack was against the baby, not Allie."

"And you think this why? Why would anyone want to hurt an unborn child?" he countered.

"The child changes everything," she said. "This was a world without even the possibility of children. And I know Allie won't be the only one. The Fallen have existed for millennia, banished by the Supreme Power to eternal exile, with not even the hope of an afterlife or any chance at redemption. All that is about to change."

"Is it?" he murmured, watching her. "Is that one of your imperfect visions?"

She shook her head. "It's only common sense. Children are hope. They're the future, proof that life goes on, that there's an afterlife in them, at the very least, whether or not there's some kind of heaven available for the Fallen. Some people hate change, even if it benefits them."

"So they do," he murmured. "Personally, I'm very fond of it. So who do you know who hates change enough to endanger the Source to stop it?"

She was clearly racking her brain. "I should have brought my lists," she said glumly.

Lists, plural. He kept his smile to himself. She was so organized, so precise, building a safe little wall around herself, stick by stick. She really thought she had a chance in hell of controlling her life.

Her hair looked like a halo of curls around her piquant face. Her eyes were huge and shadowed, and she looked exhausted. "How long have you had trouble sleeping?" he asked suddenly.

She looked at him, startled. Then she smiled wryly, and that smile was like a blow to his gut. "I should say ever since you arrived, but that would be a lie. I've never slept well."

"Why not?"

She shrugged. "Probably because I didn't sleep through the night when I was in the real world. It wasn't a very safe situation, and I needed to be alert."

"You're going to tell me about it someday," he said softly.

"Yeah, right," she scoffed. "My past is buried and I don't even think about it."

"But you still don't sleep at night."

"I don't sleep during the day either."

But she was sleepy now. He knew it, could feel her body shutting down out of sheer exhaustion. She had curled up in the chair, loose-limbed and sleepy, and he wanted her in his bed like that.

"Let me tell you my theory," he said in a soothing voice. "I wouldn't rule out everyone on your lists. Let me go over the members of Sheol who've been here since the beginning, then the ones who came later that I still remember, and then you can tell me about the newcomers. First we have Azazel. . . ." He talked on, his voice low, hypnotic, naming the Fallen, watching her eyelids droop. By the time he'd gotten to Gadrael, she was out.

He waited for her to settle into a deeper sleep. Then he rose and crossed the room, sliding his arms underneath her.

This time there was no lightning bolt between them, just a faint sizzle when his skin touched hers, absorbed quickly into his own flesh. She didn't wake. She was bone tired, he could feel it, and she settled against him easily, as if she belonged in his arms. She smelled like lilies of the valley, sweet and innocent, and he wondered what she'd taste like. He carried her into his bedroom and set her down on the bed, waiting for her to open her eyes and scream bloody murder. She didn't. Even when he settled down beside her, she didn't erupt in rage.

What she did startled him even more. She opened her eyes sleepily when he gently pulled her into his arms. "You're a very bad man," she murmured, resting her head on his shoulder as he tucked her against him.

He smiled in the darkness. "I'm a very bad angel."

But she was already asleep again, trusting him when her defenses had vanished. She was even more vulnerable than he'd thought, and he felt a pang of worry. Someone could come in and rip her bruised heart to pieces. He didn't want to let that happen.

Maybe he could toughen her up a bit without destroying her. She had a role to play, an important one, and it was too late to change course. The seer was becoming more reliable, which changed things once more. She would repeat whatever he planted in her fertile brain, and he had to gauge whether the Fallen would be in a receptive mood or a disbelieving one before he decided how to use her. If everyone believed the lies he was pushing through her, it would work just as well. Leaving the Fallen open to the chaos he was bringing.

She would be distraught at being used like that, he knew. She would hate him for doing it.

Maybe it would destroy her. He would take her gift, her body, even her love, and use them to his advantage, then walk away. If there were another way to do it, he would. He'd grown . . . fond of her,

he admitted. That suspicious way she had of looking at him, the confused, erotic thoughts she didn't
understand. The strange, inexplicable shocks that
sparked between them when he touched her.

He liked the way she looked after the Source, her
friendships with the other women, the way she stood
up to Raziel. In all, she was an estimable woman,
much more than she realized. He wished she were
going to come out the better for having been used
by him. He doubted it.

She settled so peacefully in his arms, and he
found that for once he was growing tired as well.
Angels didn't need much sleep, and he had trained
himself to make do on even less than the usual. But
in the comfortable bed, with Martha in his arms, he
almost thought he might fall asleep.

Which was even stranger. When he did sleep, it
was never with a woman in his bed, much less in his
arms. He tended to thrash around, kick the covers
off, toss the pillows to the ground, and end up facing
the foot of the bed.

He didn't feel the slightest bit restless. He almost
felt . . . peaceful. He could feel her heartbeat, slow,
steady. Feel the soft puff of her breath against his
neck. The heat of her body against his, soft and pliant. He lowered his head to rest against hers—and
slept.

CHAPTER
TWENTY

I WOKE SUDDENLY, IN A PANIC. I HAD no idea where I was. I pushed myself up in the strange bed, dazed, disoriented from my heavy sleep, and I was frightened. Someone was coming, someone bad, and I had to protect the children.

I snapped out of it, alert. It had been a long time since there had been children to worry about. Thirteen years, in fact. I was in Sheol, I was safe. No one could harm me here, no one—

I heard the shower in the background, and I realized with distant shock where I was. In Cain's bed.

How had I gotten here? I looked down at my body in horror, concentrating, trying to sense whether it was different, whether he'd . . . whether we'd . . .

The shower stopped before I could gather my senses and run, and a moment later Cain strolled out of the bathroom, a towel low around his narrow hips, and I swallowed.

All angels are beautiful. It's an essential part of the job description, and I had quickly grown inured to it. I wasn't inured to Cain.

He wasn't as tall as some of the others, less noticeably muscular. His body was thin and lithe, covered with smooth, golden skin. And that old biblical quote came back to me: "Behold, my brother Esau is a hairy man, and I am a smooth man." Jacob had been a trickster, a liar, and a thief. I doubted this man was any different.

He stood there looking at me, hands on those slim hips, a twist of a smile at his mouth. "What are you thinking about so fiercely?"

"The Old Testament," I answered with absolute truth.

He threw back his head and laughed. "You're a wonder, Miss Mary," he said. And he pulled off his towel.

Uh. No, not completely smooth. He was trying to unsettle me, and I was trying hard not to be unsettled, but it was getting more and more difficult. I managed to let my eyes drift over him with limpid disinterest, tucking my unwilling observances into the back of my mind for further examination later on. Then again, my gaze was the only limpid thing in the room.

I waited until he pulled his jeans on. "What am I doing in your bed?"

"You fell asleep while I was talking to you. I can't say I was flattered—I'm not used to women passing out from sheer boredom."

"I was tired," I said defensively. "That still doesn't explain what I'm doing in your bed."

"You were curled up in that chair in practically the fetal position. If I'd left you like that, you would have woken up stiff and aching, or you might have fallen out of the chair and woken *me* up."

"Oh, heaven forbid!" I said. "That still doesn't explain why I'm in your bed."

He shrugged, bringing my eyes to his bare shoulders. I liked them. A lot. They weren't massive like Metatron's, or as bulky as Thomas's had been. He was lean and slightly bony beneath all that smooth flesh. "I was going to put you in your own bed, but mine was closer and you were a handful. I was too lazy to go that far."

I was anything but a handful. I was too short and, apart from considering my ass and thighs too generous, I knew I was normal size. Which meant I was relatively light—and angels were very, very strong.

"You didn't do anything, did you?" I asked suspiciously.

He grinned at me. "What do you think, sweetheart? Did I leave anything between your legs?"

"Don't be disgusting."

He raised an eyebrow. "Disgusting, is it? You don't like sex?"

I'd given too much away. "Not with you."

He held very still for a moment, and suddenly I realized my danger. I was sitting in the middle of his bed, alone, at the very end of the big house, and he was only half-dressed. And then he started toward me.

I should have run. Should have scrambled off the bed and out the door before he could catch me. If he even wanted to catch me. I didn't move.

We had excellent beds in Sheol. The mattress didn't even dip when he knelt in front of me. "Oh, really?" he said mildly enough. "Let me prove you wrong."

He pulled me against him, against all that smooth, hard flesh, and I could feel the strange tingling washing over my body. I should have struggled—but he was much stronger than me; my best bet was to hold perfectly still, prove myself unmoved. Yes, that was the ticket. He could touch me, he could do anything he wanted to me, and it wouldn't matter. I could let go, let him . . .

I was fooling myself. I could let go and let him do what I wanted. I wanted him. I had chosen a life of peaceful, comfortable celibacy after Thomas, and I wanted this man so much I was burning with it. And he knew it.

"Don't," I whispered as his hands slid up my arms. They were bare, and the feel of his skin against mine made my womb clench with sudden longing. The body I had lived with all my life, the body I trusted, was betraying me.

He smiled at me, his face so close I could see the dark striations in his silver eyes. "Can't," he said. And then his mouth closed over mine.

The kiss was a wonder. He'd kissed me hard, back in that deserted room, hard and deep and demanding, and I'd been ready to do anything for him. This was soft, slow, a teasing seduction, nibbling at my lips, nipping, tugging at them until I opened for the lazy, languorous sweep of his tongue. He drew my body up against his, and my breasts were tight, almost painful against the soft cotton of my dress, soft cotton that was too thick, in the way. I wanted it off, I wanted to lie naked against him, I wanted him inside me, pushing, surging, shuddering while I held him. I wanted my too-vivid dreams to be reality. His hand slid up to cup one breast, his fingers playing with the nipple through the damnable fabric, teasing, tugging, and I wanted his mouth on me there, sucking, pulling.

He pushed me back against the sheets, gently, and I went willingly enough, not fighting. He levered himself on top of me, pushing my legs apart with his to lie between them, and I could feel the hardness of his erection against my sex. "Don't?" he whispered, mocking me, as his hand started to slide beneath the long skirt.

I fought then, a small struggle, but he held still, looking down at me out of slumberous eyes. "I don't want my clothes off." The minute the words were out of my mouth, I realized I'd given him permission of sorts. I hadn't said "Get the hell off me" or "I really don't want you." I'd been resisting so long.

I'd been dried-up and dead for so long. I wanted life. I wanted more.

He smiled down at me, a lazy, sweet smile, and shook his head. "I want to see your body."

"You don't need to," I said stubbornly. "Just go ahead and do it. You can pull up my skirts and get on with it. I don't mind."

For a moment he didn't say anything, his face a blank. And then he began to laugh, rolling off me to lie on the mattress beside me, roaring.

All my desire vanished, and I sat up, offended, relieved. I had almost made a very big mistake. I scrambled off the bed, and he didn't bother to stop me. His laughter was slowly dying, but there were tears of amusement in his mesmerizing eyes, and I stopped by the door, looking at him in annoyance. "I'm glad I could entertain you," I said stiffly. "I think I can manage this investigation on my own from now on."

I half expected him to surge off the bed and pull me back, but he simply laughed again. "Darling Martha, you enchant me," he said. "I was just temporarily blown away by the depth of your passion."

I wanted to snarl, when I'd thought I had perfect control of my temper. He really did bring out the worst in me. I couldn't think of anything to say, so I went with an old standby. "Whatever."

He laughed again, and if he had been closer I would have hit him. "I'm going to talk to a couple of people you've already discounted, just to see if I agree. In the meantime, why don't you find out if the Source remembers anything else? Rachel as well. And when you come back tonight, bring all your copious, cross-referenced lists."

"What part of me managing the investigation on my own didn't you understand?" I said crossly. "I don't need you."

His laughter faded, all amusement vanished, but the look in his eyes was unexpectedly full of a promise I didn't want to face. "Oh, yes you do, sweetheart."

CHAPTER
TWENTY-ONE

H E COULD DROWN HER, META-tron thought as he walked along the beach. Thomas's widow was very fond of the water, but she was only a mortal, after all. She could drown as easily as any human. It might be difficult, though. If he held her under, the healing power of the ocean could move through his touch to her, and there was a chance she'd be invulnerable as well. He'd never quite understood how the water worked, how it had brought him back from death but decimated Uriel's army, and he didn't trust it.

She seldom left the compound except to swim. Poison, though hard to procure, was the easiest to use, but the very idea disgusted him. He was a man of action, and poison was the weapon of weaklings. Besides, it was too variable—he'd mistimed the sleeping draft with the Source. He couldn't afford to fail again.

Breaking her neck and passing it off as a fall was clearly his best choice. If he killed her before throwing her in the water, it would appear she'd slipped and hit her head. It would be a sad accident, but no one would really mind. She was a widow, a useless appendage in the society of Sheol.

He could fly back to the house the moment he got rid of her, and it might be days, weeks, before her body was discovered. There would be nothing to tie him to her death. Cain would be annoyed if he found out Metatron was to blame, but that could be handled. Metatron shrugged. Cain would simply have to adjust his plans accordingly. A quiet little woman could hardly be that important in the complex scheme of things.

Once she was gone, there would be no one to interfere. Even Cain would eventually agree it was for the best.

"Metatron!"

He was a warrior—he never showed surprise, was never startled, though it took all his training not to jump when Cain's voice slashed through his thoughts.

He turned. Everything about Cain annoyed him—his cleverness, his speed, the way he mocked everything and everyone. But Metatron needed him too much to get rid of him. "Cain," he acknowledged in an even voice.

"You promised you wouldn't kill anyone." Cain's voice was calm, almost meditative. Metatron had the good sense not to trust it.

"I have kept my promise," he said slowly. So far.

"I wouldn't call what you did to the Source keeping your promise."

Metatron considered this carefully. Should he lie, swear he'd had nothing to do with it? He wasn't a facile liar, not like Cain, who could weave so many stories he made Metatron's head spin.

"I kept my promise."

"Are you trying to convince me someone else was responsible for drugging the Source?"

"No."

Cain's eyes narrowed. "You feel like explaining?"

"I agreed I wouldn't kill anyone. The spawn growing inside of the Source isn't someone. It's evil. She would have survived the loss, but the entire company of Sheol would have been thrown into sorrow and disarray. Those who needed to partake of her blood would feel that sorrow magnified, and therefore they'd be easier to destroy."

For a moment Cain said nothing. He was smaller than Metatron—everyone was smaller. It was odd that he seemed so powerful. "I thought we were working together," Cain said carefully.

"We are."

"Then why did you decide to do this on your own?

It put them all on their guard. Before this they didn't realize there were any traitors left in Sheol. Now they know they're in danger, and everything will be more difficult."

Metatron eyed him narrowly. "It seemed worth the risk. If the demon spawn is born, it will give them hope for the future, and we must remove that hope. It was a logical step to take."

"First off, I don't know if I'd call Allie and Raziel's child a demon spawn."

"Of course it is! The offspring of an immortal and a human? It's obscene. Like cats mating with dogs."

Cain's mouth quirked in that annoying smile, the one that always made Metatron long to hit him. "I wouldn't go that far. Secondly, the seer has become more focused. There's a chance that anything you try, she'll see ahead of time."

"If that's the case, then she might see that you aren't what you say you are," Metatron pointed out. Another reason to kill her, he told himself. But Cain was too weak to do it.

"I'm willing to take that risk. No harming women or children, if there happen to be any."

He was a fool, Metatron thought. In war you fought anyone who got in your way, man, woman, or child, ancient crone or infant in arms. He had followed orders and smote them all, and he would do so again to return to Uriel's world.

But he knew what Cain wanted to hear—and he needed his help. He could dispose of him later if he became difficult. "I'm sorry," he said, hoping he sounded sufficiently repentant. "I should have discussed it with you, but the idea came to me and I was impulsive." He was never impulsive. But Cain didn't know that.

Cain's eyes narrowed, and he shook his head. "Do not do *anything* without consulting me. I have a very carefully thought-out plan, and I can't have you stomping in and ruining everything."

"You care to share this plan of yours?" Metatron asked sourly.

"When I'm ready," Cain said. "In the meantime, leave the Source alone."

That was easy enough to promise. It was the seer who was in the way. "I won't think of anything new and not tell you," he said with mendacious honesty. After all, he'd already formulated his plan to deal with Martha. From then on, he'd be honest. If he had to.

Cain was looking at him, long and hard. Distrusting him. He would not be happy when Martha was found dead, but it would be impossible to blame Metatron. In truth, he was very well pleased with himself.

"See that you do," Cain said finally. "I'm trusting you."

Metatron almost barked with laughter. More fool he.

CHAPTER
TWENTY-TWO

C AIN STROLLED TOWARD THE
workout room that was the archangel
Michael's domain, a lazy smile on his
face, his brain moving rapidly beneath his calm exterior. He was balancing a number of possibilities, but
he'd always been good at that. Multitasking—that
was what they called it nowadays, wasn't it? He liked
it best when a thousand questions swirled around in
his mind. It filled the gnawing emptiness inside him,
kept him too busy to listen to the one insistent voice
in the back of his head, the one that never left him,
the one he refused to name.

He pushed open the door. It was late morning—
he still couldn't believe how long he'd slept with
Martha in his arms. Couldn't believe that he'd slept
at all. If there was a woman in his bed, she was there
for sex and nothing else; and once that was finished,

then one of them had to leave. Yet there had been no sex between them, merely a semichaste kiss. Well, perhaps not so chaste. He was incapable of chaste, but for him it had come close. He could tell himself it was all part of his plan to seduce her, lure her in and make her drop her guard, but that wasn't necessarily the truth. Maybe he just liked lying in bed with her, her breath gentle against his chest as he cradled her in his arms.

He was growing absurdly sentimental. Did the Fallen get senile dementia? He'd lived longer than most of them; maybe his brain was failing. Beating the crap out of someone would help his state of mind.

Michael was over in the corner, showing one of the newer angels some moves, but he looked up when Cain wandered in, his eyes turning even darker.

"Angel Cain, reporting for duty," Cain drawled.

Michael said nothing. He wasn't as thin as he'd been when Cain had last seen him, though the myriad of tattoos still swirled and danced over his bronzed skin. He was probably the most dangerous warrior in Sheol. What he lacked in bulk he more than made up for in skill. Too bad he lacked Cain's own cunning—with that he'd be invincible.

"According to our honored leader, all residents of Sheol are required to put in a period of physical training each day," he continued as Michael eyed him dubiously.

"You've been here almost a week," Michael said finally. "What made you decide to join us?"

He gave Michael his most charming smile, even knowing it was a waste. Michael wasn't one to be charmed by anyone but his new wife, the goddess Victoria Bellona. Cain would be charmed by her too, if he wasn't afraid Michael would rip his head off. "Let's not worry about the past," he said smoothly. "I'm here now."

Michael watched him out of hooded eyes, but Cain kept his expression deceptively pleasant. "You're ready to let go of the past, Cain? Why is it I don't believe you?"

Michael had moved closer, his voice low, though that was probably pointless. The dozen or so people training were watching surreptitiously as the two ancient enemies circled each other like wary dogs.

"Because you've always been a suspicious bastard," Cain said. "I have no grudge against you."

"I wasn't even there."

Cain felt the lazy smile freeze on his face. "It's in the past," he said again, and he knew Michael would hear the edge in his voice.

"Not if it still rules your life. You don't forgive any of us, do you?"

"I thought I came here for martial training, not psychotherapy." He was astonished at how pleasant he sounded—if one didn't listen too closely. *The topic is off-limits, you bastard.*

"I refused. Do you remember that much? When Uriel gave me the order to kill your wife as a lesson to everyone, I refused to do it."

"I remember everything." He shook himself. Michael hadn't obeyed the order to come with his flaming sword to cut Tamarr down. No, he'd refused and stayed behind—leaving it to Uriel to exact his own, more horrifying punishment. "It hardly matters anymore. We have a common enemy to fight now, and—"

"And you can't stop thinking about it."

Michael wasn't going to stop, Cain thought numbly. He was going to go on and on and on. . . .

"And you can't stop blaming yourself."

Only one way to shut him up. Cain didn't hesitate, slamming his fist into Michael's mouth before another word could escape. Blood erupted from his split lip, but Michael just grinned, an unholy light in his eyes.

"That's better," he said. "Now let's see what else you've learned in the last two hundred years."

A second later Cain was flat on his back, mindless fury rushing through his veins, and he almost leapt up, desperate to fight back. But he stayed where he was for one moment longer, controlling his breath, bringing his focus back into cold, crystal clarity. Michael knew what he was doing, working his enemy into a fury and then attacking his weak point.

If Cain jumped up and tried to beat the shit out of him, Michael would have the advantage.

He pushed himself up on one elbow, tilting his head to look at his enemy. "Is that the best you've got? Clearly two hundred years hasn't made much of a difference for you. Or is it your wife's pussy that's slowing you down?"

Michael moved so fast a normal man wouldn't have seen him, but Cain was expecting it, and he moved nimbly out of the way as Michael lunged toward him with a roar. "Maybe she's got your balls," Cain continued. "Because you sure as hell don't have them."

Michael slammed into him then, but Cain was ready. Nothing like attacking a man's wife and his manhood to get him in a killing rage. Not that Cain wanted to kill Michael. Azazel was his eventual goal. And not now. Not yet.

The fight was fast and brutal. He jumped and kicked Michael in the head, and the archangel retaliated with a brutal blow to the kidneys, making Cain double over. He almost threw up, but a moment later he was moving again, slamming his elbow into Michael's liver, listening to him gag in pain with satisfaction, hearing the crack of ribs splintering. Michael shoved his palm under Cain's chin, shooting his head back in what would be a killing blow for humans. Cain feinted, then kicked Michael in the arm, smashing his wrist and three fingers, a savage grin of pleasure on his bloody mouth that matched his opponent's. Michael was down again, falling hard on the cement, and Cain realized he was going to kill him after all. He was going to land on his chest and smash his ribs and heart. Michael's mouth and lungs would fill with blood and he would drown in it, and Cain couldn't stop himself—the need was too great, someone had to pay—and he moved in for the killing blow.

He miscalculated. Saw it at the last minute, that Michael had managed to turn and kick upward, his foot connecting with the side of Cain's head, and he collapsed on top of him, blood everywhere.

Silence. Complete and utter silence, and he wondered if this was what death was like. The room had been full of people, but he couldn't hear a thing. No one was moving, and maybe that was part of death too, that everyone froze in place.

Except that Michael lay beneath him, his damaged chest moving up and down as he struggled to breathe, and Cain could feel the ripping pain in his head, the agony of a broken leg that he hadn't even realized had been injured, and smell the thick, coppery tang of wasted blood, so different from the rich, spicy sweetness of a woman's blood.

He heard the slow clap from somewhere behind him, joined by another, until the entire room had erupted into applause, and Cain grinned to himself.

He knew how to make an entrance, and he knew how to make an exit.

He managed, just barely, to stand, then looked down at his vanquished foe. Michael's dark eyes were a blaze of fury, but he couldn't move, and Cain gazed at him for a long, contemplative moment.

"Are you just going to let him lie there and bleed to death?" Victoria Bellona's voice was caustic. "Or do I have to drag his sorry ass to the ocean?"

Cain turned his head. The goddess was looking thoroughly annoyed, secure in the knowledge that immersion in the icy salt water would restore her battered husband to her.

He knew it too, even if he'd been temporarily blinded by the killing lust. If he really wanted Michael dead, he would need to do it in private, where no one could save him. "I find I could do with a swim myself," he managed to say, his tongue thick behind his battered face. His jaw might be broken as well, he thought dazedly.

He reached down, and it took every last bit of strength he had to haul Michael to his feet. If anyone made the mistake of trying to help him, he'd have to kick their ass too, and he was feeling a little too light-headed. Lucky for all of them they kept out of his way.

Shoving his shoulder under Michael's arm, he started dragging him toward the doors that stood open to the sea. It was slow going, but they had time.

His clothes were red from their conjoined blood, and the thought amused him. Had he and Michael somehow bonded in their brutal, dirty fight to the death?

He saw Martha at the last minute. She was standing alone in the back, and he knew immediately that she wasn't one of those who'd applauded their epic battle. She looked sick. If he weren't lugging Michael, he would have shrugged. Life among the Fallen was about to get a lot more bloody. She'd have to get used to it.

He wouldn't have made it to the edge of the sea if Michael hadn't regained some mobility, and together they crossed the last few feet until the icy salt water caught them, pulling them out. Cain felt the darkness close over his head. He thought of Martha, with her lists and her shocked expression and her sweet mouth. Martha. He was going to have her when she came from the sea sometime; he was going to lick the salt from her skin and drink the ocean from her breasts. He was going to drown in her.

The hand that caught his ankle bit down, yanking him deeper under the water, and he opened his eyes against the stinging salt to look at Michael. If he wanted to continue the fight, then Cain was game, but he really wasn't in the mood.

Michael moved, the water slowing him, and reached out the hand that had been broken. And Cain took it.

CHAPTER
TWENTY-THREE

I RAN. I'M NOT QUITE SURE WHY. I WAITED until those two idiots came back out of the ocean, arms around each other like the oldest and best of friends less than five minutes after they tried to kill each other, waited until I knew he was all right. And then I ran.

It was my time for training, but everyone had stopped, mesmerized by the battle in front of them. Michael was a fierce taskmaster, and he wouldn't accept any lame excuse for slacking off, but right then I couldn't stand to be there. Not when their blood still stained the floor. Tory was mopping it up, clearly annoyed, and I wished I had her sangfroid. But I didn't. I wanted to throw up.

So I ran. A good long run would pass muster as training, at least partially, and I'd make up with battle tomorrow, sparring with whomever Michael assigned to me. He'd be pissed, of course, but at the moment I didn't really care.

It took a few minutes for my muscles to flow into the steady pace of the run along the beach. I hadn't bothered to stretch. It always took me like this: a transition from tense and worried to a pure, physical being, my body working, my mind simply drifting. I passed others—I had no particular need for solitude, and I didn't want to be shut away from people. I just didn't want to have to talk to them. I ran to the end of the second spit of land and slowed my pace, letting life slowly drift back in, and I finally stopped, bending over to catch my breath. I'd pushed myself too hard, and I wasn't sure why. Exactly what had I been running from?

The rocks that were massed at the edge of the water led out into the sea, almost like the stepping-stones of a giant. The last one was about two hundred yards out and huge, big enough to hold a small patch of earth and some ancient yew trees, twisted by the wind into strange, mysterious shapes. Sometimes I braved the rocks and the strong currents that flowed in this cove and swam out there. On the far side, where no one could see, were footholds. The first time I'd climbed up I had been terrified. The second I was braver. Now it was the safest place I knew.

Not even Thomas had known about it, though I'd discovered it early in our life together. Even then I'd needed time and space of my own, somewhere he couldn't reach. He'd been protective, but at times it had almost felt . . . smothering.

I climbed onto the rocks at the edge of the water, hating myself for my disloyal thoughts. Thomas had loved me, cared for me, asked nothing of me. Not even my blood. I was doing my best to honor him in his death. I'd done very well at it until Cain had arrived.

I closed my eyes. I could feel the warmth of the sun through the soft mist that always shrouded Sheol, and I let myself drift. I knew there was no way I could force a vision, find an answer when I so desperately needed one. But I couldn't help trying.

When is he going to leave? He never stays long—everyone says so. When is he going to lose interest and disappear?

There was no answer forthcoming. Even as I tried to will myself into a meditative state, the questions kept bouncing back. I knew he hadn't been the one to harm Allie, though I couldn't say why. The sneakiness of the attack was just his style. There was nothing straightforward about him; he was all smoke and mirrors. But he wasn't the type to make war on women.

Except, perhaps, me.

I took another breath, bringing it deep inside my body, trying to force my muscles to relax again after their instinctive tightening. Everything had been fine until he had arrived. Well, not precisely fine, given that we were facing possible annihilation by the Armies of God. But we'd been managing very well until he came here.

I could think of nothing that would drive him away. I couldn't even pray to a God I'd never believed in. Finding out that a Supreme Power actually existed, that he had started this complicated mess we all lived in, didn't improve matters, since he'd cursed everyone I cared about and then left us to Uriel's tender mercies. I would simply have to endure.

I stretched out on one of the rocks, the granite rough beneath my clothes, and let the sun bake into me. Watching him fight had been a horrifying revelation. For the first time I'd had a true look at the savagery beneath his taunting, teasing presence, and it had shaken me in ways I couldn't understand. I had been in pitched battles; I still bore the scars. I had defended myself and others, and if I hadn't actually killed anyone, I had been willing to. I had seen blood and horror and death all around me, and nothing had disturbed me as much as seeing Cain try to kill Michael.

Stop it, I told myself. *Think calm, peaceful thoughts.* The only way a vision was going to come was if I stopped trying to force it. I needed to relax, keep to a perfect state of peace, and maybe, just maybe, I'd get the answers I needed.

Peace. Calm. All was good, all was well, I just needed to—

The cloth came down over my head with sudden, smothering force, bringing me to instant alertness. I struck out in a panic, but the thing was enveloping me, trapping me, smelling of dust and death. I felt myself hauled up, shroud and all, into someone's arms, and I finally remembered to scream, as loud as I possibly could, as I struck out with all my strength.

I heard a muffled sound of pain; then a blow struck my head, so hard I blacked out for a moment, seeing bright lights at the back of my eyes as I struggled for breath.

My mind finally pulled itself together as I began to focus. All right, so he was stronger than I was— fighting back wouldn't help. The only chance I had was to trick him. I let myself stay limp as he dumped me over his shoulder, and I hoped I'd get a look at him from beneath whatever he'd wrapped me in.

It must have been some kind of sack—there was no light. His shoulder dug into my stomach, hurting, and it took all my concentration to keep my body loose, as if I were still unconscious, despite the panic that swept through me.

This man wanted to kill me. I knew that without the benefit of a vision—this was no complicated game: this was death and malice that had wrapped me like a corpse, and unless I did something I would be dead.

I knew where he was carrying me, probably knew the area better than he did, since this was my own private cove. He would have to make his way either back across the boulders to get to land or forward toward the sea. I wasn't sure which would be better. I could swim like a fish, but if he knocked me out I'd be helpless. Even real fish could drown.

Then again, on dry land I'd have no chance at all.

He turned toward the sea, and I let myself flop against him. He strode across the boulders, hauling me with no discernible effort, which meant he had to be strong. Then again, all of the Fallen were unnaturally strong. I tried to see if I could identify him by smell, but all I could breathe in was the musty scent of the blanket he'd wrapped me in. He could have been anyone. Even Cain. *Oh God, not Cain.*

He made his way seaward along the path of rocks with no hesitation, as graceful as all of the angels. Would he toss me into the water without making certain I was truly unconscious? It was probably too much to hope for. Would he try to break my neck before he let go? That would be the most efficient, and the Fallen were efficient.

I almost thought I could smell the sea through the enveloping folds. If I were one of the Fallen, a broken neck would heal the moment I touched the water. But I wasn't; I was a mere mortal, prey to everything that could kill a human, and I was going to die.

The hell I was.

He stopped, and I flopped gracelessly against his back. He shifted me, levering me downward, and I knew with sudden horror that he planned to simply bash my head against the rocks before he let me slip into the sea. The incoming tide would wash my blood and brains from the rock, and when, or if, they found my body, they wouldn't know what had caused my crushed skull.

I could see it clearly, a vision, perhaps, or a possibility. I felt him swing me over his head, felt the rock drawing near, and at the last second I twisted, spinning out of his grip.

Too late. My head smashed against the side of the rock, not as hard as he'd intended, and the blanket cushioned the blow. But this time I was really out, darkness snapping down around me as I sank into the cold, dark sea, sank into eternity, into nothingness, into death.

METATRON LOOKED DOWN into the inky ocean, watching the blanket disappear. He should have known he couldn't trust her. She must have seen him coming. It hadn't done her any good, though. Even if he hadn't managed to smash her brains against the rocks, he'd done enough damage that she was sinking like a rock beneath the surface, unmoving.

He'd meant to hold on to the blanket as he let her slide. It had been hard work, sewing it closed, when he'd never touched a needle in his life, but he hadn't wanted to risk her getting a good look at him. Nothing was guaranteed—he'd lived in Sheol long enough to know that the wives were surprisingly resilient. But Martha was no longer a wife; she had no protection. No one would even notice she was gone. And the blanket would hold any blood and brain that leaked out before he tossed her.

He could no longer make out the dark shape beneath the waves. He'd picked the deepest part of the water he could find, just to make certain it would take her down. His only worry now was that she'd be found before the blanket disintegrated. Too bad—he could have used it again. But it was worth it to finally close the seer's too-knowing eyes forever.

Cain might not even realize he'd been the one to do it. After all, the seer came out here a lot—it would be easy for her to slip and tumble into the sea, hitting her head on the way down.

And if he did guess who was behind it, what could he do about it? No, it was much better this way. Simpler. Cain had never been an enforcer; he'd never had to slaughter families for their blasphemies, old people who wept when they saw him. Cain was going to need to—what did they say? grow a pair?—if they were going to succeed in destroying Sheol. Or Metatron would simply have to destroy Cain as well.

She was out of sight now, taken to her grave deep beneath the surface, and he turned away, dismissing her as simply one more job completed. It was a warm, sunny day, the omnipresent mist almost transparent. All was well with the world.

I WAS DROWNING. I knew that—I had water in my lungs already, and the wet folds of the blanket trapped me as I sank, deeper and deeper. I began to struggle, pushing at it, kicking my legs free, wriggling, until it finally slipped over my head. It didn't help. The ocean was pitch-black; I couldn't breathe, my skin was numb from the cold, and part of me wanted simply to let go.

I kicked. I'd gotten turned around when my assailant had thrown me in the water, and I was still disoriented from the blow on my head. I would swim in one direction, moving toward the surface. If I went the wrong way and drowned, so be it. If I ran into the man who'd tried to murder me, he could finish the job with my blessing. I was tired of fighting.

I moved like a seal through the water, upward,

sleek and fast, and light began filtering down. I might even make the surface before my lungs exploded, I thought dazedly, without relief or despair. I kicked again, moving, moving, and a figure coalesced in the deep water in front of me. Thomas?

It wouldn't take much. Just a slight adjustment, and I could move down to the deeper part where he waited for me, the enveloping, smothering presence that I hated and missed. Oblivion, peaceful, lovely, the embrace of the water all around me. Why shouldn't I give in?

Because no matter how hard I tried to be calm and serene and meek, at heart I was a fighter. I kicked, hard, and a moment later my head cleared the surface, and I began to choke.

I was out beyond the last boulder, out of sight of anyone on the shore. The choice had been made—at least for today I would survive. I managed to swim to the ledge on the ocean side of the rock, the last of my energy spent in pulling myself up. It was narrow, and I could barely hold on as I coughed and choked and spat up seawater. And then I lay there, unmoving, letting the sun warm my iced-over skin, letting my breathing slowly return to normal.

My throat and my lungs burned. There was blood on the ledge, and I realized my head was bleeding with unnerving enthusiasm. I had no idea how badly I'd been hurt, whether I was going to die there on the ledge, my body dragged out to sea when the tide came in, or deposited neatly on the shore for someone to find.

I didn't care. The sun was warm as I lay there; the soft afternoon breeze brushed over me. I let go, sinking into a blessed, comforting darkness.

AZAZEL WAS ALONE in the assembly hall, reading through the volumes of scriptures that had been passed down. The volumes of lies, Cain thought with a cool delight. When Azazel found out the truth, it would shatter the very beliefs he'd held so dear, with which he'd once governed. It was tempting to wait for his revenge, to make it more complete.

But Azazel was alone now, his back to the door, and the residents of Sheol were busy with their various duties, far away from the meeting room. He could ease in and break Azazel's neck, and he'd be paralyzed, unable to crawl to the sea for healing. He would die, his lungs filling with his own blood, and Cain would watch him and think of Tamarr and justice long overdue.

He slipped inside the door, silent and deadly, ready to attack, when a sudden wariness slid inside his concentration. Azazel lay before him, a perfect target. But something was wrong.

Martha. He had no idea how he knew it, but he'd

been tuned in to her from the moment he arrived in a burst of well-controlled flame. Martha was in danger.

He looked at Azazel's back, so vulnerable; he wouldn't get this chance again.

But he heard her cry out, in fear, in pain. The water. She was in the water.

He turned and left, closing the door to the assembly room quietly behind him.

COLD WATER SLAPPED my face, waking me, and I tried to sit up, immediately tumbling back into the water. The sun was almost at the horizon. I had no idea how long I'd been there, and I didn't care. I needed to get back.

I held on to the ledge, testing my strength. Apparently I wasn't going to die. I reached up and touched the side of my face. Something was crusted there, presumably dried blood, and I winced in pain. I should go, swim around the rock and try to make it homeward, but something stopped me. How could I be sure my would-be murderer had gone? The last thing I wanted was to walk straight back into his filthy hands.

I pulled myself up onto the ledge, now submerged by three inches of water with the incoming tide, and started up the side of the cliff. Most of the steps were easy enough—it was almost as if natural stairs had been worn into the rocks, leading to the copse of trees at the top. Only a few were difficult, and when I'd first discovered the path I'd tumbled back into the ocean any number of times before conquering it.

I couldn't afford to fall again—this time I might not surface. I moved slowly, my hands clinging to the rocky outcroppings, a mantra muttered underneath my breath: "Please, please, please." I didn't know who I was talking to, didn't even care. It simply helped me keep moving.

When I finally saw the twisted trees looming overhead, I almost let go in my relief. I practically soared up the last few steps to land, belly flat, on top of the rock, gasping. Safe.

I was about to push myself up when something stopped me, some preternatural sense that danger was near. I stayed where I was, considering it. Of course danger was near. Sheol was a small place, and whoever had attacked me couldn't have gone far. No one had flown overhead. . . .

Which reminded me I still wasn't safe. I managed to inch my way up the last rise to the copse of trees, protected by their twisted, sheltering branches, and I heard the soft rumble of male voices from the shore mixed with the sounds of the ocean, the water slapping against the rocks, the wind in the trees. I couldn't recognize them. I only knew that *he* was there. The one who had tried to kill me.

I could sense his malevolent presence so strongly that it made me shiver. Danger lay just over the rise of the rock.

I could get back to shore. I just needed to rest for a little bit, and then I could swim back in, make my way to my room, and go find a nice, big tub to soak in.

The voices stopped. I had to risk it, had to see who was trying to hurt me, or there was no way I'd be safe. I wouldn't be able to prove anything, but at least I'd know whom to keep clear of. And if I found out who'd done it, I'd figure out why. As far as I knew, I wasn't a danger to anyone.

I inched closer, the rock scraping my skin. Closer and closer to the edge; I would just take a swift look before ducking back down, hoping against hope he wouldn't see me.

One more foot and I'd be there. I pushed, and rose up.

He was walking away. I could see only his back, but I knew who had stood there, watching the waves.

Cain.

He must have felt my eyes on him, for he stopped, turning back to stare at the rock, but I'd dropped back down so he couldn't see me. I laid my face against the rock, and for some reason, I cried.

What an abysmal idiot I was. I knew he was danger personified. I knew he was manipulative, conscienceless, a liar and a trickster. A predator of the first order. So why was I crying? Had he blinded me with lust when he'd kissed me, fooled me with false tenderness when he'd held me? Was I so gullible that I'd actually believed him?

Apparently I was. At least no one was there to see the collapse of my foolishness. I could wallow in misery, safe on my own little island, and it would be my secret. When I dove back into the water, the sea would wash my tears and my idiocy away, and I would emerge whole again.

If I'd ever been whole in the first place. Thomas had rescued and then smothered me, but I'd begun to heal. Only begun, I realized now. I was still broken—Cain had proved that to me.

CHAPTER
TWENTY-FOUR

THE LAST LIGHT HAD ALMOST VAN-
ished by the time I dove off the rock,
the water enveloping me in its icy
embrace, and for a brief moment I considered letting the tide carry me out to sea. But I was made of
tougher stuff than that, so I swam toward shore with
slow, easy strokes, telling myself I was leaving everything behind—the pain, the fear, the vulnerability—
and ready to build a new, stronger skin.

I was shivering by the time I reached the shore.
It never grew that cold in Sheol, but the tempera-
ture dipped once the sun set, and the breeze was
strong tonight. No one was in sight, and instinctively
I knew there was no danger near me. At least that
sense had sharpened, though I didn't really need it.
All I had to do was see Cain to know I was in trouble.
I'd known that from the beginning, but somewhere

along the way I seemed to have forgotten. How else could I have ended up in his bed, ready to surrender?

I wrapped my arms around my wet body and hurried along the shore, back toward the house. I got more than a few curious looks as I reached the compound, and I saw Tory start toward me, but Michael caught her arm, distracting her, and I rushed into the main hall, still dripping water.

It would dry, and I didn't care. I'd missed dinner, and I was hungry, but I could eat in my room. I stopped briefly in the small kitchen off the dining room anyway, before continuing on my way, the larger butcher knife hidden beneath my flowing, sodden garments. All I wanted was a deep, hot bath, but I would dream about food while I soaked, and it would be waiting in my room when I returned.

Each apartment in Sheol had a bathroom with a shower. The tubs were in separate rooms, since few people used them, and there was a large, spa-like room near the annex that hadn't been used in years. I was going to get into that tub and stay there until my skin wrinkled—it would take that long to warm my bones.

I could feel that I was safe—Cain wasn't in his rooms, and I had no sense of danger. I had no idea whether it had anything to do with my visions or not, but things were becoming clearer, the sense of danger, the presentiment of evil. I only hoped I could trust it.

I stopped in my room long enough to grab clean clothes. I was icy cold, sandy, and sticky, and for some reason I still wanted to cry. The sea was supposed to wash all that vulnerability away, I thought, automatically shoving my wet hair away from my face and then wincing as I felt the place that had taken the brunt of my fall. At least I had stopped bleeding.

The bathing room was spacious, the tub closer to a Japanese soaking tub than a modern bathtub. Locking the door, I turned on the water, set the knife down nearby, then stripped off my wet clothes and stepped under the shower to rinse away the surface layer of grit and sand and blood.

My chest hurt, and I looked down to see the scratches from crawling over the rocks. My knees were bruised, my fingers battered from my desperate climb. In fact, I was a total mess, and if immersion in the ocean hadn't helped, then a hot bath wouldn't fix things either. But at least it would warm me up.

The lights were too bright overhead when I stepped out of the shower, so I crossed the room and switched them off. There was a skylight over the tub, and the moon was almost full, shining down with a silvery light. I set the knife down on a nearby table and let out a shaky sigh of contentment. Perfect.

The water was like a lover's caress, warm and comforting, flowing around me as I sank deep into its welcoming arms. I slid down, full-length in the huge tub, and ducked my head underwater, feeling it swirl around me. The cuts and abrasions stung for a moment, then slowly began to calm, and when I pushed back up I felt renewed.

I leaned my head back, staring at the empty sky overhead. Not so empty. I glimpsed a graceful silhouette flying overhead, dark against the bright moon, and my body tightened in sudden fear. I knew, I *knew* who it was—the one who had tried to kill me. It had to be Cain. I could feel the malevolence even from here, and I stared up at him, willing him to come closer. Instead he flew up, high, high into the sky, and I leaned back, relief and sorrow washing over me, secure in the knowledge that at least for now I was safe. Cain was gone, though who knew for how long.

I could already feel my wet hair curling around my head, but I didn't care. For now I was safe, and I could stay in this tub forever, staring at the distant moon.

I sensed rather than heard the footsteps outside. The bath chamber was off a different corridor from my room, a corridor with nothing else. There was no reason for someone to be walking here.

But someone most definitely was standing outside the door. I closed my eyes, trying to sense who was there, but there was no hint of danger, no feeling of ill will, and I relaxed. Cain was too far away to hurt me. It must be Tory or Rachel or even Allie checking on me.

I almost called out, but something stopped me. The door handle turned, and I felt a ridiculous frisson of fear. And then it opened.

I should have known locks wouldn't keep him out. What I didn't understand was how he could get here so fast when moments ago he was flying upward into the darkest heavens. I wondered if I could reach the knife before he did. I didn't move.

Cain shut the door behind him, and I heard the soft click of the lock. So even on the off chance that someone could hear me scream, they wouldn't be able to get to me in time. I didn't bother sliding lower in the tub—in the shadowy room he wouldn't be able to see anything, and besides, if I was about to die, modesty was of little comfort. I met his gaze across the room and waited for panic to fill me.

It didn't come. Maybe I was past being afraid. Maybe some unnatural calm had come over me, now that the gloves were off. Except that I'd been in danger before, been in the midst of a pitched battle, and I'd been scared to death. Why was I so calm now?

He came into the room, all lazy grace, and picked up the large knife from the stool that was just out of reach. He held it up, examining it. "Are you any good with a knife, Miss Mary?"

His low, sinuous voice sent a shiver of reaction through my body. How sick was I, to be aroused by the face of death? I never would have guessed I was that perverse.

"Not very." My voice came out a little rough, and I cleared my throat. "It was the easiest weapon I could find."

"Against whom?" He sounded only casually interested as he balanced it in his long, clever-looking hands. Beautiful hands. Deadly hands, whether he'd been the one who'd tried to kill me or not.

"You."

The single word sat there between us. He didn't look surprised. "Not that effective a weapon, my sweet," he murmured. "You'd be better off with a thinner blade. Easier to plunge deep into flesh." He moved, so swiftly his hands were a blur, and the knife was spinning through the air, coming toward me.

I couldn't move, watching it, mesmerized, in slow motion like an old movie as it sped straight for my heart. And then it landed in the wall just past my head with a solid *thunk,* and I let out a gasp.

"On the other hand," he murmured, "I am very good with a knife. If I wanted to kill you, this knife would be embedded in your throat, and no one would ever know I'd been here."

I was shaking. The room was awash with shadows, and I hoped he wouldn't notice the water rippling around my nervous body, but he was an observant man. He came closer, hooking the stool with one leg and pulling it under him. "You don't have the sense of a newborn kitten, do you?" There was just a trace of annoyance in his voice. "There are a number of bathing rooms in the compound, and yet you seek out the most isolated one, where no one will have any idea where you've gone, where no one can hear you scream."

"Why should I scream? What do I have to be afraid of?"

"I could make you scream," he said softly.

"Don't!"

"Don't what?"

"Don't play with me," I said fiercely.

His smile was cool, almost terrifying in the moonlight. "But, Miss Mary, that's exactly what I want to do. I want to play with you until you scream and cry and beg."

"You sick fuck."

He looked genuinely confused. "Not particularly. There's nothing that perverse about wanting to take you to bed and give you the best sex of your life. Though considering what I know about Thomas, that's not much of a challenge."

Now I was the one who was confused. "What are you talking about?"

"Sex. Fucking. Making you come so hard you

can't move or cry or speak for days, and then doing it all over again. What did you think I was talking about?"

I said nothing. I felt more at sea than when I had been trapped on the rock partway out into the ocean.

His eyebrows snapped together with sudden annoyance. "For God's sake, Martha, don't tell me you really thought I was going to hurt you?"

I barely noticed that he'd used the right name. "It's a logical enough assumption, since you tried to kill me earlier today."

He grew very still. "Did I? Why don't you explain to me how that happened, since I don't seem to have any memory of it."

"You know perfectly well what you did! You threw a blanket over me, smashed my head against a rock, and threw me into the ocean to drown." Before I realized what he meant to do, he'd caught my chin in his hand, turning my face toward his, and his eyes were narrow, dangerous. He reached out and I flinched instinctively, but the fingers that pushed the hair out of my face were surprisingly gentle, the whisper of a caress as they brushed past the wound on the side of my face.

"And what makes you think I did this to you?" he said softly.

I wanted to turn my face into his palm, idiot that I was. I didn't. "I'm a seer, remember?"

"A piss-poor one. Did you have a vision that I

was out to kill you?" He didn't sound the slightest bit aggrieved at being falsely accused. Probably because he knew the accusation wasn't false.

"I knew. I *knew*. I was swimming in the water, out deep, dizzy and disoriented, trying to find something to hold on to. And I knew the man who had tried to kill me was still there, watching. By the time I managed to climb up on the rocks and get a good look, you were just turning away."

There was an odd expression in his eyes. "Down by Luther's Cove, you mean?"

"You don't deny it?"

I wished I could see what was going on behind those opaque eyes. "Oh, no, I don't deny it. In fact, I was down there looking for you. Someone told me they'd seen you head off in that direction, and my senses, while not nearly as infallible as yours"—the irony there was offensive—"told me I'd better check up on you. I even called your name, but you didn't answer. You probably heard me and instead stayed there in hiding, afraid I was going to finish what I'd supposedly started."

"Weren't you?"

"Oh, most definitely," he said softly. "But I was thinking about what we'd started earlier in my bed. The truth is, I wasn't alone out there. Someone else appeared to be waiting for you to make a reappearance."

"Who?" I snapped.

His thin smile wasn't pleasant. "I'm not sure it's a wise idea to tell you. You'll probably be convinced that he was the person who tried to kill you, and he might be entirely innocent. I'll look into it."

"Don't you want me to trust you?"

"You'll never trust me, Miss Mary, and we both know it. Why should I waste my time?" He rose from the stool, wandering around the room, and belatedly I remembered I was sitting naked in the deep tub. Granted, the moonlit room was in shadows, and the milky water hid a great deal. Being naked was the least of my worries, I reminded myself. "So you came back here, convinced I was trying to kill you, and you decided to go take a bath in a deserted part of the compound. With a knife for protection, except you forgot to take it with you when you got in the tub."

"I couldn't very well bathe holding on to a knife," I shot back.

"You could have—should have—put it under your feet. The knife is stainless—it won't rust. Instead you sat here like a plucked chicken already in the stew pot, waiting for me to come in and turn up the heat."

"Lovely image."

"Better than a bloodbath." He turned, leaning against the door, seemingly at ease. "So how come your uncertain powers didn't warn you that I was outside your door? Does your self-preservation juju only work in the open air?"

I opened my mouth to snap back at him—then stopped to think about it. I wasn't afraid of him. The realization astonished me. At least, not afraid he was going to kill me. It was always possible I was the sick fuck, crazy enough to face death at my lover's hands and not care about it, but I didn't think so. In fact, I knew he wasn't going to pull that knife from the wall and plunge it into me. He wasn't going to put those beautiful hands around my neck and hold me under the water. He might disrupt my life, break my heart, but he wasn't going to hurt me physically.

He must have seen the slow realization dawn over my face, even in the shadows. He nodded. "That's better."

I didn't bother to deny it. "Then who . . . ?"

"Leave it to me." He came closer, plucking a towel from the pile by the door. "Time to come out."

I gave him a scornful look. "Not while you're here."

"I can always get in with you," he said blandly, and I was smart enough not to call his bluff.

"At least turn your back," I said, holding my hand out for the towel.

I expected more of an argument. Instead he simply reached down into the warm water, caught my arms, and hauled me up out of its protective depths, wrapping the huge towel around me before I could panic. It was dark, I reminded myself. He couldn't see anything, even with the skylight overhead.

I yanked myself out of his arms, catching the towel tight around my body. "Go away."

"After I make sure you're safely tucked away in bed."

"I don't need you to tuck me into bed," I snapped.

"You sure about that?" he murmured, his low voice sliding deep inside me, warming me, disturbing me. He walked past me and plucked the knife out of the wall, then handed it to me, hilt first. "This isn't much of a defense, but it's better than nothing."

"I can defend myself. I'm a trained warrior." My voice was defensive.

"So is everyone else in Sheol, and someone here wants to kill you," he said, and there was no arguing with his logic. "Indulge me, in this at least. I intend to take care of your little problem, but in case it proves more complex than I expect, I wouldn't want to leave you here defenseless."

"I'm not—"

"I beg your pardon. Without a weapon." I couldn't see his expression in the shadows, which meant he couldn't see me, a small mercy. He opened the door to the hallway, then turned back to me.

"I don't need an—" The words were lost as he made an impatient noise and swooped me up into his arms, striding out of the room and down the hallway. It took him only a matter of moments to reach our corridor, kick my door open, and carry me inside, and a moment later he'd dropped me onto the bed so that I bounced, scrambling for the bath sheet that covered me.

"Stay put," he said. "I'll be back."

A moment later he was gone.

CHAPTER
TWENTY-FIVE

THE BITCH HAD MANAGED TO SAVE herself. Metatron speared upward, fury vibrating through him as he hurled his body into the darkness, every muscle rigid. How dare she? She was a woman, worthless, just one of the temptresses who had brought the Fallen to their miserable existence, and yet she'd managed to trick him. He'd been convinced she was dead, and if Cain hadn't shown up at the beach and refused to leave, he would have made sure of it, finished the job if necessary. Instead Cain had stood there questioning him, and in the end he'd had no choice but to retreat, angry and frustrated but reasonably certain she was dead.

She wasn't.

At least he could take cold comfort in the reasonable assurance that Cain didn't suspect him. Cain would trust his word.

He already knew that Cain was irrational when it came to the seer, and he wouldn't agree that she needed to be silenced before she interfered with their plans. Cain thought he could control her. Cain was a fool. Women were irrational, weak, ruled by their emotions. There was a reason there were no female angels—they were unworthy.

Cain himself had begun all this, back in the beginning of time. He'd been the first to take a human woman to his bed, and even the example Uriel had made of him hadn't stopped the others. When this was done, when the Fallen were brought back under Uriel's sway, then it would be time to finish Cain, destroy him utterly for the chaos he had instigated.

Metatron embraced the breathless ice of the night sky, celebrating the emptiness that echoed in his soul. There was no room for passion, for weakness, for distraction. His job was to serve Uriel; if he hadn't failed him, let Azazel and that witch he'd married best him, he'd still be at the archangel's side. Those two would have to die as well, though Uriel might not give the order. Metatron would see to it before he could be countermanded, assuming Cain didn't gut Azazel first. One didn't disobey Uriel lightly, and Metatron needed to earn back his place with him. But anything that happened before that time would be fair game.

He flew higher, darting and soaring like some

maddened phoenix, until the rage left him and all that remained was cold determination. He could almost hate the seer for the fiery emotions she aroused in him. He despised losing control. It was difficult enough trying to guess what Uriel would want him to do in order to return to his good graces and his side. Emotions—hatred, anger, impatience— interfered with that.

He slowed, began the measured drift back toward Sheol. He would try again, and next time he would leave nothing to chance. He would have to wait a few days, just to allay suspicion, but with any luck the seer would suspect Cain. He was the logical culprit, the newcomer who couldn't keep away from her. If Metatron had managed to drive a wedge between them, that could only work to his advantage.

He dropped down onto the sand lightly. The moon had set, the stars barely visible through the omnipresent mist. That was another annoyance—it was always too bright in Sheol. It shouldn't be, surrounded as the place was by the fog that kept it hidden from everyone; but compared to the world that Uriel ruled, it was blazingly, blindingly bright. It gave him a headache.

He walked up the slight slope to the main compound. He had three rooms on the third floor, a luxurious combination that he both despised and enjoyed. Soft beds and rich foods were for the weak, and he was used to a harder, leaner existence. He would welcome his return to it, but in the meantime he allowed himself the indulgence. He considered himself a spy in the midst of the enemy, and spies were often forced to live in less than optimal circumstances. If he had to endure luxury, so be it.

He didn't notice the figure lounging by the seawater pool until he was almost past it, and Cain's voice, soft and deadly, came out of the darkness. "Enjoy your flight?"

Metatron froze, then willed his body to relax. He was bigger than Cain; there was no question he could defeat him quite easily. But he still might have need of him. "I like the night air," he said cautiously. There was no way Cain could know what he'd done. The seer hadn't seen him, and no one could guess he'd been behind the attack. After all, he'd given his word, and lying was always difficult for the Fallen.

"Do you?" Cain's voice was deceptively pleasant. "I do as well. Fewer witnesses, for one thing."

Caution was deeply ingrained in Metatron—he thought slowly and methodically, seldom impulsive. "Did you wish to discuss strategy? You have yet to explain to me how the seer will be of benefit, and time is running out."

"So you decided to break your oath and murder her? Because I hadn't given you a good enough reason not to?"

Metatron didn't flinch beneath the whiplash tone, and he didn't bother to deny it. "You seem to have a blind spot where the seer is concerned. She's a danger. Her visions are growing more reliable, and sooner or later she's going to see something that will ruin all our plans. If you really want to destroy the Fallen, you're going to have to make some sacrifices. Though why the seer would be a sacrifice eludes me."

"And I'm required to explain everything to you?" There was no mistaking the silken menace in Cain's voice, but Metatron didn't blink.

"If we're going to succeed in bringing Sheol back under Uriel's rule and destroy the Fallen, we must work together."

Cain was silent for a long moment, and Metatron waited. He couldn't see Cain's face in the darkness, but he was reasonably certain Cain would make the wise choice. He wanted to destroy the Fallen as much as Metatron did.

"I chose the seer for a reason," Cain said finally. "Her visions are cloudy, uncertain. If I bond with her, I can manipulate them."

"You can't bond with her. She isn't your mate," Metatron protested, shocked.

"Things aren't always as they seem in the world of the Fallen. Trust me when I tell you I will suffer no ill effects when I take her to bed, no ill effects when I take her blood."

"She won't agree," he said flatly.

"Such a lack of confidence in my powers of persuasion. She'll beg for it."

Metatron breathed a sigh of relief. Cain was sounding as cold, as ruthless and determined, as he could wish. He'd been wrong to doubt him, wrong to think he was weak. He would be able to bend the seer to his will, and if he couldn't . . . well, there would be any number of chances to finish what Metatron had started out by the rocks.

"Then what have you been waiting for?"

Cain's tone was dismissive. "That decision is up to me."

"Don't wait too long," Metatron warned. "Or I may have to go ahead with my original idea."

"You touch her and I will kill you."

The words were spoken so gently that for a moment Metatron didn't recognize the seriousness of the threat. When he did, he laughed derisively. "You're no match for me. I'm far bigger and stronger than you."

A moment later he was slammed backward onto the stone paving, Cain on top of him, a knife held tight against his throat, and he froze. "Yes," Cain said softly, "but I'm faster."

He could do it, Metatron thought, staring up at him without emotion. Cain could slash his throat and then hold him down so he couldn't reach the healing waters. Metatron choked, the action making the edge of the knife dig in, and he felt blood begin to trickle down the side of his neck onto the stones beneath him.

"I should kill you on principle," Cain continued in a light voice, and now Metatron could see his face, the absolute chilling emptiness in his eyes. "I've always worked alone, and I don't like having surprises get in the way of my plans."

Metatron held very still, resisting the impulse to point out that they'd been his plans originally. He viewed the possibility of death with equanimity. He'd died once already, and he had complete faith in Uriel. Uriel would reward him for his efforts, even if Metatron didn't succeed.

Cain sat back, removing the knife from Metatron's throat. "We can decide to work together for our common goal, or we can dissolve our partnership. I need to know I can trust you not to go behind my back and fuck up my plans."

The more Metatron lied, the better he got at it. "All right," he said. "But I need something from you."

The expression on Cain's face didn't suggest he was in the mood to offer any concession. "What?"

"That you stop screwing around and finish with the seer," he said impatiently, using words he'd never used before. "Fuck her senseless, drain her blood, do whatever you need, but I don't want to worry about her tripping us up. She sees too much, and she knows you're not to be trusted. She's never trusted me. If you don't get her under your control, and fast, she'll destroy everything."

Cain rose with one easy move, and the knife disappeared beneath his clothes once more. Metatron would have to remember he carried one. Hand to hand they were no match, but Cain had always been very, very good with a knife.

"I was planning to. If you hadn't been so hamhanded, it would already be done. I'd gotten her halfway toward trusting me, and now she thinks I might have been the one to try to kill her. And Martha is not the kind of woman who gets aroused by danger."

Metatron shuddered. The thought of the Fallen and their mates . . . commingling . . . filled him with disgust, but this time he recognized the necessity. If Cain could fill the seer's mind with the visions he wanted, it would lull the Fallen into a sense of complacency, and they would never know what hit them.

Cain held out a hand to him, but Metatron ignored it, jumping to his feet swiftly. "We can't afford to make any more mistakes. Time is running out, and we need the Fallen to be irreparably broken before Uriel leads the Armies of Heaven here, or there's no telling what might happen."

Cain glanced up at the pitch-black sky. "I plan to take care of it. After all, I've been without blood or pussy for weeks now."

"Don't!" Metatron's protest was instinctive, his disgust overwhelming.

"Afraid of a little word, Metatron? You don't like pussy? Well, I know you don't like pussy, but do you have a problem with the word? I can come up with all sorts of other terms, like c—"

"You're foul."

Cain's slow grin was infuriating. "I'm healthy. And fortunately, the smart choice, Martha, happens to coincide with my personal preference. Are you going to want a blow-by-blow description, or simply word that the deed is done? *Blow-by-blow* being the operative term."

Metatron controlled his reaction by sheer force. "I'll take your word for it."

"And exactly what are you going to do for me, Metatron, old friend?" Cain inquired in a silken voice.

It was easy enough to lie. He was getting quite good at it. "I won't make any more moves against the seer. I'll leave that to you."

"And since your word has proven worthless, I won't ask you to swear to it. Just remember that if you hurt her I'll kill you. And I fight dirty. You wouldn't even see me coming."

"You do not need to tell me you have no honor," Metatron said stiffly.

"No, I don't, do I? I suggest you remember that."

CHAPTER
TWENTY-SIX

THE DREAMS CAME AGAIN THAT night. I was in the ocean, but this time it was warm, embracing, and strong hands were on my ankles, pulling me down. I went willingly, knowing my lover was taking me, my lover who was Death.

His golden hair flowed around his beautiful, cruel face, and I couldn't breathe until he put his mouth on mine, and suddenly the water was no danger at all as he pulled me deeper and deeper, holding me against his body as we danced. I held on to him as I'd wanted to, my arms around his waist, my head against his shoulder, as he dragged me down, and I wanted to weep with sorrow and joy. This was what I was born for. This was what I would die for.

His hands caught my hips and brought my legs around him, and he was hard, so hard. The light was strange and eerie, and no one could see but my lover, and I could release the control I kept over my body, let the fierce, hot desire wash over me, wash over him. I needed his touch, I needed him inside me. He could dominate me, he could worship me, he could control me or let me take charge. He could violate me, take me any way he wanted, sacred and forbidden, as long as he took me.

There was fire beneath the water. I knew it was impossible, but I didn't care; I was as drawn to those flames as I was to Cain. He pulled me toward it, and I felt the pleasure-pain of it licking between my legs, felt the spiraling burn of desire spread through me, claiming me, drowning me in the flames and the sea, and when he pushed inside me I burst into a thousand tiny stars, sparks settling slowly into the depths.

My eyes flew open. I was lying flat on my back in bed, cocooned in the velvety darkness of the deepest part of night. Every square inch of my skin tingled, my nipples were so hard they hurt, and the ache in my womb was a hard, physical thing. What was he doing to me?

And then it came again. *Come to me.* Like a siren call on the night wind, but I was no longer listening. Now I knew.

It was Cain, the trickster, manipulating me, playing games. Maybe even mocking the repressed sexuality of the poor, deluded widow, playing games with her dreaming mind and laughing at her. I rolled over on my stomach and buried my face in my pillow, moaning, this time in shame.

I wanted to kill him. At the very least I wanted to slap the smile off his charming, devious face. Hell, I wanted to stab him.

I sat up on the bed, leaning back against the rough wall. It felt as if I'd switched off a light, or broken a phone connection. In the muffled distance I could almost hear him calling me once more: *Come to me.* Resolutely I closed my mind to him. He wasn't getting anywhere near me, into my dreams, into my body. And as much as my muscles tensed, I wasn't going to get up and knock on his door, even on the pretext of slapping him.

The hell I wasn't. I pushed off the bed, fury vibrating through me, intensifying with the now clear call from his seductive voice. I walked across the floor, opened my door, and strode over to his, knocking with deceptive softness.

"Come in," he said. I didn't move. *Come to me.* I remained rigid, holding behind my back the pretty Japanese vase I'd snatched off a pedestal. Nothing but the best for Cain.

A moment later I heard him move, could almost imagine the languid beauty of him as he came toward the door. It opened, and he stood leaning against it, a slow, sensual smile on the face that I still, ridiculously, wanted to kiss. "There you are," he said, and the timbre of his voice slid beneath my skin, another arousal. Magic tricks, like the wall of flame, all illusion and no substance.

"Here I am," I agreed pleasantly. "You called me?"

A wary look came into his silver eyes for a moment. "I don't think so," he lied smoothly. "But you're welcome, nonetheless. Any the worse for wear after your adventure?"

Adventure? He called a murder attempt an *adventure*? My simmering rage came close to bubbling over. Not enough to change my mind and decide he was behind it—time and wisdom had convinced me otherwise. No, he didn't waste his time with straightforward murder attempts; instead he burrowed into someone's mind to torment and mock her while he undoubtedly got his own rocks off.

I smiled sweetly. "Are you inviting me in?"

"Of course," he said, opening the door wider. And he made the critical mistake of turning his back on me.

He was a lot taller, but the vase was big, and I crashed it down over his head with all my strength, listening to the satisfying crack as it shattered against his hard skull, watching him go down onto the hard floor in a boneless heap.

Unconscious. Blood seeping into his golden hair. Lifeless.

The sudden cry of pain came from me as I sank to the floor beside him, pulling him into my arms. What had I done? This wasn't a movie—I could have killed him with my stupid fury and hurt pride. He was a deadweight as I cradled him against me. The warmth of his blood trickled down my chest, soaking into my clothes, and I began to cry like a stupid baby, rocking him. *Don't be dead, don't be dead,* I prayed silently.

I'm not dead. The words were clear and wry. *But I'm going to have one hell of a headache.*

I looked down at him, ready to sob with relief, and then realized he hadn't spoken out loud. His eyes were open, watching me, and this time the words were audible. "Hell, Martha. Can't you take a joke?"

I dropped him on the floor, and his head bounced slightly as I tried to scramble away; but his head was a hell of a lot harder than even I had suspected, and he caught me and yanked me back. "I liked it better when you were holding me," he added.

"Dream on."

He laughed, the heartless bastard. "I think we've had enough of dreams, haven't we?" And before I realized what he was doing, he'd tugged me down to his mouth.

The sizzle I felt every time we touched was still there, more a quiet vibration than an actual shock. I knew I should have slapped him, but his mouth was so sweet beneath mine, and he wasn't dead, and neither was I, and for a brief moment I just wanted to savor it. I put my hand out to cradle his face lightly, to thread my fingers through his long, silky hair, and then I yanked, hard, pulling his mouth away from mine.

He rolled out from under me before I could follow up with any more mayhem, bouncing lightly to his feet, then stared down at me with a sudden frown. "You're bleeding."

I glanced down at the blood on my shoulder. "No, Sherlock, that's your blood."

"No, Watson, you're kneeling in shards of pottery. Clearly your last-minute remorse wiped out your common sense."

I scrambled to my feet as well. He was right—a piece of the vase was stuck in my leg, and I yanked it out ruthlessly. "I'll survive." It was then that I realized what I was wearing. In deference to the warm night, I was dressed only in a thin shift, one that covered all the important things, like scars and breasts and hips, but hung only halfway to my knees and left my arms and too much of my chest bare. And he was looking at the blood trickling down my leg with an expression that made my stomach twist in what had to be disgust. But didn't feel like it.

I should walk away. I'd made my point, there was nothing more to say. But I said it anyway. "So, was any of it real? Or just dreams?"

"A little of both." He watched me warily. "I didn't take anything you weren't willing to give, by the way. In case you've decided to call me any nasty names."

"Like dream rapist?" I shot back. "It doesn't seem much different from putting a drug in someone's drink."

"Doesn't it? You had a choice. You always had a choice, and you chose me. Just as you did tonight."

I stared at him, momentarily speechless. "I think," I said meditatively, "that I really hate you."

"No you don't. I can prove it. Come to me, Martha." It was the first time he'd said those words out loud, yet they echoed through my body.

"I don't think your magic juju works when I'm awake."

"It doesn't. It's just me asking. Come here, Martha. Or turn your back on me. It's your choice. It always has been."

I stared at him. "And it doesn't matter which one I choose?"

His smile was rueful. "Of course it does. I'm ready to explode from wanting you. You're making me crazy—I can't concentrate on why I'm here; all I can think about is getting inside you, and each dream only makes it worse instead of taking the edge off. I'm drowning in you, in your scent and your touch and your taste. Come to me, goddamn it." His voice was ragged at the end of this, and I was hot, trembling.

"No," I said. Just to see the darkness flood his face. "You come to me."

He moved with the timeless, effortless grace of all the Fallen, and before I could rethink my foolish offer he'd pulled me into his arms, wrapping my legs around his hips as he kissed me. I had no choice but to twine my arms around his neck and hold on tightly as he ravaged my mouth, kissing me . . . completely. If one could come from being kissed, this was the kiss that would do it. His mouth was warm, wet, and I opened beneath the pressure of it, tasting his tongue, his want, his demand, with a fierce need of my own. He carried me through into the shadowy bedroom, and his skin was hot beneath my hands. I knew what would come next: gentle kisses, sweet encouragement as he set me down on the bed. He would coax and charm me until I finally relaxed, and then—

I felt the wall against my back, hard, and his hands were up under the shift, on my hips, ripping away the scrap of underwear I wore. He braced me against the wall as I felt his fingers between my legs, testing me, slipping in the wetness of my arousal, and then he fumbled with his jeans. I heard the rasp of a zipper in the darkness, and a moment later he was pressed against me, large and hot and real, and there was no sweetness, no gentle persuasion, there was only the hard thrust of him, pushing in, deep, so deep that I wanted to cry out in sudden satisfaction. Wanted to cry out for more.

But his mouth still covered mine, his tongue pushing into my mouth as his cock pushed between my legs, and the sizzle between us turned into a small shudder of satisfaction. He began to pull out, and I wanted to cry. It wasn't enough, I needed more of him—and then he thrust back in, deeper than before.

I was digging my fingernails into his shoulders, but he didn't seem to mind. He pulled out again, and this time his thrust reached all the way home, to the tip of my womb, and I cried out against his mouth, climaxing again, harder this time, so that my entire body seemed to convulse. He held still, letting me ride it out, and then he began to move when I didn't think I could bear any more, pushing through the clinging walls of my sex, a hard, steady thrust that pushed me back against the wall, his hands under my butt now, cradling me, holding me as he worked me, taking his time. He tore his mouth away from mine, sinking it onto my shoulder, and I felt his teeth grazing the tender skin at the base of my neck. I knew what he wanted, the completion of this rough, heavy joining, and I could only blame him for the fact that I wanted it too. But I was past speaking, lost in the insistent push and power of his body in mine, deep, impossibly so, and it should have hurt, but I was so slick he could move easily enough within the clinging tightness.

I didn't expect anything more—I was still trembling with the aftermath of the shattering climax I'd just had—when he started to move faster, harder, and he put one hand between us, touching me, rubbing me, and this time I did scream, I couldn't help it, as a wave more powerful than death caught me up and flung me into the night air, and I was sobbing, clawing at him, holding on to whatever I could as the maelstrom knocked me off my feet.

He joined me, rigid, trembling in my arms as I felt him come, felt the liquid warmth inside me, and I wanted him to take me, all of me, my blood, my life, everything was his. But I was beyond speech, beyond thought, as another climax hit me, out of nowhere, and the world disappeared.

Everything swung dizzily around me as I felt him move, carrying me the rest of the way across the room, lowering me onto the bed. "Don't move," he said roughly. As if I could. Every muscle in my body had turned to rubber. I sank into the welcoming softness of his bed, his scent all around me, and fell asleep.

WHEN CAIN CAME back, she was lying on her stomach, one hand curled protectively under her chin, dead to world. He looked at her, immediately hard again, and shook his head at his own absurdity. He was supposed to be using her, manipulating her. Instead he seemed to be at the mercy of his over-powering need for her.

It was lust, pure and simple, he told himself. If lust could ever be pure. For some reason she called to him as no one in memory had, and there was no rhyme or reason to it. She refused to be charmed by him, when he had most women at his feet with only the slightest effort. She was quiet, reserved, and saw right through most of his games. And he couldn't get enough of her.

And the oddest thing of all—he'd been so caught up in the clenching power of her body that he'd forgotten all about her blood. The climax that had shaken him to his very core had been like nothing he could remember feeling, and even with the scent of her blood against his face, dancing beneath her skin, coming inside her had been enough.

Thinking about her blood now made him even harder, though. She was a blood virgin—that had been common knowledge—and she'd fight him like hell over it. She was a hard woman to convince. And the longer he stood here, the harder he got.

He looked down at his hands. They were shaking slightly with his need for her. What the hell was wrong with him? What had she done to him?

He wasn't a fool, and he knew the answer. One that was unacceptable. Any form of weakness was, and if he could deny it he could force it out of existence. He wanted her. He didn't have to look any deeper into the whys of it. He wanted her, and now that he'd taken her the first barrier had been broken, and he could have her until he tired of her. He could fuck himself senseless in the sweet, milking clasp of her body, and eventually he'd have enough.

Even if it he couldn't imagine that ever happening.

He wanted to slide his arm under her stomach, pull her to her hands and knees and push inside her. He wanted to pound away at her until this blistering need finally disappeared. In the shadowy light he could see the scars crisscrossing her body. As he'd expected, they traced across her back as well, the cruel lines fainter here, fading. He wanted to kiss those lines as well. He wanted to put his mouth all over her body. He wanted everything from her.

He climbed onto the bed carefully, so as not to wake her. He lay on his side and pulled her against him, wrapping his body around hers, his cock hard against her backside, demanding, wanting to feel her breasts in his hands, her blood in his mouth.

She sighed, curling into him. Trusting him in her sleep. He rested his head against hers, breathing in the scent of her hair, her skin, her blood. And prepared himself for a long night of torture before, inexplicably, he fell asleep as well.

CHAPTER
TWENTY-SEVEN

MY FIRST THOUGHT WAS THAT something wonderful was happening. Like the Christmas days that had always been just a little bit better. Almost immediately it was followed by a flood of panic. The sense of disaster lurking. I held very still, opening myself for the vision that was trying to make its way into my barely conscious mind, and then reality came rushing back. Where I was. Who was with me. What I had done.

He was asleep, his arms holding me against him. He was hard, and I could feel my body heat in instant response. Even the blood seemed to leap in my veins at the realization that he was all around me. I wanted to turn in his arms, wrap my legs around his hips, and pull him inside me. I wanted to press his mouth against my neck and have him take everything.

I moved very carefully, sliding out of his arms, and for once things went my way. He didn't wake up. It was getting close to full daylight, and I looked down at my body. I could see my scars clearly, and there were bruises forming at my hips where he'd held me so tightly. It had been little more than a hard, fast coupling, like nothing I had ever endured before.

And I was lying to myself again. The only way endurance came into it was in keeping up with him. I could still feel the power of the climaxes that had ripped through my body, and the memory shamed me.

I'd faked it with Thomas. I knew that now. He'd been so patient, so careful, so gentle, and I'd felt nothing more than warm affection and gratitude. Now, with one rough encounter, I seemed to have graduated into a full-blown sexual human being, hot and needy, and I hated myself for it.

I wanted to hate Cain, and while I knew there were a dozen reasons that hatred was justified, my sexual response wasn't one of them. That was mine to own. It made no sense that Cain had suddenly been able to turn on a switch that I'd wanted to keep forever hidden, but he had, and I could only blame myself.

I found the torn shift I'd had on when I'd stormed into his room last night, but there was no sign of the underwear he'd ripped off me, and I wasn't about to go searching and wake him up. I tiptoed through the silent bedroom toward the door, carefully avoiding the shattered bits of vase that littered the floor. Had I really smashed it over his head? Had last night really happened?

I got to my room and headed straight for the shower. I was sore between my legs, and touching myself as I washed reminded me of him, stirring the powerful surge of longing once more. I used cold water, the icy stream a punishment far different from the embrace of the cold ocean I longed for, and I half expected him to be waiting for me when I emerged, but my room was silent and empty in the dawn light. I told myself I was glad.

I needed someone to slap me. I had been touched by terrible, ugly men. I had been made love to by a gentle, beautiful man. One was hateful and degrading. One was sweet and cherishing. Last night had been elemental, rough, overwhelming, and everything had changed. Why now? Why had I let this happen?

Maybe it was the shock of the previous day. It wasn't often that someone tried to kill me; little wonder that I had wanted, needed, some proof of life. Sex was the very antithesis of the death someone had wanted to hand me, and making love with Cain had been an act of defiance, of claiming life.

Making love? I wanted to snort at my own absurdity. There was nothing about love in what I had done with Cain. Just a spasm of powerful, physical response. Biology, that was it. Nothing more.

I should use Cain's word for it, but it was too ugly. I wouldn't call it anything but a mistake, one I wouldn't make again. For all I knew, I'd made that mistake with the very man who'd tried to kill me. I had told myself it wasn't Cain; now, in the cool light of day, I wondered if I'd been foolish once more.

Of course I had. I had made mistake after mistake. The worst being the fact that I still wanted to go to him, climb back in bed and wrap myself around his body.

I dressed quickly in severe, dark clothes, pulling my hair back into a tight knot before looking at my reflection, and then couldn't stop the laugh that bubbled up. I had a black eye and a scrape along the side of my face, which my ruthless hairstyle exposed for all to see. I also had a glow that even I could recognize. There was no other term for it. I looked well fucked.

I reached up to release my hair to cover my too-revealing face, then changed my mind. It would be interesting to see how people reacted to my bruises. Would anyone give himself away?

Or had I already faced the man who had done this, climaxed with his hard cock inside me? If so, why hadn't he finished it? Finished me?

My plan for the day was simple. I would spend it with Allie, safe on the top floor of the main compound, away from everyone, and we would talk about the baby and not worry about the storm that was fast approaching. I would tell her I'd slipped on the rocks, or something equally lame, and with luck she wouldn't notice anything else. I wouldn't have to face Cain until I was ready to, and that was a small comfort. I could put what had happened between us in a dark place in my mind and ignore it, concentrating on what was really important.

For the first time, the most glaring question came to me. Why? Why would someone want to hurt me, silence me, kill me? The answer was obvious and immediate. Because I saw things. I had stopped anyone from hurting Allie. With luck, I would see other dangers before they could happen. Someone must be afraid I would see what he or she was going to do, and it had to be something very bad.

My visions were still unreliable. I hadn't foreseen my own danger, from either the man who'd tried to kill me or the man who'd taken me up against a wall. What kind of gift was that, when it couldn't even give me a simple heads-up? *Don't walk alone on the beach—someone's going to try to drown you. Don't walk into the man's room in the middle of the night, wearing hardly anything, and start a confrontation when you know sex has been seething beneath the surface since you first saw him.*

But then, I had never been able to make my visions obey my needs or give me answers to questions that were vitally important. Maybe if I could find out who'd tried to kill Allie, I would discover who had tried to kill me as well. Or maybe the two events were entirely unrelated. Most people had secrets, and my erratic visions could expose things people needed to keep hidden.

There was nothing I could do but watch my back. And keep as far away from Cain as possible in this tight little society, until I knew for sure just how dangerous he was. I couldn't afford a repeat of last night. I didn't think my heart could bear it.

As if my heart had anything to do with it. I wasn't a coward, but right then I needed to be. I headed toward Allie's safe aerie before anyone could stop me.

SHE WAS HIDING from him. Cain had half expected she would, and for now he should be willing to let her be. Last night had been a mistake—he'd been planning to seduce her slowly, so that he could insinuate himself into her visions more thoroughly. Instead he'd banged her like the horny bastard he was, and he knew she would run. It didn't matter how many times she'd climaxed, and while he'd been too busy to count, he knew she had kept track. She was terrified of her own sexuality; he'd botched it, and she'd gone into hiding.

It was for the best. He had no intention of touching her again until his own irrational longing was under control. As long as she was safe, he could keep his distance.

At least, he should. He could no longer deny that he was obsessed with her, anathema that the admission was. He didn't want to need anyone or anything; he'd spent most of his endless existence alone and inviolate, and he preferred it that way. Physical release was easily found—it hadn't been idle boasting when he'd told her he could have anyone he wanted. He knew how to flatter, how to charm, how to flirt, how to seduce, though she'd been absurdly resistant to all his patented tricks. Until it had all exploded into a few rough moments up against the wall, and all his masterful skills had simply disappeared in his need for her. He'd lost control, and he hated himself for that.

In retrospect, he should simply have taken her to bed the first chance he got. He'd been so bemused by his reaction to her that he'd been instinctively cautious, looking around for anyone else to use in her place. By waiting, he'd fueled his lust instead of defusing it, so that now she was a dangerous distraction. Each time he'd entered her dreams and taken the sweet release of her body, he'd made his own longing worse. Even taking her last night hadn't been the release he'd expected. He'd put it off for so long that a taste wasn't enough. He needed to feast on her. His need made no sense to him, but denying it was getting him nowhere. It simply was.

But time, pushed along by Metatron's ham-handed attacks on Allie and Martha, was running out.

Cain would destroy the safe, smug little world of the Fallen, rip away the masks and lies that covered them, so that they might rise, stronger than ever and with no lies to weaken them, and wipe out the Armies of Heaven. And he would kill Azazel, who had led the Fallen and done nothing when Uriel had murdered Tamarr.

Now it seemed he would have to kill Metatron as well, for putting his hands on Martha. It was the least he could do, as penance for the pain he was going to cause her.

Once the smoke cleared and the dead burned, including Azazel, he would let her go, release the bond. He'd leave again, and he wouldn't come back until he'd forgotten all about her.

She was mortal, after all. In a hundred years she wouldn't even be a memory.

CHAPTER
TWENTY-EIGHT

AFTER ONE LOOK AT MY FACE, Allie had said nothing. If I'd had the energy to worry, that would have been cause enough—Allie stomped in where angels feared to tread, and tact had never been her strong suit. I must have looked as shell-shocked as I felt.

She even managed to beat me at cribbage, which she never could. For some reason I'd become unable to count to fifteen. But Allie was more than the source of blood for the Fallen. She was the source of strength and solace as well, and as the morning passed we ate ice cream and pastries and lasagna and every possible comfort food we could think of, and we laughed and even cried a bit. I finally began to feel my shattered soul recovering.

I got through without seeing Cain once. It was what I'd planned, so it made no sense that I felt oddly deflated. I managed to sneak into my room while everyone was at dinner; I locked the doors, drew the curtains, turned off the lights, and curled up in my bed like a child afraid of the boogeyman. I didn't know what I'd do when he knocked on the door.

He didn't come. Not to my door, not to his own. I tried to reach out with my mind, to sense where he was, but as usual my stupid gift came up with a big fat nothing.

The only way I could find him was through sleep, but even that proved elusive. I tossed and turned, but the memories kept coming back, brief and visceral. His mouth on mine; his hands on my hips, holding me; his hand between my legs, stroking me; bringing me to a swift climax; his cock against me, pushing into me.

I rolled over on my stomach, groaning. He'd started something I'd never wanted, and I didn't know how to get rid of it, how to make it go away. I hadn't wanted sex, hadn't liked sex. Now I was obsessed with it.

When I awoke the next morning I was frustrated, grumpy, and bleary-eyed from lack of sleep, but at least I'd managed to keep the erotic dreams away. If staying awake would do it, I'd go without sleep for weeks or months or however long it took for Cain to leave.

I was strong, and I wasn't going to give in to weakness. Never again.

METATRON MOVED PURPOSEFULLY along the hallway. The women were talking, and while he despised gossip, this time he listened.

"Did you see Martha?" the demon Lilith demanded.

Victoria Bellona answered. "I did, and I wanted to hug her. She finally went to bed with Cain. It's about damned time."

"Not necessarily the wisest choice," Lilith murmured.

"Oh, come on, admit it. He's walking sex. And no one deserves it more than Martha."

"But he'll leave. He always does," Lilith said.

"Maybe not this time. I bet Allie will know more." A moment later they were rushing up the stairs, and he watched them go with disgust burning in his heart.

It mattered not that it was part of Cain's mysterious master plan; it still filled him with contempt and fury. The obscenity of lust ate at his soul, and the knowledge that Cain had given in, had writhed naked with the seer, was so foul that he needed to cleanse his mind.

And the only way he could do so was with blood.

He couldn't afford to let Cain stop him again. No one else would pay any attention, but Cain was watching too closely. He had to be distracted.

There was one thing in Sheol that would override Cain's careful plans, a score he had waited millennia to settle. He could settle it now.

"Azazel's looking for you," he announced when he found Cain in the training room.

"Azazel can go fuck himself," Cain growled, his attention on a sparring pair. "Keep your arm up, Gadrael," he called out, then glanced back at Metatron. "Are you his message boy now?"

It was all too easy. "He said you were afraid of him. That you were looking for a way that you didn't have to fight him."

Cain had grown very still, all his attention on Metatron now. "He told you that?"

"No. I heard him talking to Raziel. The message he sent to you was 'Get over it.'" He stepped back, waiting for the explosion.

At first he was disappointed in the result. Cain said nothing, slowly rolling up his sleeves to reveal surprisingly powerful arms. And then he caught sight of Cain's face, and was satisfied.

"Did he really?" Cain inquired in a silken voice. "And do you have any idea where I might find him?"

"Haven't seen him. He usually ends up on that ledge he likes, where he can watch over everyone."

"You mean spy on everyone," Cain said. "I have to leave," he called out to the sparring partners he was supposed to be observing.

"What the hell?" Michael demanded. "This isn't optional, Cain. We're fighting a war."

"It's not my war," he said shortly, and headed for the door. Metatron followed him, needing to be certain Cain had taken his elaborate and not-too-subtle bait.

"Where are you going?" he demanded.

Cain turned and gave him a dulcet smile. "I'm going to find Azazel," he murmured. "And I'm going to cut out his heart and eat it."

I ATE BREAKFAST in my room, giving in to cowardice for the moment, and looked over my lists, trying to make sense of them. The more I stared at them, the more incomprehensible they seemed, and I closed my eyes, only for a moment.

I had trouble napping in the middle of the day—sleepless nights were bad enough. If I lay down to rest, it would make the insomnia even worse. But I could no more stop this than I could fly.

I dreamed—not of sensual lassitude, but of walls of flame and blood and death, until, at the end, I saw Azazel. Dead. I could hear Rachel's wail, so strong that all the women in the universe wept, and I felt the bleak impossibility of it, too real. Azazel was dead, murdered by a raging madman.

Cain, holding a knife, covered with the spray of Azazel's lifeblood, a savage grin on his face.

I tore myself out of sleep with a hoarse gasp, sweating, shaking, sick to my stomach. This was no bad dream fed by the minutiae of my own life. It was a vision, and it was going to happen if I didn't stop it.

I scrambled out of bed. I had no idea what time it was or how long I'd slept. I only knew I couldn't be late for what looked like an execution. I grabbed the nearest thing I could find, one of Tory's discarded dresses, and ran from my room.

I didn't bother to stop at Cain's. He wasn't there. The likelihood of me being able to stop him was slim at best, and if he was truly a determined assassin, then I'd just be collateral damage. Which still didn't explain why we'd had sex. Why he'd want to have anything to do with me.

Unless he thought he could manipulate my visions? Good luck with that. My visions defied control, predictability, even reality. They were neither one thing nor another, the gift of a satyr, cruel and useless most of the time.

But not this time. This time I had seen clearly, and I would stop it from happening—or die trying.

The ground floor was empty, and I headed straight out toward the beach. I hadn't seen much in the background of the vision, but in retrospect the misty blueness of the sky had arched above everything, and the blood had splattered over shrubs as Azazel's body lay among the flowers. And Rachel kept screaming, the sound piercing, agonizing, ripping at me.

No. It hadn't happened yet, and I would stop it. If I had to kill Cain myself, it wasn't going to happen.

The beach was deserted as well, and I looked at the soft swells longingly. The water healed the Fallen. If I could, I'd drag Cain into it and hold his head under; maybe whatever sick rage had prompted such a horrific act would be cured.

I started to run toward the cove, fool that I was, and as I moved I felt a shadow over my head. I looked up, squinting against the brightness of the sky, but I could see only a silhouette, one of the Fallen, wings spread wide.

I sped up, the sense of disaster rushing through me in sickening waves, searching the deserted landscape with desperation clawing at me. There was no sign of them, yet I couldn't shake the terror that washed over me.

And then I saw them.

CAIN LANDED ON the ledge beside Azazel, touching down lightly and folding his wings into nothingness. Azazel was perched on the edge in his favorite spot, watching the endless ocean, but Cain had no illusions that he'd taken him off guard.

"You've been a hard man to find," he said lightly, dropping down beside the man he was going to kill. "Where have you been?"

Azazel kept his gaze fixed on the horizon. "I had things to do. Are you here to kill me?"

"Of course."

Azazel nodded. "I always knew you'd be coming for me eventually. I wondered what took you so long."

"Maybe I wanted you to sweat it."

Azazel turned to look at him. "Do I look like I'm sweating?"

Cain felt the familiar murderous rage build inside him, and he pushed it down. He needed to be calm, rational. Uriel was coming, and he could put off his revenge no longer.

He gave Azazel a sour smile. "You don't feel anything at all, do you? You stood by and watched as Tamarr was ripped to pieces, and not only did you do nothing to stop it, you didn't even blink as she died in screaming agony. You felt nothing. You're a cold, dead bastard, and my killing you won't change a thing."

"Then why do it?"

Cain's left hand tightened around the knife. "Because you're here."

He brought the knife out, and it glittered in the sunlight as he surveyed it. Yes, it was a good choice. He'd always been talented with a knife, and he liked the intimacy of it. He wanted to feel each blow and think of Tamarr.

Tamarr, whom he couldn't picture anymore. He'd lost her face first, more than a millennium ago. Then her voice. Then everything about her but the memory of his love. Love that he would never feel again.

Azazel was watching him, perfectly relaxed. "Will killing me make you feel better, Cain? Will it fill that black hole inside you? Because I don't think so. I think you're angry and confused and lost, and you've been thinking about revenge for so long it's become automatic. And you're wrong. I felt something when Uriel killed your wife, even if I didn't show it. I was sick, and furious, and broken."

"Then why didn't you do anything to stop it?" he spat. "Why didn't you say something, for God's sake?"

"You idiot," Azazel said in an almost genial voice. "We couldn't. Uriel lined us up and then made it impossible for us to move, speak, or even react. We were silent sentinels to what he was doing, and it was meant to scare the shit out of us, keep us from ever making the same mistake. And if you doubt me, remember the bonds that held *you*. They weren't physical, but they held you back, so you could only watch and scream. We weren't given the option of screaming."

"I don't believe you." He gripped the knife more tightly. He'd cut Azazel's throat first, then cut out his tongue—anything to stop his lies.

"You know it's the truth," Azazel said flatly. "You just don't want to believe it. I know you've been planning something—you want to destroy all of us, the ones you blame for letting Tamarr die. But deep down you know it's your own guilt you're trying to assuage."

"Thanks for the amateur psychology," Cain snarled.

Azazel's smile was cool and disdainful. "So, are you working with Uriel to bring us all down? If you're going to kill me, there's no harm in telling me."

"Working with Uriel? What kind of idiot are you? You think I would go to all this trouble to cut your heart out when the man who actually murdered my wife gets away with it? No, Azazel. I'm going to teach the Fallen how to win against Uriel. Once you're dead, I'm going to show them that their rules and their lives are based on nothing but lies, and when they accept that, they'll have nothing left to lose. And that's the only way to beat Uriel at his own game."

Azazel looked at him. "Clearly you've been planning this for a long time."

"I've had millennia."

"And you don't think the Fallen might mind if you butcher me?" Azazel seemed no more than vaguely curious.

"I'll tell them you knew the truth about Sheol, and deliberately misled everyone."

"And what exactly is the truth?"

"That there is no such thing as the blood bond. You kept that quiet so you could control things through the so-called Source, whoever had the misfortune to be your wife at the time. You knew we were invulnerable to fire, but you convinced everyone it was a deadly poison, one more thing to keep them under your thumb."

Disbelief was clear on Azazel's face. "And you're telling me it's not? I've watched members of the Fallen sicken and die from the mere touch of a flame. You're crazy. Next you'll be telling me the sea doesn't heal us."

"It does. The only reason fire kills the Fallen is because they believe it will. The same with blood. It's a way to keep the Fallen faithful, keeping your tight little society under your control."

"Interesting," Azazel murmured. "You're forgetting one salient point, however."

"What's that?"

"That they are no longer under my control. I gave them up, disappeared. Raziel now governs the Fallen."

"He's your stooge."

Azazel laughed. "Don't let him hear you say that. He's easily annoyed, and he's on edge, with the baby coming."

"One more piece of proof that the rules are an illusion. All it took was a little of your wife's brainwashing, and we suddenly have a miracle pregnancy."

"'We'?" Azazel echoed. "I didn't think you still considered yourself part of the Fallen. I thought you wanted us all dead."

"Only you, Azazel. I wouldn't be here if I wasn't trying to save them."

Azazel nodded. He glanced down at the knife, shining in the sunshine. "I'm afraid I'm going to fight back. If you'd come for me before I found Rachel, I would have been an easy target."

"Exactly," Cain said, his voice cold and terrible. "You need to feel the loss the way I did."

"Trust me, I have," Azazel murmured. "Losing Sarah almost killed me."

"Of course it did," Cain scoffed. "And yet you managed to fall in love again, have your happy life once more."

"You could as well, you know." Azazel's eyes showed no fear, none of the usual distance. There was something infuriatingly close to compassion in them. "You've spent millennia on a cold, empty quest for revenge, and trust me, you won't feel any better once you finish with me. No matter how many Nephilim I killed, I couldn't bring Sarah back, and I couldn't dull the ache within me."

"More lessons, Azazel? Keep them. The blood bond doesn't exist. Women are interchangeable."

"Our Martha is a faceless fuck? Yes, I know you finally bedded her. I just don't understand what took you so long."

"Shut up."

"She's a weak point in all this, isn't she? If what you say is true, if the mating bond doesn't exist, if women are interchangeable, then it won't matter that she's down there on the beach, watching us."

Cain jerked his head downward, and he could see her, a small, solitary figure, staring up at them. It was too far for a human to see clearly, but she would know anyway, and he could feel her panic, feel her inward scream at him, to stop what he was doing.

He ruthlessly shut off that voice, turning back to Azazel. "Do you really think a temporary fuck would make any difference to something I've planned for thousands of years?"

"No. But I think Martha would."

"Wrong. Are we ready to do this, old man?"

"You're older than I am."

"Only in years. You were born a coldhearted ancient."

"Perhaps." He nodded. "You know I'm going to fight you."

"I would expect no less. I even know you carry a knife, so you're not unarmed. There's nothing to stop us. If I die, so be it. But I won't. You will."

Azazel glanced down at the beach again, but Cain kept his gaze averted. He couldn't allow a momentary weakness to distract him from justice.

"It's possible," Azazel said in a measured voice. "But I'm afraid you're going to have to choose."

Something was clawing at Cain, trying to break through the silence he'd imposed. A rough fear. He couldn't afford to pay any attention, and he narrowed his eyes as he took in Azazel's deceptively relaxed gaze, the knife tight in his hand. "Choose?"

"Between Martha and your revenge."

"I told you, I don't give a fuck what Martha thinks—"

"Martha won't be thinking. Martha will be dead, unless you go after her."

Unwillingly he turned his face back to the narrow stretch of beach, and everything inside him froze.

CHAPTER
TWENTY-NINE

I HADN'T EVEN FELT HIS APPROACH. HIS feet were silent on the shifting sands, and I was so intent on the drama being played out on the ledge high above me that I didn't notice the shift in wind, the scent of sweat, the malevolence on the air, until his heavy arms caught me from behind in a deathly embrace, one huge forearm across my throat, blocking off the air, the other around my waist, squeezing me.

I couldn't cry out—my throat was being crushed, slowly but inexorably, as I was lifted off my feet, and I kicked backward in rage and desperation. My struggles meant nothing to the vicious giant behind me, the same man who had tried to smash my head against the rocks, the same powerful angel who felt nothing. Metatron.

I could feel consciousness fading, and with it, my

life. I tried to turn my head, some stupid, sentimental remnant of me wanting to look at Cain when I died, but the heavy arm around my throat kept my head motionless. Thick, cottony darkness was closing in around me, and my struggles were weakening even as I clawed at his arm in desperation.

What a lousy gift, I thought dizzily, that it couldn't even warn me of my impending death. And then I could think of nothing at all, my mind a silent scream, Cain's name, as I fell into the doubtful comfort of endless sleep.

A moment later I was flung through the air, landing on the sand. I lay there, struggling for breath, knowing I was going to die anyway, that he'd crushed my throat and my lungs and there was no way I could breathe, when suddenly everything came back with a whoosh, and I realized the air had merely been knocked out of me when I went flying. I lay still, struggling to regain use of my muscles as I watched the two angels fight in a furious battle to the death.

Blood was everywhere, and I wanted to cry out, to scream a warning before Metatron's huge fists crushed Cain, but I'd underestimated him. Cain was faster, smarter, and possessed of such a murderous rage that he made Metatron look like a lumbering giant. Blood spurted from Metatron's neck, and he sank to his knees in the sand, clutching his throat, as Cain closed in on him. I tried to call out, to tell him no, but some small, savage part of me wanted this. Wanted violence in my name. Wanted some kind of proof that Cain actually felt something for me.

There was a sudden darkness as Metatron's huge wings extended, and a moment later he was soaring upward, fast and high into the sky. I rolled onto my back, expecting to see Cain fly after him.

A moment later I was caught up in his arms, held against his bloody chest as he peered into my face, looking for signs of damage. "I'm okay," I tried to say, but there was only a whistling rasp of sound as I choked.

He pushed my hair from my face with a surprisingly tender touch, and I could see the relief in his eyes. "You're okay," he said, and I wanted to snap that I was trying to tell him that, but I gave up. "And you can't talk," he added with a faint curve of his mouth. "I can't think of a better combination."

I closed my eyes. Everything hurt, particularly my stomach and throat, but he was right, I was okay; and for the moment I didn't have to do anything but let him hold me in the warm sunshine, his hands tender.

I don't know how long it was before I felt another presence, and I opened my eyes to see Azazel land lightly on the beach beside us, his wings folding behind him, a grave expression on his face. "I couldn't catch him."

"Just as well," Cain said grimly. "I want to be the one to kill him."

Azazel nodded, looking down at me. I should have made an effort to sit up, but it was just too comfortable being held. I wasn't even going to think about why, think about the man whose strength was slowly filling me. I was going to let go of everything.

"How is she?"

"She'll live," Cain said briefly, a bit heartlessly, but his hold on me was still incredibly gentle, so I didn't object.

"So are you ready to finish what we started, or would you prefer to wait till you've recovered a bit from fighting Metatron?"

Cain gave him a snarl—surprising, when his usual manner was effortless charm. "I can kill you and Metatron with one hand tied behind my back."

"Yes, I saw how successful you were with Metatron," Azazel said. "I'm more than happy to let you try to kill me now if you're ready. I just want to point out a few things."

"Get the fuck out of here," Cain snapped.

"In a moment." He moved closer. "When the time came to kill me or save the woman you insist doesn't matter to you, you chose to save her. What do you think that means?"

All I could hear was *the woman you insist doesn't matter* and I tried to push away from him. It was a waste of time—I still felt weak and shaky, and even at full strength I was no match for him as he held me more tightly.

"It means I can always kill you another day."

"You and I both know that isn't true. That chance won't come again anytime soon. Yet you went to save Martha. I'll believe the things you've told me about Sheol, but you're wrong about one thing. There is such a thing as bonded mates, and Martha is yours."

Cain ignored him, continuing to stare down at me as if I really mattered. "She's a means to an end," he muttered.

"But your end is now out in the open. You don't have to use her anymore. Why are you still holding her?"

"I can still kill you," Cain muttered, and I was ready to second the motion.

Azazel simply shook his head. "I'll bring what you said to Raziel and the council and we'll consider it. In the meantime, why don't you take the woman who doesn't matter to you somewhere and take care of her?"

And then we were alone. I waited for Cain to drop me on the sand and take off. Even if he did care just the tiniest bit, Azazel had thrown down the gauntlet, and Cain would have to prove him wrong. He'd been using me, which was no surprise. So why was it suddenly hurting so badly?

I felt the sudden tension in his muscles the moment before he rose, but it was an effortless gesture, even with my weight still in his arms. A moment later we were up, up into the misty blue of the Sheol sky, soaring through the heavens, and all I could do was swallow.

Flying had always terrified me. The few times Thomas had insisted on taking me out had been miserable disasters, and Azazel had known that. He'd challenged Cain to carry me anyway, the bastard, and I held my breath and closed my eyes, certain the ground was going to come thudding up to meet us.

He held me loosely, comfortably, and I considered turning and clinging to him for dear life—then realized that I wasn't afraid that he would drop me. Even with this casual embrace, I knew I was safe, and the sensation was both disturbing and oddly comforting. I opened one eye first, then the other, and realized we were moving through the shreds of late-morning clouds, soaring, the salt scent of the ocean drifting up to us. Wind was tugging my hair away from my face, and I dared to look up at him as he flew. He'd saved me, he'd held me, he'd kept me with him, and now he was taking me to safety. For now, that was enough.

When he finally set down, it had taken longer than a straight shot would have. I looked up at him questioningly as he dropped down into our joint courtyard, and oddly he seemed to know what I was thinking. "I needed a little breathing space," he said, almost an apology, except that Cain didn't apologize. He charmed, he manipulated, he lied, but he never apologized. "I thought you wouldn't mind."

If it had been Thomas, he'd have been covered in scratches from my panicked hands. But he wasn't Thomas; he was so clearly different from my gentle, loving Thomas, who had never been the right angel for me. I didn't know why Thomas had been convinced I was his mate, why he'd brought me here when I was frightened of everything, but he had. And now I understood why. It was for Cain.

I shook my head, my voice still lost, and tried to get him to put me on my feet. He ignored me, striding toward the French doors that led to his apartment. I tugged at him, gesturing toward mine, but he shook his head.

"No," he said, carrying me into his rooms and kicking the glass door shut behind him with such force I was afraid it might shatter.

He set me down on the bed so gently that I felt tears stinging my eyes, and I tried to blink them away. That only drew his attention, and he stared down at me for a long moment. "I want you to rest for a bit," he said. "Though I'd be just as happy if you didn't recover your ability to speak for a while. You're very restful when you aren't arguing."

If I'd had more energy, I would have stuck out my tongue at him, but as it was I simply lay back, watching him out of hooded eyes.

"I'm going to clean up, and then I'll be back," he said. "You sure you're okay?"

I nodded, none too enthusiastically. Clearly he was taking Azazel's orders to watch over me seriously. Of all the things I hated in this life, pity was one of the most despised. Particularly pity from someone I longed for with all the maturity of a childhood crush. I might as well stop denying it; I was obsessed by him. When I was dying, he was all that I could think of; and even now, when I wanted to smash something over his head again, I still trembled at the thought of his touch.

On instinct, I reached up and carefully touched the back of his head where I'd bashed him, and there was a spark of electric tension between us. He winced as my fingertips glanced across the bump. "Yeah, it's still there," he said with a grimace. "Next time you want to bash me over the head, why don't you pick something a little flimsier and a little cheaper?"

I flipped him off, trying to put all my communication skills into that single age-old gesture. He just laughed again, drawing a soft blanket over me.

"Sleep, baby," he said, and I realized that was the first honest endearment he'd used.

I decided to sleep.

UP, UP, UP into the icy darkness Metatron soared, his face a mask, his heart a stone. He had failed. Never in his life had he not managed to complete a task set before him, whether one of his own devising or Uriel's bidding, with the sole exception of killing Azazel. He'd failed not once but twice to kill the seer. He'd failed to rid the Source of her spawn, and in the end he hadn't even been able to obliterate Cain, a man smaller than he was. The icy air had stanched the bleeding from the wound on his neck, and he knew that once he reached Uriel, he would be either welcomed or banished into nothingness. He deserved no less. He had failed himself and he had failed Uriel.

He was returning to the afterlife with information that he would offer freely, whether Uriel took him back or not. He hadn't been driven from heaven; he had merely been killed in combat and left behind. Uriel would not be pleased that he hadn't made his way back sooner, but he could always say he had hoped to gather information to bring down the Fallen.

If Uriel let him stay, let him lead the armies once

more, he would dare to ask for the Source. In all of this she was blameless, and Uriel might be disposed to be generous. If not . . .

That was to be decided later. First he had to talk his way back into the dark, celestial glories of the afterlife. He just hoped Uriel was in a good mood.

CHAPTER
THIRTY

I T WAS DARK, A DEEP, COCOONING NIGHT, and I was safe. I lay in the arms of my lover, naked and warm, skin to skin, and I sighed, moving closer. I was curled around him, my head on his shoulder, my arms around his waist as I listened to the rise and fall of his breathing and waited for what this new erotic dream would bring. In my dreams nothing was forbidden, and I wanted ecstasy to wipe out all the bad things. I wanted his mouth all over me; I wanted to taste him, take him in all the forbidden ways; I wanted to scream and cry and melt with him.

His hand slid up my arm to cup my face, turning it up to his, and in the moonless night I could see only the familiar glitter of his eyes looking down at me. His fingers were long, hard, stroking my skin, and I realized with sudden shock that this wasn't another dream. I was in his bed. Naked.

For a moment I froze, and he simply pulled me closer, skin to skin, his mouth against my ear. "It's all right," he whispered. "I'm here."

I wanted to tell him that was exactly what was wrong with the situation. He threatened everything I cared about. But it was too late. His hands were sliding down my back now, molding me against him, and it was only reasonable that I lift my mouth for his kiss, slow and hot and sweet. It was . . . amazing, the laziest, most thorough of kisses, starting with the soft pressure of his mouth on mine, feathering against my lips until they were trembling. His tongue delicately traced the seam of my closed lips, pushing. I knew that if I let his tongue inside me I would do anything, and for a moment I resisted. He bit me then, a soft, reproachful nip, and I gave in, letting his tongue push into my mouth, touching mine, sliding, and I closed my eyes and fell into the wonder of it, kissing him back.

For some reason I expected him to be in a hurry. After all, our first coupling had been rough and quick, and even Thomas had been relatively straight-forward and businesslike about the whole thing. But in the blessed privacy of the pitch-black night, Cain took his time, moving his mouth across my cheek to my ear, biting the lobe gently in a surprisingly erotic move. I'd never considered my earlobes to be an erogenous zone. Trust Cain to have known.

He kissed me again, and this time he coaxed my tongue to move, to dance, to slide against the rough texture of his in a slow, languorous joining that made my skin sizzle. Or maybe that was just the remnant of the strange effect he had on me. He moved his mouth down along the side of my jaw, my neck, pausing at the base where my carotid artery pumped with a steady, aroused throb, and he breathed in the smell of it. I could feel his want, his need, palpable. I could feel my own need, overriding my fear, and when he placed another small, erotic bite there, heat flooded my body.

I opened my mouth to stop him, but no sound came out. I had forgotten that Metatron's murder attempt had left me mute.

Which meant I couldn't tell him no tonight. It was no longer my decision; I could hide in the darkness and take what I wanted and then pretend it had nothing to do with me. For a moment I was tempted, so tempted, to pretend this was out of my control.

But it wasn't. It was exactly what I wanted, just as I had accepted those invading, arousing dreams. I had welcomed his body into mine many times already, in that half-life between waking and sleeping. I would welcome him now.

He pushed me back against the mattress gently, leaning over me, and I went willingly. I knew what would happen next—he would push inside me, and

I would take him, hold him in my arms as he shuddered against me.

But he made no move to cover me. Instead he cupped my breast, and I arched against the surprising reaction it brought. My breasts had never been sensitive, yet the light touch of his fingers against my nipple was unbearably arousing. His mouth followed, and I found I could make noise after all, a low, sensual moan of reaction as he licked my breast, then closed his mouth over me and sucked. I reached up, needing to hold on to something as sensations bombarded me, and I caught his strong biceps, digging my fingernails in. He bit me then, lightly, growling low in his throat, and heat washed over me, a fierce conflagration I was more than ready for.

I would have cried out when his mouth withdrew, but he simply moved to the other breast, giving it the attention I craved, this time sucking harder, biting harder; and to my astonishment I felt a spasm of pure sensation rock my body, making my womb clench. I had climaxed from his mouth on my breasts. What kind of wanton was I?

The best kind, his answer came out of nowhere, voiceless, but I knew it was Cain. It was all right. *Every woman should be a wanton with her lover.*

Are you my lover?

What do you think? Even in my head he sounded sardonic, but I didn't mind. That was Cain.

And I could have him any way I wanted him, I knew that instinctively. I could lie passive and responsive, letting him pleasure me, cover me, make love to me. I didn't have to do a thing.

Suddenly that wasn't enough. His mouth was drifting across my stomach, and for a moment I worried that he could feel the faint unevenness of the scars that marred my body. And then I forgot all about it when he moved lower, pressing his mouth against the soft curls that protected my sex.

Instinctively I closed my legs, and he laughed. *You aren't getting away with that.* He pressed my legs apart, gently, inexorably, and after my initial resistance I let go, letting him move down, lick me between my legs, a slow, erotic sweep of his tongue, as if he was savoring the taste of me. *Yes, I am,* the words came.

Stay out of my head, I protested silently, and I felt the soft brush of his laughter against me.

I'm going to be everywhere inside you, angel, he said. *And you're going to want me there. Stop fighting what you want and claim it.*

Arrogant bastard, I thought, glad he could hear me. *And* I'm *not the angel, you are.*

Most people would disagree, he said, and then the conversation vanished as he put his mouth against me, licking my clitoris with such precision that I made a raw sound of pure need, a tiny, shivering orgasm sweeping over me once more.

You're too easy, he said, and I froze, ashamed once more. *Stop it,* he added, lifting his head, and his cool fingers replaced his mouth, stroking me, sliding inside me, and I was wet, and ashamed, and wanted to pull away even as his wicked fingers kept my arousal at a fever pitch. He slid upward, pulling me into his arms, trapping me there when I wanted to turn away. His mouth was at my ear, and this time the words were spoken, distinct in the noiseless night.

"You are a responsive, beautiful woman, Miss Mary." He felt my immediate stiffening, and he laughed. "Yes, love, I know you're Martha. Plain-speaking, straightforward, working in the kitchen while everyone else gets the goodies. But for me you're Miss Mary, lush and private and mine. And when I lick your pussy, I want you to come."

The words shocked me.

"And when I fuck you, I want you to come so hard you scream," he said. And his words were another forbidden arousal.

Then do it. My silent demand hung in the night air, but to my surprise, he simply laughed.

"Too soon for that, darling," he said against my throat. "This is going to take all night."

I shivered in anticipation, not certain if I was aroused or afraid. Or both. His hand was still between my legs, stroking softly, and he pulled me to him with his other arm. I pushed my face against the smooth warmth of his chest, hiding from his too-observant gaze, relaxing into the slow, sensuous touch of his long fingers against me, inside me. I had climaxed twice with him, an astonishment, and I knew there was nothing I needed to do right then. I didn't have to pretend to have an orgasm; I didn't even need to struggle to achieve one. In a strange way, it felt as if coming twice meant I had already done my duty, and I could just curl up against him, letting him touch me as much as he wanted to, rubbing my face against his hot skin like a kitten while I enjoyed being stroked and petted.

"Now, when did sex become such a chore?" he whispered in my ear as the rough tips of his fingers teased my clitoris, and I jerked, startled at my own fierce reaction. "You don't have to prove anything. There aren't any rules in this bed." He moved his head slightly, so that his breath was hot and arousing against my ear as two fingers slid inside me, deep, a slow, erotic sweep that had me tightening my hold on him.

He was still listening to my thoughts. I didn't ask him how he could do that—Thomas never could. I opened my mouth to tell him not to, but once more I was mute, nothing more than a rough sound coming out, and I shut it again. I wasn't going to think about anything. I was going to keep my mind a white-cloud blank. I was going to—

I spasmed, arching off the bed, burying my face against him as another climax rocked me, and he held me, hard, prolonging it so that I froze, breathless, my entire body trapped in a tight knot of explosive power.

He eased me out of it slowly, gentling me down, and I was vaguely aware of an anger that he understood women's bodies, that he understood *my* body so well that he could arouse and shatter me with ridiculous ease. As I sank back against him, my face wet with inexplicable tears, part of me wanted to punch him, hit him, hurt him, simply for knowing me too well.

He threaded his hand through my hair, his mouth brushing away my tears. "You think too much," he said, this strange, half-spoken, half-thought conversation part of my resentment. "Just take the pleasure and stop fighting."

I could. I could let him do anything he wanted to me, let it take all night. He could stay in charge, manipulating me, pleasuring me, controlling me. Or I could see what I could do to shake his complacency.

I reached my hands up, cupping his face, and for the first time in my life I did the unthinkable. I kissed a man. All my life I had been the one who was kissed, the receiver of pleasure, never the giver. All that was about to change.

I pressed too hard at first, pushing him back, and

then I softened it, tasting him, letting my tongue trace the outline of his lips, slide between them to taste his tongue. His quiet sound of surprise hit me low in the belly, and I smiled against his mouth. I was liking this, far more than I'd ever expected.

I slid my hands down over his smooth chest, letting my fingers trace the outline of his taut muscles, the sleek heat of him, the hard points of his nipples, and on impulse I leaned down and licked one. He jerked in response, and I liked that even more. I licked the other one, and then fastened my mouth over it, as he had done to me. It was tricky—there wasn't much to latch onto—but his response made it worth the trouble, his muttered curse music to my ears.

"You're wading in dangerous waters, Miss Mary," he growled low in his throat, and the name felt like an endearment. I let my hand move down over his flat stomach until I reached the beginning curls of hair, and I hesitated. Nothing to be afraid of, I told myself. It was a body part, just like any other. It had been inside me already—it was time to learn it. I reached down and slid my hand over his cock, determined not to jerk away.

It was astonishing—smooth and silky to the touch, hard as iron, hot and almost pulsing in my hand. My fingertips traced the veins that stood out, drifted over the head, already damp with arousal, and slid down to cup his testicles, heavy and hot in my hand. He groaned, and I wondered if he was listening to my thoughts, but he said nothing, and I smiled. I'd finally managed to shake him from his self-assured control.

I moved my mouth down, kissing the flatness of his navel, letting my tongue dance in the silken trace of hair, and suddenly I wanted more. I wanted to taste him; I wanted him in my mouth, at my mercy; and before I could think twice I shifted my head down and took him, bringing his hard cock deep into my sucking mouth.

He cursed, a string of foul, utterly arousing words, and his hands twined in my hair, not holding me there, simply caressing me as my tongue learned the contours, the texture, every bump and ridge. His skin was different there, tasted different, and I experimented, bringing my mouth up to encircle only the head, then sinking back down to encase as much as I possibly could, then repeating it, and suddenly the pleasure wasn't for him, it was for me, arousing me impossibly, so that I was shaking, sweating, wanting so much from him, wanting this surrender. The taste, the silk, the suck of him, filling me . . .

He pulled my head away, and I fought him for a moment, then gave in, let him pull me up and cover my mouth with his, his kiss hungry and demanding; and I realized with shock that I'd almost brought myself to another of the seemingly endless orgasms simply by using my mouth on him. Who would have thought that such a forbidden act could bring such pleasure? My state of arousal was so high that it wouldn't take much to put me over the edge again, but I tried to hold back as he pushed me down onto the mattress, following me, moving between my legs.

He was covered with a film of sweat, shaking slightly, and I wanted to laugh in triumph. *I thought this was going to take all night?* I sent the thought out to him, not yet trusting my voice.

"It will," he said, sounding faintly grim. "But right now I can't wait anymore, you witch." He positioned the thick head of his cock against me. Now that I'd felt it, touched it, tasted it, the thought was even more arousing, and I was shaking too, waiting for the heavy thrust that would claim me.

Instead he pushed in slowly, so slowly I wanted to scream. I could feel everything as he sank in, and he felt bigger than ever, moving through the slickness of my own arousal, no pain, just a slow, inexorable claiming that was making me shake and shiver and arch against him, trying to hurry his possession, trying to pull him in, but his control was back, and he refused to be rushed. "I want you to feel this," he whispered against my ear. "I want you to be so caught up in you and me that there isn't room for anything else. Not doubt, not control, not trust or

Thomas or any of the thousands of reasons you don't want this. I want you to think only about why you do. Why you want me inside you. Why it feels like you'd die if you didn't feel me inside you. And then you'll understand what I've been feeling for the past week, every time I look at you."

I tried to punch at him, but I was too caught up in the sensations rocketing through me, and I simply clutched the sheet below me, arching my hips for the final thrust that brought him into me completely.

Instinctively I squeezed the walls of my sex, trying to draw him in even deeper. He cursed again. "Martha, you're going to kill me," he said.

My name. And he began to move, slow, steady thrusts that shook my body, shook the bed, shook him. I wrapped my legs around his hips, reveling in the feel of him, and we began the slow, inexorable dance of love and the little death that felt cataclysmic. He felt so damned good.

I closed my eyes and let it flow over me as he rocked me, rocked us into a deeper kind of sensuality than I had even guessed existed. When his hands slid under my butt, bringing me up even higher, I managed a surprised sound as the momentary discomfort brought an odd stab of even stronger arousal, and my sudden, ungovernable need made me almost panicky, my fingers reaching up to dig into his shoulders, clawing at him as he moved faster and faster, until we were both covered with sweat and he was slamming into me, hard, so hard.

And then he froze as time stood still, and he stared down at me, wild and lost and loving, and this time when I exploded he came with me, hot semen flooding me, his indrawn breath the only sound he made as he shook in my arms, rigid.

He collapsed against me, and I knew the wetness on his face was sweat, not tears, but I could fool myself, couldn't I? Stray, lingering convulsions rippled through my body, and at each one he groaned, his cock twitching inside me in reaction.

It wasn't enough, and I couldn't imagine what my lingering sense of need meant. I was drained, exhausted, trembling in his arms as he kissed my face, my mouth, my neck, and then I knew what I needed. He had filled me with his life's essence. I needed to give him mine. I wouldn't be complete until I did, and the last bit of fear dissolved into a different kind of lust. The lust to give, to be taken in an entirely different way.

I reached up, my hands weak and shaking, and caught his head as he started to move downward on my body. I brought him to my neck, and I could feel his mouth, hot and demanding, his tongue licking my skin, his teeth, just a tease; and with sudden despair I realized that was all he would do, until I told him otherwise.

I said the damning words. "I love you," I managed to squeeze out the merest breath of sound, but it was in the air, alive, shocking. "And I think you love me. I want you to take me. Take . . . my blood."

I don't know what I expected. He didn't hesitate, the permission unleashing whatever trace of restraint he had left. He bit deep, hard; and for a brief moment the pain shocked me, only to be followed by the most exquisite pleasure imaginable, almost better than sex. Almost. I wrapped my arms around him, holding him close against me as he drank, sucking at me, and this time the final climax was no surprise at all.

CHAPTER
THIRTY-ONE

CAIN WOKE FIRST, THE BRIGHT light of day streaming in the French doors, illuminating everything. Martha lay curled in his arms, relaxed, trusting, and he could see the dried traces of tears on her face. He'd always wondered why women cried when they had sex. The most blissful moment life had to offer shouldn't bring tears as well, but for the first time he had an inkling of just why. There were the rare times when the pleasure was so intense it seemed too much to withstand. He couldn't remember when he'd felt that way before, but there had to have been numerous times. If he stopped to think, he'd come up with them, but right then he didn't want to think about anyone but Martha.

He should pull away from her. She thought she was in love with him. Even worse, she thought he loved her. Women didn't understand that great sex could be just that. And the sex had been beyond great. It had been bone-shattering. But he couldn't afford to be sentimental. The shit was about to hit the fan, or had already, and he couldn't waste time lying in bed with her. The night had been long, he'd been hungry, and she'd managed to keep up with him. He wasn't sure which of them had passed out first, and his morning hard-on was getting worse the more he thought about it. The damned thing was going to fall off if he didn't give it a break. He pulled out of her arms carefully, letting her settle back in a gorgeous sprawl of limbs.

He paused in the act of leaving the bed, staring down at her. The sunlight showed no mercy, and he could see the scars clearly now, when before they'd been only shadows. She was lucky she was still alive.

He let his eyes trace the lines, dug deep by the Nephilim's razorlike claws, and to his surprise he realized they only made him want her more. He'd never thought scars would be a turn-on—but then, everything about Martha was a turn-on, and he couldn't figure out why.

Maybe he'd simply been too long without sex. He'd lost interest in it—there were just so many ways you could do it, so many different kinds of women. Of course, last night Martha hadn't seemed like a kind of woman. She had seemed like *the* woman, mysterious, erotic, elemental. And instead of losing interest, he'd been inspired, more so than he could ever remember. Even now he was thinking about how soon he could get inside her again, whether she'd want to ride him again, whether she'd—

She stirred, and he would have leapt off the bed if she hadn't reached out and touched him, her hand brushing his chest, staying him. And then her eyes flew open as she realized it was broad daylight, and she immediately tried to close in on herself, hiding her scars from him.

It was simple enough to take her arms in his hands, put his knee between hers, and make her open up again. "Why are you trying to hide?"

She started to speak, but only a rough, breathy sound came out, and she cleared her throat. This time he could hear her, but her voice was raw and rasping. "The scars," she whispered. "They're ugly."

"They're hot," he said, and leaned down to lick his way along the line that was carved between her breasts.

She froze, rejecting the notion; but she'd gotten well past her shyness last night, and a moment later she softened, and in the heat of the morning sun her nipples hardened. He closed his mouth over one, just lightly, giving it a soft tug, then released it to look down on her, smiling. She looked well loved. She had love bites on her breasts and thighs, slight bruises on her hips where he'd held her, and the more noticeable mark on her neck where he'd drunk from her. No, she looked well fucked, he reminded himself. And he wanted to do it again.

He had better things to do, more important things, but right then he couldn't remember any of them, and he was moving his head up, about to cover her soft, kiss-swollen mouth with his, when the pounding on his door ripped him away from her.

"You are called to stand before the Council of the Fallen," the archangel Michael's voice thundered.

"Shit," Cain said, rolling off her and getting to his feet. "We'll continue this later." His voice was soft, just for her, though he expected Michael heard it anyway. They all would know she'd spent the night with him, even if they'd missed their previous encounter. He was going to have to face all the overprotective power of the Fallen and their wives, when he didn't feel like answering anything, at least about Martha.

Another round of pounding, and Cain swore. "You'll have to wait, Michael. I'll come with you, but I'm going to take a shower first, unless you want me to show up to your fucking council naked."

"You would," came the contemptuous, muffled reply. "Five minutes."

"Ten."

"Five," Michael said. Cain noticed he didn't demand entrance, further proof that they knew he wasn't alone. Fine. He glanced back at Martha. She'd wrapped herself in a sheet, though whether to protect herself from intruders or to hide the scars, he wasn't sure. He considered all the things he could say to her, and dismissed them. She was the last thing he should be thinking about. Turning his back on her, he disappeared into the shower.

I SLIPPED FROM the bed, wrapping the sheet around me like a toga. My body ached, inside and out, and my soul hurt. I knew what was coming, as surely as if I'd had a vision. Maybe I had, and had deliberately forgotten it.

I headed for the French doors, knowing I could get to the safety of my own room that way. I expected to feel a little light-headed from blood loss, but in fact I felt almost powerful, if a little . . . battered. Either he hadn't taken that much or I was stronger than I thought.

I slipped out into the bright morning sunshine filtering through the haze overhead, and for a moment I thought about Metatron spearing upward, trailing blood. Where had he gone? Had he made it before he bled out? I hadn't seen how bad his wound was— I'd had more important things on my mind than the man who, inexplicably, wanted to kill me.

But maybe it wasn't so inexplicable after all, I

thought, closing the door behind me as I stepped into my small room. The only danger I presented was through my visions. Clearly Metatron had been afraid I would see something that would stop whatever his personal agenda had been. The question was, had he left for good? Or did I have to keep looking over my shoulder in case he showed up and figured the third time was the charm?

I headed straight for the shower. I had no intention of letting Cain face the gathered might of the council alone. I had no idea why they intended to question him, but the truth of what had happened last night had finally hit me. I'd told him I loved him. I'd told him he loved me. He'd taken my blood. Which meant, very simply, that we must be bonded mates.

The knowledge shook me. For one thing, according to the ancient laws that governed the Fallen, a human couldn't bond twice. Thomas had never truly been my mate. That knowledge was a physical hurt. I'd withheld everything from him—my sexuality, my blood, my complete trust—while he'd given me everything. Now I'd even withheld my bond with him, the final betrayal.

And for what? For Cain, who had never spoken of love, of caring? For a charming liar who had probably taken me on a whim?

He hadn't said the words. Yet he'd drunk from

me. Taken my blood in the ancient bonding ritual that proclaimed us united until the end of my comparatively short life. Which meant that I did matter to him, no matter how it appeared.

And last night it had felt like I mattered very much. Even if any words he'd spoken, both aloud and in my head, had been faintly mocking, his actions had been the opposite. Surely no man touched a woman like that without love?

I washed quickly, wincing at my abraded skin, the tenderness between my legs, the ache of muscles seldom used. I reached for the usual enveloping white clothes, but something stopped me at the last minute, and instead I grabbed Tory's emerald-green dress. I pulled it on, letting it settle around my hips, and stared at my reflection in the small mirror, the one I usually avoided. I was looking at a stranger.

The green made my skin luminous and my hazel eyes deepen. Or maybe sex made my skin luminous. The scar curved down over my breast, disappearing beneath the low neckline of the dress, but this time I wasn't going to hide it. I towel-dried my hair, then shook it, letting the riotous curls loose around my face. My lips were swollen from his kisses and my eyes had a dreamy, sated look; when I walked into the assembly hall, everyone would know what we'd been doing. I didn't care. I was his bonded mate, and he wasn't facing them without me.

I'd hoped to finish in time to walk with Cain and Michael, but they had already left, so I followed them as quickly as I could down the long, winding hallways until I reached the main part of the house.

The doors to the assembly hall were closed, and Tory was waiting outside, a troubled expression on her face. When I reached for the handle, she stopped me. "You don't want to go in there."

"Of course I do," I protested, astonished. "What are they going to do, torture him?"

"It doesn't have anything to do with you," she said, a little too forcefully. "They want to find out the truth behind why he's here."

I gave her an exasperated look. "I didn't think he'd be hauled before the council because he seduced me. As a part of Sheol, everything concerns me."

Tory looked startled. "You slept with him again?"

"Yes. I thought everyone had figured that out," I said, trying my best to sound nonchalant even though I could feel my cheeks flush. "And it's more than that."

"How could it be more than that?" Tory said warily.

"He drank from me. I'm his bonded mate." I felt strange saying the words, as if it wasn't quite real.

If anything, Tory looked even unhappier. "I think we should go back to your room. You should wait and see what happens."

"What are you talking about?" I was beginning to feel very uneasy, my skin prickling the way it did when I felt a vision coming on. "What's wrong?"

She didn't answer, and I wasn't going to wait. I pushed past her and pulled the door open.

No one even noticed my presence—everyone was riveted to the drama playing out at the front of the room. Cain stood there, and for a moment I let myself drown in his beauty, in the acceptable knowledge that he was mine. He had been, even before he'd arrived here, ever since he'd begun showing up in my visions; no matter how much I tried to fight it, the truth was inescapable. He was mine, and I was his, and it was all right to love him.

I let go of the very last of my doubts and defenses as I looked at him. I loved him. No matter how secretive, annoying, and manipulative he was, he drew me like the moon tides drew the ocean, and the connection was as deep and implacable. I loved him as I had never loved Thomas, and all the shame in the world wasn't about to change that simple fact. It shocked me, both the knowledge and the unshakable *rightness* of it. I loved him.

I moved through the throngs of people crowded into the room, slipping past them so that he could see me, know I was there. He would find the bond just as unexpected and troublesome as I had, I thought, but he would know it for the truth. If he took the blood of anyone but the Source or his bonded mate, he would die.

"So you want us to accept that we have spent countless millennia believing a lie?" Raziel snapped in a voice like a whiplash.

"Yes." Cain's own voice was cool and controlled.

"You tried this once before, the last time you graced us with your presence. You insisted we could walk through fire, and Ezekiel was fool enough to believe you. He died screaming."

"Because he didn't believe. Uriel's curse is nothing but brainwashing. The Higher Power commanded us to become blood-eaters, and there's nothing we can do about that. But the rest of it is nothing but lies. We are impervious to fire. Our women can drink blood as well and suffer no harm, only lasting life. They can bear children—haven't you wondered why your Source became pregnant?"

"It was with Rachel's help," Allie said, sitting at Raziel's right. She looked pale, and I was filled with a sudden foreboding. "The Lilith has ancient powers, and she—"

"She may have helped, but the only reason you got pregnant was because you weren't convinced you couldn't. You didn't fall into the usual category of the Fallen's so-called bonded mates—you'd survived on Raziel's blood, you weren't alive by the usual standards. In fact, it was Raziel's resistance you had to overcome. If the Fallen believe that children are impossible, they release no sperm."

"So-called bonded mates"? What did he mean by that?

Raziel wasn't finished. "So you expect me to direct someone else to touch an open flame and see if he manages to survive? I don't think so. We tried that. And where exactly is your confederate? No one has seen Metatron since yesterday morning."

"Metatron is gone," Azazel said from his seat between Allie and Rachel. "And good riddance."

Raziel turned to him, and if there was any doubt who was the Alpha, that was now put to rest.

Azazel spoke quietly and respectfully. "Metatron was trying to kill Martha. Clearly he was afraid of what her visions might reveal."

Raziel turned to Cain. "And how was Metatron working with you? Was he part of your plan to destroy the Fallen?"

"Metatron was a tool, imperfect though he was, until he attempted to think for himself. He decided getting rid of the seer would aid him. And he was behind the attempt on the baby."

"And where is he?" There was no missing the murderous look in Raziel's eyes.

"Gone," Azazel offered succinctly. "Cain stopped him from hurting Martha, the two of them fought, and Metatron escaped."

Raziel looked at him, unappeased. "And how do you know all this? You and Cain have never been particular friends."

"We were having a discussion up on the ledge when we noticed Martha and Metatron together. Cain went to rescue her, and I was close behind."

"What kind of conversation?" No one mistook the silken tone of Raziel's voice for anything but menace.

"A private one," Azazel replied.

"I was about to kill him," Cain offered lazily. He glanced at Azazel. "If you think I'm going to accept any favors from you, you're mistaken. If Metatron hadn't chosen that moment to go after Martha, Azazel would be dead."

"You chose Martha over revenge?" Raziel said, disbelief strong in his voice. "That's not like you."

Cain could see me if he bothered to look. I had moved to the front of the room, the deep green of my dress a splash of color that he couldn't fail to notice. "I had planned to use her," he said without the slightest trace of guilt. "It's easy enough to move within her dreams, and I was going to implant what I needed."

"You were going to implant your ridiculous idea of truth about fire and blood and Uriel?"

He shook his head. "No. She's been such an ineffective seer that I was going to implant the opposite. If she insisted that fire was dangerous, you were more likely to go in search of flames to test the theory."

It felt like a slap in the face. Not only had he used me, he'd planned to do far worse, playing on my wretched incompetence. No wonder Tory had tried to stop me. She had followed me in, standing right behind me, and I would have turned away, but I couldn't move, mesmerized by the pain I knew was coming.

"Unfortunately for you and Metatron, her visions have become a great deal more reliable."

Cain shrugged. "I could adjust my plan either way. It's too late now. I can feel Uriel coming, and I expect Metatron will be by his side once more. And if you don't listen to me, you'll all be dead in the next twenty-four hours."

There was a murmur of distinct unease from the crowd, but Raziel was unmoved. "So you're telling us we're impervious to fire, even though all evidence has been to the contrary. Has the sea lost its efficacy?"

"The sea still heals you."

"And we must still be blood-eaters?"

"Yes. But you can drink the blood of anyone you choose. The myth of bonded mates is just that, a myth. You can drink from one woman at night and another the next day and suffer no ill effects. In sex, you're no longer constrained by archaic rules. There are no bonded mates. You can screw who you want, bleed who you want."

I could feel myself growing numb, unable to turn away.

"And I suppose you want me to sacrifice my people to prove that's true," Raziel said. "A problem if, as you say, Uriel's arrival is imminent. I would lose two warriors if I tested your claims about fire and blood."

"I drank from Martha last night. I'll take someone new today and be fine. More than fine, I'd be stronger than ever. We all know that blood gives us power, but there's a limit to how much we can take without hurting the donor."

Donor, I thought frozen. Not mate. What an idiot I'd been.

"This way you can take from several woman without hurting them, and become more powerful than Uriel would even suspect."

"I don't believe a word you're saying," Raziel said flatly. "Prove it."

Cain looked around the room. His eyes caught mine for a moment, and then moved on, as if I were nothing more than a . . . a donor. "Anyone want to volunteer?" His voice was wry, mocking. Clearly he didn't expect anyone to offer.

Tory pushed past me. "I do, you bastard," she snarled. Michael was close behind her, and she grabbed the knife he always carried, slashing it across her wrist.

She held it out to Cain, bleeding, furious challenge in her eyes, when all I wanted to do was slink away. I believed him. I believed every word he said.

But I was frozen, particularly with Michael's body behind me, practically vibrating with tension, and I realized he was in trouble as well. Watching your mate feed another would be enough to drive one of the Fallen to the brink of madness. Even Raziel hadn't quite got used to it.

Cain looked at her for a long, assessing moment. And then he caught her arm in both hands, holding her steady, and put his mouth against the bleeding gash, sucking.

The room was completely silent as he took from her, pulling at her in an almost sexual act. And then he looked up, his eyes meeting mine over Tory's narrow wrist, and he didn't slow down, didn't back off with a polite lick. He watched me as he drank from another woman, and I couldn't move, encased in ice and sorrow. And a sudden, unexpected, entirely healthy rage.

I could feel the tension running through Michael as he stood behind me, and I realized I should just let him go. He'd crush Cain like a bug, and I'd cheer him on.

A moment later Cain dropped Tory's arm, looking at Raziel with eyes glittering in triumph. "Nothing," he said. "Except," he added, looking at Tory, "you're delicious."

That was enough for Michael, who shoved me aside, heading for Cain with a murderous roar, and I wouldn't have stopped him, really I wouldn't, except my skin was suddenly covered with a thousand tingles, the pain hit my head and stomach at the same time, and I collapsed on the floor in a dead faint.

CHAPTER
THIRTY-TWO

I WAS OUT FOR A ONLY MOMENT. WHEN my eyes opened, Tory was on her knees beside me, holding me, the entire place was in an uproar, and out of the corner of my eye I saw Cain. Michael was holding him, and it almost looked as if he was holding him back, keeping him from coming to me, but I knew that was a lie. Everything about him was a lie.

I tried to pull my stupid brain together. The vision had come in shards, like a shattered mirror, and for a moment I wasn't sure what went where. And then it coalesced.

"They're coming," I said hoarsely.

No one made the mistake of asking what I meant. Raziel surveyed Cain with unbridled contempt. "It appears we're going to have a chance to prove your word sooner than we thought. Everyone who is able, go to the armory and prepare. Tory, help Martha to her room—"

I struggled to my feet. For once no doubt troubled me; the vision now was clear and terrifying. "I'm fine. I can fight. But they're coming with . . . fire." Unwillingly I glanced at Cain, expecting a look of triumph on his face.

There was nothing but calm acceptance. He'd gotten what he wanted. There would be no more lies—at least, not right now.

He was the least of my worries. I turned and looked out over the quickly dispersing Fallen, and my eyes caught Rachel's. "It's time," I said quietly.

"Time for what?" Tory demanded, but Rachel was already pushing her way toward us. Toward the front of the room, where Allie sat frozen in sudden terror.

"No," she whispered, but I could hear her, hear her fear.

I broke away from Tory and went to her, catching her trembling hands in mine. Allie, the Source, who was afraid of nothing. "It's going to be all right," I said firmly.

Raziel was across the room, conferring with Michael, and Cain had disappeared entirely. I shielded Allie from view as best I could, and Rachel joined me. "We need to tell Raziel," she said.

"Don't you dare," Allie said. "We're under attack. He needs to focus on saving the Fallen, and I can't have him distracted."

"Allie, the baby is coming," Rachel said quietly. "Don't you want him there?"

"I'd rather have Sheol still standing once the baby arrives," she said somewhat breathlessly, as another contraction hit her. "I need help getting back upstairs."

"You can't possibly make it up all those stairs in active labor," Rachel protested.

"Hate those stairs," Allie gasped. "But I can do it."

"Hold on." Rachel disappeared.

Allie looked up at me, her eyes filled with sadness. "I'm so sorry, Martha," she said. "He's a heartless bastard."

"Don't worry about me." I brushed it off. "I've been through worse." I couldn't remember when at that particular moment, but I was sure it would come to me. "Concentrate on the baby. It's coming, and it's going to be fine. I promise you."

She squeezed my hands, some of her panic leaving her. "Since you know so much, why don't you tell me what sex it is?"

I laughed. "You'll find out in a few hours," I said. "Be patient."

Rachel was back, with Tamlel by her side. Calm, trustworthy Tam, who simply scooped Allie up in his arms and strode toward the open door. Rachel started after her, but I stayed where I was, knowing what I had to do. She turned and looked back at me, a question in her eyes.

"I have to fight," I said. "You know you can bring this baby into the world without me, and I'm going to be needed."

She nodded, accepting. Strange, how everyone suddenly believed me after all the years of doubt.

"If you get the chance to accidentally gut Cain, please do so in my honor," she called back over her shoulder.

I laughed. It surprised me. I wouldn't have thought I could ever laugh again. At least the thought of Cain's demise was enough to cheer me. "I'll keep it in mind," I said.

There was a moment's concern on Rachel's face. She knew me too well. "You're going to survive," she said. "Aren't you?"

"The battle, or Cain?" I shrugged. "Haven't you noticed that my visions are entirely worthless when it comes to my own life? I have no idea what's going to happen. I just know I need to be out there."

She couldn't hesitate any longer, but she crossed the room and pulled me into a fierce hug. "Don't die," she ordered. "We're going to get our revenge on Cain."

"I'll do my best."

And I was alone, the assembly room deserted. I sank into the seat Allie had vacated. That lovely, refreshing fury had died, leaving sorrow in its place, and I leaned back, blinking. I couldn't afford to cry—

and besides, he wasn't worth crying over. When I did cry, and it would happen sooner or later, I'd be crying over my own stupidity, my willingness to believe the impossible. I had looked into his eyes and known he loved me. And what hurt most was that I had deluded myself. He'd never said anything. And for this I had betrayed the memory of Thomas on every level.

They were drawing closer. I could feel them, the Armies of Heaven, ruthless and cruel, and this time Uriel himself was leading them, the boogey monster of Sheol, the most hated and feared despot. We were going to face him, and I didn't know if we were going to win or lose.

I rose. I needed to get out of this stupid dress, the one I'd thought would dazzle my newly bonded mate. I headed straight for my room and ripped the damned thing off, tearing it down the middle with more strength than I knew I had. I dressed in my usual loose white clothes. They would show the blood, but I could move freely in them, and right now I was in the mood for blood.

I needed to see Cain once more before this started. Not to talk to him—God knew I had nothing to say. I just needed to look and congratulate myself on coming to my senses. In love with him? That was ridiculous. I barely knew him. And he'd been playing mind games with me the entire time, intent on using me in the worst possible way.

One look at him and I'd be primed to kill.

There were only a few people left in the armory, but Tory was waiting for me. She looked at me warily. "You're not mad at me, are you?"

For a moment I felt something sting my eyes, but I blinked it away. "Don't be an idiot."

She held out her arms, and I had to go into them or she'd think I was lying. She'd done what she had to do to prove what a lying bastard Cain was. She'd done it to protect me, and I loved her for it. But I didn't want to be held.

I went anyway, hugging her tightly, trying to keep it together. And then I pushed her away with a shaky grin. "We're both going to make it," I said.

She grinned back at me. "You bet. Want me to spike Cain if I get a chance?"

I shook my head. "He's not worth it. If the Armies of Heaven don't get him, then someone else will. We've got more important things to think about. "

Tory nodded. "What do you want for a weapon?"

"I don't need one."

"Martha—" she began, but I shook my head.

"Trust me."

"Wouldn't you be better off in the infirmary with Rachel?" Tory's voice was curious.

"Rachel's not in the infirmary. She's with Allie. The baby's coming."

"Shit."

I nodded. "Yeah, shit. But you know they'll do fine in the infirmary, even without Rachel. They don't need me."

Tory wasn't looking happy. "So you're going to walk out on the battlefield unarmed?"

"Trust me, my mood is dangerous enough."

That coaxed a laugh out of her as she was strapping on the leather armor used by the front line. She was a warrior goddess, in her element. "Let's go, then."

The Fallen were lined up on the beach, armed, ready. It was a small army but a dangerous one, with the archangel Michael, the quintessential warrior, in the lead, with Raziel and Azazel beside him. Cain was there as well, though his face was turned away, and I started to head toward the back when Tory halted.

"I'm not leaving you," she said flatly.

"You need to be with Michael," I protested.

"Yes, I do. But I'm not leaving you."

"You want me to go to the front lines where I'll be a sitting duck?" It seemed like the perfect argument.

"I'll protect you."

We were wasting time arguing. The sky was growing dark with the approaching angels, and I was filled with a remembered dread. I had lost everything the last time I had faced combat, and I could still remember the screaming pain of the Nephilim's claws on my skin. But I knew Tory. She wouldn't relent. "Okay."

They were watching the sky, and only Michael noticed when Tory slipped in beside him, taking his hand and squeezing it. Cain was still turned away, talking to Raziel, and the sound of his voice made me freeze. *Just turn around,* I thought. *One look at your lying face and I'll be able to let go of this stupid infatuation you manufactured. One look.*

"They're planning to use fire," he was saying. "The only way you can possibly win is to believe the fire won't hurt you."

Raziel's eyes narrowed as he saw me, and Cain turned. There was a moment of silence as he looked at me, his face unreadable; unbidden, the memory of last night came back, his face as he looked into mine, his unspoken words against my skin. *Love me.* And I did.

It was no delusion I could wash away in the face of his trickery. No infantile crush. For once my visions had been cruel and unyielding when it came to my own life, and I looked at him and knew with a certainty stronger than anything I'd ever felt in my life. Whether bonded mates existed or not, he was mine.

The heavens opened.

Fire rained down on the beach, and everyone fell back in sudden panic as flames erupted, higher than the house, higher than an angel could fly without getting singed and poisoned, if the old laws were true. The first wave of angels came behind, landing on the beach with wings furled, out of reach of the water that had proven their downfall. We could see them through the flames—lined up and ready, cutting off any escape.

The noise and heat from the fire were overwhelming, but I could hear Cain's voice. "The fire won't hurt us. We have to go through it, bring the fight to them, or we're all going to die."

"He's lying!" someone shouted. "We can move back, come at them from the side—"

"Don't be an idiot," Cain spat. "I'll go first." He drew his sword, and suddenly he looked very different. Like an ancient warrior angel of old, beautiful and lethal, fearless in the face of death.

"We already know you're impervious to fire," Raziel said coldly. The flames flickered against his skin, giving him an unearthly glow. "Gadrael is right—this could be a trap."

Michael cursed suddenly, pulling away from them. "This is bullshit," he said succinctly. He grabbed Tory and kissed her soundly, then turned and headed for the flames, sword drawn.

Everyone watched in breathless silence, the only sound the crackle of the inferno that was slowly approaching us. Michael didn't hesitate. With a battle cry he charged through, Cain right behind him, and we could see them through the flames, untouched, as the Armies of Heaven came to life.

"What the hell are you waiting for?" Raziel shouted. "Go!" And with that he raced after them, followed by the rest of the angels.

For a brief, vain moment I hoped Uriel's armies would be trapped between the flames and the water that had proven so deadly to them, but already the bloody, dangerous angels of heaven broke through, meeting the Fallen as they charged.

And then it was a battle once more, smoke and noise, screams of the dying, blood everywhere. I stood frozen in the midst of it, barely able to see through the billowing black smoke, as around me the wounded fell. I came to with a jerk as I saw a dark angel standing over Gadrael's fallen body, about to finish him off with a spear to the throat, and I screamed at him, racing toward him. Gadrael's sword had fallen by his outstretched hand, and I scooped it up and leapt on the angel, screaming like a banshee.

He fell. The sword had pierced his armor, pierced his heart. I had slaughtered Nephilim, those hideous, barely human creatures, by the dozen, but I had never drawn my sword against another human being. An angel, no less. And he was dead at my feet.

I heard a choking noise, and looked to see Gadrael coughing up blood. The angel had been thorough with his handiwork—Gadrael had been cut up so badly, there was no time to get him to the infirmary, no way to get him to the sea. I knelt beside him in the sand, cradling his bloody head in my lap, murmuring soothing words. The Fallen might survive, but I was human.

"Hold on," I said urgently. "Someone will come and help get you—"

"Not . . . enough time," Gadrael said, his breath wheezing through a slashed lung. "Get the Source."

The Source, who was right now giving birth, far above the battlefield. I stared down at Gadrael in despair. I was going to hold him as he died, and there was nothing I could do.

I looked around me for any kind of help, but people were fighting for their lives. Through the curtain of fire I could see them now, the pitched battle, and I took only a moment to acknowledge that in this, at least, Cain hadn't lied. The Fallen had survived the fire.

And Cain had survived on the blood of two different women. I had no idea whether my blood would provide the same healing power as Allie's, but I had no choice. I took the sword and cut my wrist, an expert slash, and held it to his mouth. "Drink."

He clamped his mouth shut, like a child refusing spinach, and shook his head.

"He's been right about everything else, damn it," I said. "Take my goddamned blood." And I reached out and held his nose, so that he had no choice but to open his mouth.

I felt his teeth as he latched onto me, the pain short-lived, and I watched him drink. There was no pleasure in it, not as there had been when Cain had taken my vein, but there was comfort in knowing that I could save at least one man.

A moment later he rolled away from me, jumping to his feet and grabbing the sword I'd used. He stared at me in amazement. "My wife is going to kill me," he muttered, and charged back into the fray.

Everything passed in a smoky daze—I had no idea whether it was minutes or hours. I moved among the wounded, sinking down, giving them my blood, sending them back to fight once more as more and more of Uriel's army descended and were cut down. The sky was black with smoke and with wave after wave of dark soldiers, and I knelt in the sand, tears running down my face. We could never prevail against them, not when they outnumbered us so heavily. Half of our warriors were human women, trapped behind the wall of fire, watching numbly.

Suddenly just enough of the smoke lifted and I could see Cain, covered with blood, a savage grin on his face as he fought a huge angel. It was Metatron, slashing and hacking at him, and panic froze me in place. I had no proof, no sense that Cain would survive this battle, and Metatron was enormous, determined. I could kneel there and watch him die, and there wasn't a damned thing I could do about it.

I wanted to scream, but I covered my mouth to stop it. There was no way he could hear it through the noise of battle, but I knew that he would anyway, and it could distract him at a crucial moment. I watched, motionless, as Metatron forced him back, back, even as Cain slashed at him, and I wondered if that was desperation thrumming through his lean, strong body, or determination.

And then the world went sideways as Cain tripped over a fallen soldier, sprawling backward; he wouldn't have time to recover. Metatron was moving in, his blood-splattered face like granite, descending upon him for the final kill, and I knew that if Cain died I would die too, I would simply cease to exist. I watched in helpless horror as Metatron leapt to finish him off.

In time to meet Cain's upthrust sword slamming into his chest, twisting. Metatron went down, boneless, sprawling on the sand beside Cain.

I let out my breath in relief—until I realized that Cain hadn't risen to stand over his fallen enemy. He lay still, spent, and I knew with sudden certainty that he was dying. Alone. Without me.

I rose. Humans couldn't walk through flames. Fallen angels shouldn't be able to either. Cain didn't know all the answers, and in this insane world of Sheol anything was proving possible. I started toward the flames.

"What the hell are you doing?" Tory caught my arm. She wasn't human, but neither was she one of the Fallen, and she'd been trapped on this side of the battle as well, fighting off the soldiers who managed to break through.

"Cain. He's hurt."

"What the fuck do you think you can do about it?" she yelled back.

"Save him," I said, ripping myself away from her grip. "Or die trying."

I ran toward the flames.

HE WAS DYING, and he didn't really care. He'd finished Metatron, that piece of business paid for, and he couldn't think of anything else he needed to do as the noise of battle raged around him. Metatron had fought well, better than he'd expected, and the killing blow he'd landed beneath Cain's ribs was testament to that fact. It was all right. He was ready for it to end.

Odd—he would have thought Tamarr's face would finally come back to him when he was dying. But all he could see was Martha, her halo of unruly curls around her stubborn face, her delicious mouth. He laughed as he lay dying. It was just like him to think lustful thoughts as he finally blinked out.

"You asshole." He was hearing Martha's voice as well, though those weren't exactly the loverlike sentiments he would have wished for his final words. He opened his eyes to tell the phantom just that, and then froze. It was Martha in the flesh, covered with soot and blood and grime, kneeling beside him, fury in her eyes as she shoved her wrist at him. "Drink."

"How did you—?"

"Do you think you know all the answers? Drink, or I swear I'll let you die on a pile of rotting corpses. And don't worry if you taste a few other men at my wrist—I'm sure you don't mind sloppy seconds."

He stared at her in disbelief. And then he caught her arm, yanking her down, and kissed her, hard.

For a brief, golden moment she kissed him back. And then she shoved him away. "I thought you were going for my neck."

He was fading now, but it was worth it. To die with Martha's kiss on his mouth was as good a way to go as any.

"Asshole," she muttered again. And he could taste the warm, sweet, life-giving drops of her blood against his lips, his tongue, and he swallowed, taking her.

THE WOMEN FOLLOWED me like a horde of ancient Celts, screaming blue murder, moving through the blaze as if it were as insubstantial as the mist that shrouded Sheol. I heard them as I fed Cain, heard them as I cradled his head in my arms, but I didn't watch. Either we'd prevail or we wouldn't—right then I couldn't stand any more bloodshed. This was the last time I would see Cain, the last time I would be with him. Assuming we both survived, I was leaving. Going back to the ugliness of the real world, maybe. Raziel would have some idea of a bolt-hole until I recovered. But for now I could hold him and look down at the lying bastard and love him as I knew I shouldn't.

Slowly, slowly, the noise grew softer, the deafening clang of metal against metal dying back, the thuds and grunts fewer, the screams of the dying fading into nothingness, and I wondered if I was dying as well. I realized with absent despair that we were bathed in a golden light, and I looked up, expecting to see some kind of eternity waiting for us. Instead I saw the sun beating down on us, with no cloud of dark angels blocking the light. I stared around me dazedly, to see that the wall of flames had disappeared and I was kneeling in the middle of a bloody battlefield strewn with hundreds of bodies, though I recognized none of them. They were all soldiers of Uriel's.

Who had now seemingly departed. There was a sudden shout of triumph, followed by a roar as the army of the Fallen raised their bloodied weapons in triumph, and I looked down at the man whose head I cradled so tenderly.

He was looking up at me, a bemused expression on his face.

I dropped his head in the sand.

A moment later I reached Tory, throwing myself into her arms as we hugged each other, laughing and crying—when the familiar sensation washed over my skin, and I froze.

Tory stared at me. "What's wrong?" she demanded. "You've seen something. Are they coming back?"

"Eventually," I said in an absent voice, breaking free of the sudden trance. "It's not that."

"Then what the hell is it?"

"Listen!"

For an impossible moment there was complete silence on the bloody sand. And then, like purest music, the sound came floating out into the sunlit air, carried down from the topmost floor.

The healthy cry of a newborn baby.

CHAPTER
THIRTY-THREE

RAZIEL STARED DOWN AT HIS sleeping son, a look of complete amazement on his face. It had been three days since he'd been born, and Raziel still couldn't get over the absolute wonder of him. Ten fingers and toes, a sweet milky smell that Martha insisted went with all babies. And Allie was fine, if exhausted from the short, hard labor, smiling at him so benevolently that he wondered if she was the same woman who took delight in pricking his pride. "He's beautiful," he said in a voice of wonder, knowing he only echoed what every father in history had said when gazing upon his child.

"Shhhhh," Allie said. "Martha's asleep."

He frowned, but lowered his voice anyway. "Why do we have to worry about Martha getting enough sleep? You're the one who just had a baby."

"And she's the one who's been walking him while he cries so I can rest. Between that and her visions and Cain and serving as a source, she's been a mess. She finally drifted off a little while ago, and I want her to sleep as long as possible."

Raziel glanced over at the seer. She was pale, paler than he'd ever seen her, curled up in a chair by the window, one hand under her face in a protective gesture. "Cain's not going to be a problem for much longer—he's leaving."

"Of course he is," Allie said in a dangerous voice. "The rat bastard."

"He saved us."

"Rat bastard," Allie repeated firmly.

There was a soft knock on the door, just enough to startle the seer into wakefulness, and she jumped up. "Sorry," Martha mumbled. "I don't know why I fell asleep. Are you up for visitors, or should I send them away?"

"Depends on who it is," Allie said.

"Michael and Tory," she said promptly.

Raziel stared at her. "How do you know that?"

Martha had a sudden hunted look on her face, but she managed to shrug. "The vision thing," she said finally. "It's gone haywire. I'm getting constant flashes of things that don't really matter. The good thing is, it no longer makes me sick." She shook herself, as if shaking it off. "You want us all to go away?"

"Of course not," Allie said immediately. "Bring them in."

Raziel watched the seer as she went to the door. She'd lost weight in the three days since the battle. She was bruised and had stitches across a long gash on her wrist, and everything about her looked pale and battered.

He handed the baby back to Allie, a little afraid he might drop him, and turned to greet the archangel. "You've come to see the new baby."

"No, I've come to gaze upon your shining face," Michael said dryly. "Of course we've come to see the baby." He gazed down at it, nodded as if to say "That's a baby," and stepped back for the women to fuss. "What are you going to call him?"

Raziel glanced at Allie. "We were thinking Luca."

"Bringer of light." Michael nodded, approving. "In honor of the First."

"Yes," Raziel said. He hesitated, then drew Michael aside. "You know, it was the damnedest thing."

"What was?"

"In the heat of the battle, just when I knew we were going to defeat them, I thought I saw something. As far as I could tell, Uriel was nowhere around. But something else was."

Michael was looking at him critically. "Don't tell me you're having visions?"

"Of course not!" he protested with an uneasy laugh. "You didn't see anything, did you?"

"Besides blood and death and flames? No. What did you think you saw?"

"Lucifer." He said the word softly, half hoping Michael wouldn't hear it. But the archangel had frozen at the name. "Uriel's angels were retreating, the last of them cut down where they landed. I was looking to see if Uriel was with them, and I swear I saw Lucifer, sort of floating there. Shimmery, like a mirage, and he was trying to tell me something. And I have no idea what."

Michael was looking like he'd seen a ghost as well. He began to curse softly beneath his breath, this man who, before the arrival of his wife, had never cursed at all. "I've seen him too. Not in battle. Earlier."

Raziel just stared at him. "We've spent millennia trying to find him, and you just now decide to tell me this?"

"I didn't remember."

"Don't give me that—seeing Lucifer isn't something you'd forget."

Michael was looking grim. "No, it isn't. Unless something deliberately interferes with the memory. It was in the Darkness. We couldn't have escaped without him. He's trapped there, or at least part of him is. He wasn't physical there either."

"Shit," Raziel said. He glanced back at his newborn child with regret and longing. "We're going to have to go after him. Into the Darkness. We have to bring him home."

I SLIPPED OUT of the room as Michael and Raziel carried on a hushed conversation. They were talking about Lucifer, the first of the Fallen, the long-lost savior of us all. And it was us, all of us. I was one of the Fallen, and I would live forever. Our mortality was another of Uriel's convincing lies. With blood we would never grow old, sicken, or die. If we shouldered the curse of the Fallen, drank the blood of our mates, we would be as they were.

But without the wings, which was patently unfair, I thought, testing to see if I still had a sense of humor. It was there beneath everything, slightly singed but intact. We would have no need, no craving, for blood, but if we did drink it, it would keep us young, which was probably an excellent arrangement for most of the bonded mates in Sheol.

And they *were* bonded. Cain, who thought he knew everything, was wrong about that one as well. It was independent of whose blood was taken—when one of the Fallen mated, it was an unbreakable bond, strong and true. Unless, of course, it was made in deceit and treachery, in which case all bets were off.

He was leaving. I knew he would. In fact, I'd been glued to Allie's side for the last three days in hopes that he'd take off before I had to see him again. It had all been too much, the shock of betrayal, followed so closely by the battle. I'd given too much blood on the battlefield, ending with Cain, and I felt weak, dizzy, unable to face anything but the soft and sweet baby Allie let me hold.

But I'd hidden out for too long. He hadn't gone yet—it was one of the many things I knew. My formerly imperfect visions, painful and rare, had now become a constant companion, an almost comfortable one. I knew where people were, what we were having for dinner, how cold it was going to be. It was as if I'd been living in a house full of shuttered windows. Now all those shutters had been flung open, and I could see everything.

Including Cain, in his room, getting ready to leave.

I even knew where I was going, despite my better judgment. I was going to him, though I wasn't sure what I'd do when I got there. I still had an intense longing to smash something over his head, but it hadn't done any good the first time.

It was a warm afternoon, lovely, as all afternoons in Sheol were lovely. I didn't bother to knock, pushing open the door to his room and walking in as if I belonged. He was standing by the French doors, staring out into the garden, and he turned, startled, wary.

"I'm not going to hit you," I said. I didn't want to hit him. I still had the faint hope that after all this time, all this betrayal, I wouldn't care anymore. I looked into his beautiful, deceitful face and knew I would care for an eternity.

"That's good. I'm not quite recovered from Metatron's handiwork." His voice was light, relaxed. Deceptively so. I could feel the tension thrumming through his body as it vibrated through mine. "At least I killed the bastard."

"I thought he was your confederate."

He hurt you. At first I thought he'd spoken the words out loud, shocking me. And then I realized I'd once more heard his thoughts. Or had I just imagined what I wanted to hear?

Cain shrugged. "He wasn't good at following orders." *I wanted to make him suffer.*

I stared at him, then tried to shake off the unreasonable hope that was beginning to fill me. I could see it, as I could see so many things now, but I was afraid to believe it, even if my other visions had become almost infallible. *Not this one,* I thought. I was never right about me.

But I looked at him and I knew. I was on a precipice, and I had a choice to make. I could let him go. Or I could fight.

"What do you think you're doing?"

He raised an eyebrow, no sign of the inner turmoil I could feel so strongly coming off him in waves. "I'm leaving." *I don't want to.*

I took a deep breath, and did the bravest thing I had ever done, harder than facing the Nephilim or the Armies of Heaven. "I don't think so."

He looked at me for a moment, his silver eyes wary. "What did you say?"

"I said, 'I don't think so,'" I repeated in a determined tone. "Aren't you tired of running away all the time?"

"I'm not running away," he protested. And I heard him again, the words clear, the words he couldn't say.

I love you. Leaving you tears me up inside, but I can't stay here and keep on hurting you. I love you. Let me go.

I shook my head. "You're running away," I said again, "and it's time to stop." I moved across the room to him, standing close enough to touch him, afraid to. I straightened my shoulders. "Your place is here."

He just stared at me, and then that familiar lazy grin lit his face. The one that he used to charm everyone. The one that from now on would be only for me.

"Is that so?" His voice was cool, distant, but I was no longer fooled.

"You were right about some things and wrong about others, you know."

"Why don't you enlighten me?"

"You were only partly right about the fire. You didn't know the wives could go through it as well. You didn't know that we could be immortal either."

"You'll have to understand I was concentrating on saving Sheol. I wasn't thinking about the future, and women were far down on my agenda."

Try again, big boy. You can't fool me anymore.

I knew he heard me by the startled expression on his face. But then he dismissed it.

"Of course you weren't thinking about the women, you asshole." My spoken voice was loving. "You were wrong about bonded mates. The blood may have nothing to do with it. You've proven you can drink from anyone and survive. But that doesn't mean the bond between a Fallen and his mate isn't strong and unbreakable."

"Doesn't it?

Damn, he was being stubborn. "No, it doesn't. And I have one more important piece of information for you. I'm your bonded mate, even if you're too pigheaded to believe it. I'm yours. No one else's. I'm going to be immortal, and we may as well not waste centuries until you grow a brain and realize it."

"Really?" he said, not giving an inch. "Do you have anything else to say?"

All right, so this wasn't going so well. Maybe I was wrong, maybe I'd botched it, maybe the voice in my head was wishful thinking. Maybe it would be better if I sat down and burst into tears, but I was trying to maintain a scrap of dignity if he decided to be a blind idiot. "Yes," I said. "I love you. So man up, or angel up, or whatever, and love me."

He didn't move, his eyes sweeping over me with lazy deliberation. "Your visions tell you that?"

"Yes. And my heart."

"Well," he said in a measured voice, "looks like your visions finally got it right." He came to me then, pulling me into his arms. "I love you, Miss Mary. I'm no good for you, but if you'll have me, I'm yours. Forever."

"I'll have you." My voice was steady, my heart racing.

He kissed me then, all the trickery and all the defenses gone. Cain, the rebel, the trickster, the wanderer, my mate.

He had finally come home.

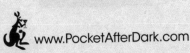

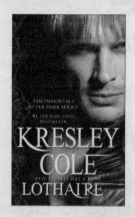
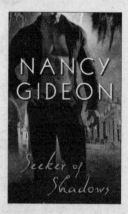

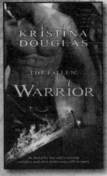
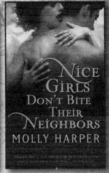